A LITTLE HOPE

A Novel

ETHAN JOELLA

SCRIBNER

New York   London   Toronto   Sydney   New Delhi

Scribner

An Imprint of Simon & Schuster, Inc.

1230 Avenue of the Americas

New York, NY 10020

This book is a work of fiction. Any references to historical events, real people, or real places are used fictitiously. Other names, characters, places, and events are products of the author's imagination, and any resemblance to actual events or places or persons, living or dead, is entirely coincidental.

Copyright © 2021 by Ethan Joella

First Scribner hardcover edition November 2021

SCRIBNER and design are registered trademarks of The Gale Group, Inc., used under license by Simon & Schuster, Inc., the publisher of this work.

For information about special discounts for bulk purchases, please contact Simon & Schuster Special Sales at 1-866-506-1949 or business@simonandschuster.com.

The Simon & Schuster Speakers Bureau can bring authors to your live event. For more information or to book an event, contact the Simon & Schuster Speakers Bureau at 1-866-248-3049 or visit our website at www.simonspeakers.com.

Interior design by Wendy Blum

Printed in Italy

1   3   5   7   9   10   8   6   4   2

Library of Congress Cataloging-in-Publication Data has been applied for.

ISBN 978-1-9821-7119-3
ISBN 978-1-9821-7121-6 (ebook)

For Rebecca, Gia, and Frankie.
Because, because, because.

Contents

1.

Rain Day

Freddie Tyler wakes at six and watches her sleeping husband breathe for a moment. The dog lifts his head from his place at the foot of the bed and jumps off to join her before she slips out the door. Downstairs, she flips the switch by the fireplace and flames spread out among the river rocks.

The coffee sputters and drips as she opens the back door for the dog, Wizard. Freddie relishes the rush of autumn air against her ankles, watches the dog trudge through the dewy grass, goes back in to feed the cat, which has been waiting in the kitchen.

She shouldn't be worried.

Freddie has always loved mornings. She likes the margin she gains when she's the first awake. She likes the way the back lawn outside the window looks rested and raked. She likes the way half the kitchen is dark. The sun through the skylight makes lazy shadows of trees across the wood floors, and she wanders around the house as if she has just discovered it.

Beyond the yard's back fence are two wooded lots, and she wishes she and Greg could buy them so no one ever builds there. The trees are starting to turn, just blushing now with hints of red, and she pictures a deer somewhere tiptoeing its way around. She imagines knowing those lots would always stay the same, knowing they could make that happen. But this isn't a good time to talk about the future.

She breathes the way she heard Greg breathe in bed. She stands by the counter and places one hand on her chest and feels its steady swell and release. She imagines the clean air filling her body. She thinks of their daughter, Addie, breathing in her room, knows she will have to wake up in less than an hour.

These past few weeks Freddie has had a need to save, to hang on to everything—Addie's drawings, receipts, and even land that hasn't been built on. She wants to put yellow caution tape around everything good.

Her intentions for mornings are always optimistic. Yoga in front of the French doors. Or taking Wizard on a walk to Woodsen Park, pausing so she can glimpse the fallen leaves and observe the quiet houses: the papers still in driveways, the cars still tucked in, the lights in windows slowly coming on.

She waits for the coffee and even thinks of writing again.

Freddie used to be a writer. *Used to* the way someone refers to once being a gymnast or having lived in London. How did she let that part of herself get away? The part of her who spent so many hours as an undergrad sitting in a circle of dramatic people workshopping pieces—*pieces* was what the professors called everything. *The piece you submitted.* She even published stories and poems years ago, in decent journals.

Could she find her writer self again, at almost forty? It

hasn't really left her, has it? She is still always, always recording information in her head. Maybe she could write a poem today. Maybe the first paragraph of a *piece* on grief—or potential grief. She knows what she will say. How grief comes in shyly, like a new season. How grief is something else before it is grief. She could write about detecting grief.

She shakes her head. This could all be nothing. This thing with Greg might keep being nothing.

She pours her coffee and remembers the clothes in the dryer and thinks if she just folds five things, the pile won't be so big, and there will still be enough time for yoga. For dog walking. For the beginning of the essay on grief or nongrief. She wipes the spot where the coffee has spilled. She folds two kitchen towels, a pillowcase, a T-shirt of Greg's, and a pajama shirt of Addie's that Freddie holds to her face for a second. She looks longingly at Greg's shirt, the collar frayed, but she thinks of Addie, who doesn't know anything about this. Addie, who thinks a bad day is when *Curious George* isn't on. She feels a swelling in her throat when she thinks of her tiny daughter but shakes her head, clearing the thought. But this little pajama shirt with the horses on it bothers her. It's too brazen in its innocence: horses without bridles, meadow flowers, small squiggles of clouds and birds in the sky. Whoever made this shirt must think nothing bad can happen to anyone.

It's not fair.

She looks around and sees the bananas she bought on the way home from work yesterday. The green has just vanished, and they sit in front of the subway tile backsplash. The con-

3

trast of bright yellow against white stuns her. She used to write about beautiful things: mountains, old red bridges, fields of geese.

On the refrigerator, Addie's drawing of a pumpkin with trailing vines and a thick stem. Freddie sees Greg's appointment card and she straightens it: October 17. One week away. She doesn't think she can wait a week, but then she wishes seven days would last forever. Greg. Her Ken doll, she always called him.

Greg. Still real, still sleeping upstairs in their bed.

Nothing has happened.

Wizard waits at the door to come back in, and she wonders for a moment if Mrs. Crowley could get by without her today. But there are those bridesmaids' dresses—five of them in that awful paisley print—and that miserable Bob Vines who owns the Regent Theater in town wants his pants ready for pickup tomorrow. Now isn't the time to call in sick.

Even if a sick day meant the walk with Wizard, the undisturbed yoga, the newly hatched plan to pick Addie up from school early and go to Shake Superior (Connecticut's newest restaurant chain) for a midday burger and fries, convincing Greg to meet them afterward, could all happen. Maybe they could go to Woodsen Park and watch the kite club, the group of retired men who meet there to fly box kites. They could even drive to the farm with the donkeys and buy gourds and cider. There is a whole world out there—in their small city of Wharton and beyond—that they miss every day.

She crosses her arms. She wishes it would rain. A rainy

day would make it easier to call in to work and say she's not coming.

Her mother always loved the rain. She would sit in the small kitchen with the cherry tablecloth, and smile hopefully at Freddie's father, a farmer, who would look out the window, shrug, and sit beside her, his knee touching her knee. "A cozy day," her mother would say, and it would be. They'd read the paper and later he'd watch *The Price Is Right* while she did needlepoint in the living room. "No point in working in this," her dad would say, and the fire would swell in the stone fireplace, and their grandfather clock would chime, while outside the rain coated the fields of alfalfa, the tool shed.

She would give anything to stay home today—to have one of her parents' rain days.

She planned to write full-time when Addie started school. Now with Addie in first grade, Freddie finally has the day to herself. She meant to write after the conference in Vermont a couple of years ago with Lance Gray, the famous poet.

"You see things," Lance said in that session. He pointed right at her. Others had told her she was perceptive.

"Such a caring, sensitive girl," her mother used to say.

Freddie expected to make tea every day, get the house together, volunteer in Addie's classroom. To write. She imagined afternoons seeing the school bus turn the corner outside the office window, and hitting *save* on her laptop, sighing a satisfied sigh from another day's work. *You see things.*

But when Mrs. Crowley advertised for a seamstress a few

hours a week, Freddie saw the Help Wanted sign and decided to give it a try. "It'll be good to show up somewhere," she said to Greg, who shrugged. She imagined this routine forcing her to make the hours count—that she would get her writing done between dropping Addie off and heading to the cleaners. She feared being unmoored—that the whole day would get away from her. She thought a part-time job would put parameters around her hours, like the lines on a map.

Greg loved the writer in her. He would put on his reading glasses and skim over her drafts and nod and smile. He frowned when she told Mrs. Crowley on the phone that she could start the next day.

This was in August, when they found some irregularity in his bloodwork after his physical, and he started to notice some symptoms. Maybe Greg worried she was trying to make money in case he didn't pull through. Maybe she was—even though money probably wasn't a problem at this point. Greg's boss, Alex Lionel, had treated Greg very well—stock in the company, a generous salary, a new Mercedes a few years ago. Their house was paid off, and they were savers. They were always planning for a spectacular future—a good college for Addie, trips to islands and Europe.

You see things.

To write, she always thought, you have to dive deeper. Maybe she wanted to stop seeing things. Now she likes the certainty of hemming and sewing. She likes that she can usually start over, yanking thread away, if she needs to.

Mrs. Crowley paid Freddie well to alter clothes from

Wharton and the town over, even the town beyond that. After word of a capable seamstress got around, the jobs piled up. Who would have thought? This only started from her mother teaching her to sew, and from her time in college helping out with the costume department.

Now she's with Mrs. Crowley four days a week in that store with all the clothes in plastic swishing around on the automatic rack, the smell of wool and silk, the radio set to NPR or the BBC. Crowley Cleaners is spacious and tidy with its streak-free windows and immaculate entry floor mat. Mrs. Crowley, a tough widow with her "My, oh my" and "Yes, dear" responses. Her shaky handwriting, her efficient bookkeeping. Her weekly checks made out to Frederica Tyler.

Freddie likes being needed.

If she tries hard enough, she can almost forget writing. Forget her goal to put a portfolio together before the holidays, to apply to the Iowa Writers' Workshop. It was a silly idea anyway. How would she ever get to Iowa? The program always seemed like a stamp of legitimacy. She wondered what kind of *pieces* they wrote, what they discussed in small groups.

She hears the toilet flush and the water running. Greg brushing his teeth, as he always does, before breakfast and coffee. When he comes down, his charcoal hair will be slicked in place, his face will be cleanly shaven. He never looks wrecked the way she feels.

Wouldn't she know if he really was ill, if the first round of medication the doctors started him on in August wasn't working?

She plunks an English muffin into the toaster and puts out two cereal bowls. She sighs as she looks at the clock—how do the minutes just rocket by? She tiptoes up the stairs, and waves to Greg as she stands outside the bathroom. He is wearing the black silk robe that he wore for a Halloween costume several years ago—before Addie, before everything. Now it comes out in colder weather. "Hey," he says.

"Well," she says, "the Clark Gable robe has reappeared." He had been going for an old Hollywood smoking jacket look with the costume, had grown a mustache and held a pipe.

He models it. "I think I'll enjoy my breakfast in it." His chest underneath looks solid. He is the most solid person she knows. Once, when they were dating, he pushed her car, the transmission dead, down the street to a safe spot.

"You should wear the robe to work." She looks back at him once more. She can't help it. She tries to memorize him.

Greg splashing hot water on his face. Greg's hand gripping the razor, his other hand in a fist as though he could beat up anything. Greg with his hazel eyes, Wizard lying on the bathroom floor looking up at him.

She touches her daughter's door and is gripped by something aching and slow. Turning the knob, she hears the sound of the humidifier. Addie is so perfect, lying there next to her worn stuffed penguin, her arm slung off the side of the mattress, her Pottery Barn Kids sheet with the parakeets. Freddie should turn off the humidifier, which usually wakes Addie. She should raise the shade. She steps closer to her beautiful girl, her eyelashes so long and still. Freddie cannot bear this, she thinks.

Greg, she thinks. She bends down to kiss Addie's head, backs up, and leaves the room.

From across the hall, Greg raises his eyebrows when she returns Addie-less. "I don't think she needs to go," she says.

"She has school," he says. "She has art today. She loves art."

"I know." Freddie clears her throat. "But she's sleeping so nicely . . . I'm not going in either." She wiggles her toes in her slippers and looks him in the eyes. "Let's all be together." She wants to put her head on his shoulder and weep, but he would hate that.

Greg dries his hands on the white towel. He touches a spot of blood on his neck, a shaving nick. "I have work," he says, and walks past her. "We didn't plan this."

Plan? Does he want to talk about plans, really?

She stays in the hallway and watches him walk down the stairs. She thinks of the small pajama shirt folded on the kitchen table.

She notices the clean line of his neck, how square his shoulders are. She notices his black robe, the way it bounces as he walks. He has to step over the cat, which lies on the middle step. She thinks he shakes his head briefly as he lifts his knee and clears the cat. And then she notices with the last few steps that he holds on to the railing more tightly than he ever has. As if he's bracing himself for something. As if he looks out the window and sees rain.

2.

The Best Applicant

He has come to appreciate gray. Most of the offices at Garroway & Associates are some form of gray: gray tweed chairs in the lobby, gray seagrass wallpaper, swathes of gray carpeting, men and women in gray suits, gray computer monitors, and grayish paintings with orange sunsets. Greg Tyler likes the fog-and-steel feeling the whole place gives him.

In the hallways, light jazz music plays from the satellite radio station, and once in a while, Greg thinks how lucky he is. This is the kind of place he always dreamed about working in when he took finance and marketing courses at BU, and here he is in this office with a view of downtown Wharton. It overlooks the statue with the wishing fountain, the Regent Theater, the big solid Wharton Library where his daughter, Addie, likes to take the marble stairs two at a time, and in the distance, trees and the bridge over the Naugatuck River.

When he was in college, he wore a cologne called Gray Flannel, and he almost thinks he rehearsed somehow for this. Didn't he always know he'd end up here? Didn't he see himself with this office bigger than most, a polished desk and a phone system that looked like it was designed by NASA? Didn't he see himself out with clients with a company credit card, going for drinks at Hamilton's or a long meal at The Dock, where they would pass around spreadsheets and project plans and toast a new merger? Didn't he see this future even when he drove that Volkswagen with the bumper hanging off, even when at twenty he had to work as a bar runner at Sidecar for eighty-five dollars a week? Didn't he raise his hand as high as he could in classes and turn in his papers early because he felt somehow he was inevitable? He believed in this future. He knew he would keep pushing, keep staying late, keep accepting projects and paperwork, always smiling, always unruffled, and saying, "You got it" to whoever handed him anything. He thinks of himself then and can't help smiling. Nervy little shit.

He hands a file to Pamela, who has worked at the same gray desk for almost four decades, more or less. "I'll get right on this," she says. She wears bright lipstick and a starched blazer. He wonders if he will be able to say he did anything for forty years, have a job that long, a life that long.

He will turn forty in four months. That is, he *should* turn forty. Four months has turned into a century, it seems. He can't even think about four weeks. Four months would take him to February. He hopes to be shoveling snow. He hopes to see Addie in her hat and mittens, their dog bounding in newly fallen flakes. His driver's license has to be renewed then, too. He wants all these things. He wants February so badly.

He tries to keep his feet over the pattern divots in the carpet because every so often he feels as though he could swerve, that dim sensation gripping him. So he puts one black shoe down and then the other and tries to look like he's calm. He is one of the VPs here, and he does not have to hurry. Perception is reality, right? No one knows anything except his boss, Alex Lionel, and Greg has barely missed a half day since the diagnosis last week.

In August, after a routine blood test, they called him in, said they were concerned, said it was in the precancer or *smoldering* stage, and it might not progress any further. He hated both terms: *precancer* reminding him of prealgebra, and *smoldering* reminding him of a cheap romance novel.

They told him back then a round of experimental drugs might keep it at bay, keep it from becoming anything. But last week, he and Freddie got the bad news: it wasn't at bay, it was no longer *pre-*, it was more than smoldering. He will always remember that date, October 17, as the day his life was upended. The *ticktock* diagnosis, he calls it in his head. If he's not lucky, it's tick-fucking-tock.

But he can still do an hour at the gym after work most nights, and he swings Addie around when they're playing the space ejector game, and except for his wife's pitying looks and her "*Now* can we start addressing this?" prods, he's holding his own. Sometimes in a whisper, in a quick hiss, he hears the name of his disease rush through his head: *multiple myeloma.* Cancer of the plasma cells. He hates the name: the double *m's*, the way some hospital staff members trip over the pronunciation. He hates his plasma cells that failed him. He hates that his disease is mostly unknown—it could be like anemia or high blood pressure for all anyone knows. None of the serious name recognition of brain cancer or heart disease.

"I would call it a bone marrow defect," his doctor said that first day.

"Bad bone marrow," Greg tsked, mock-slapping his thigh.

"It would do you well to not minimize this," the doctor said.

"Will it make my bone marrow less defective?" Greg shrugged after he said this—yes, yes, he knew he was cracking, and he could feel Freddie's tearful eyes glaring at him. The oncologist with his white hair and starched gingham shirt reminded him of a doctor in a Hallmark Channel movie. If he stops for a moment, he can list the titles on the doctor's bookshelf. He can describe the exact turpentine-and-lemon furniture polish smell that the office had. But he hasn't stopped, and he doesn't plan to. A rolling stone and all that. But he felt something that day about Freddie, some confession in her crying that she loved him and needed him so much. He always knew this, but it was validated in that moment. He remembers leaving the doctor's office and thinking *I am loved* before anything else.

Now it's Alex, his boss, in Greg's office doorway, leaning to the side. Alex, with his face tanned from golfing, thinning hair, thick gold wedding band, an air of expensive cologne, shining cuff links. He hates these new eyes Alex has for him, and the way he never suggests the club anymore, or a long lunch at Martin's Steakhouse—the way he tries not to dump too much on Greg's plate. Some days he wears suspenders or a bow tie. When Alex bought Greg a Mercedes when he promoted him to VP, he said, "Once in a lifetime, kid. Don't get too used to me buying you stuff." Alex who can't do half the push-ups Greg can, but he will probably live to be ninety.

"Mr. President," Greg says. "To what do I owe the pleasure?"

"Just checking on you." Alex clears his throat. He steps in slowly and crosses his arms. He pretends to be looking at the black-and-white photo on Greg's wall of Addie and Freddie— Addie riding the carousel a year ago at Woodsen Park, the ballet dress she insisted on wearing that day, her soft bangs, eyes squinting from the sunlight. Freddie standing beside her grinning, long blond hair looking so beachy then, gold hoop earrings, her expression carefree. When was the last time his wife grinned? When have her eyes sparkled like this? Not for two months, at least. Greg thinks of how he just wants to tell her to relax, *let me worry about this.* He used to be able to make her happy so effortlessly (tickling her sides when she was making a salad, or coming out of the bathroom in his silky black robe), but now with all this, he has to worry about her constant fear.

He is weary already, and he hasn't even started fighting this thing. And now Alex is worried, too? Greg feels like some tragic man in a Greek myth who saddens everyone he meets.

"Checking on me? What am I, a soufflé?" He selects *compose* on his email. "I'm just in the middle of writing Edie at Home Walls."

"Greg, what does Freddie say?"

Greg stiffens. He looks up from his computer screen. The empty email window beams at him. "About what?"

"Are you going to keep doing this?"

"Doing what?"

"*Doing what*," Alex says. "Avoiding your illness."

"Illness."

"Yes, your illness."

"You make me sound like Emily Dickinson in a white nightgown." For some reason, he always pictured the poet in bed in a nightgown, scribbling on parchment.

"Oh stop."

"You stop." *Et tu, Alex*, he wants to say. *Don't you know me better than this?* Nothing has happened yet. He's still trying to figure things out. Until then, can't Freddie and Alex call the dogs off and let him be? He feels betrayed. *Haven't I proven myself to be more than a quivering sick man? Didn't I oversee a huge merger less than a year ago? Didn't I save clients who were all but signed off on leaving? Haven't I kept Freddie and Addie wanting nothing?* Just over a year ago, he ran two marathons in one summer. Can't Greg be the one to tell them when to worry? Don't they know he will wrestle and clobber this thing? That is who he is.

Alex goes to the door. "Pamela, Mr. Tyler and I are going to have a quick meeting."

"Sure, Mr. Lionel. Anything you need?" she says outside.

"We're fine," Alex says, and closes the door softly.

"Thanks for not broadcasting my *illness*." Greg pushes back his desk chair and looks out the window. The leaves are that fully awake color that will only last a day or two. A woman below pushes one of those horrible double-jogging strollers, and he wonders if he will lose the ability to move something like that, to lift the dog into the car, to carry fence posts on his shoulder.

"I want to know what the doctor says, and what we're going to do. The doctor doesn't say to do nothing, I assume."

"Yes, he says I should make jokes about it and keep showing up at work."

"Then you need a new doctor." Alex takes off his glasses. His eyes look strange without them. He rubs his cheek and sits in the leather chair in front of Greg's desk. "What are we talking here—chemo, radiation? Stem cell transplant?"

"All of the above, my friend. You should see the binders I get to read, and all the appointment cards we have on the fridge. It's just a parade of great stuff waiting for Greggy."

"I'm sick with worry about you."

Greg's stomach flips. "Stop."

"Stop?"

"Yeah, stop." He pauses. Looks down at the computer. He pushes his keyboard hard, hard enough to make it skate across the desk, and puts his arms behind his head. "I'm not worried, so you shouldn't be."

Alex does a half laugh, half sigh. "You're not worried?"

"No, do I look worried?" He tries to flex his chest, his arms, as though he is standing at attention for some type of military inspection.

"Yes, I think you do."

"I shouldn't have even mentioned this to you." He shakes

17

his head. "You're treating me like that egg experiment I did in high school."

"I want to help. I'll get you in to any specialist. I'll hire a consultant who can explain every medical term at your appointments. Shoot, if I have to fly you to Switzerland, I will. I think of you as a son. *You know that.*" His voice wavers with emotion when he says this.

Greg shakes his head. He sees fear in Alex's eyes, he sees uncertainty. And after what happened to Alex's son all those years ago, Greg realizes saying that word is a big deal. *Son.* He feels honored. This makes his eyes burn, and he swallows hard. "Then you should know me better."

Alex gets up. "Should I call Freddie? Should I talk to her instead?"

"No."

"That's what I thought."

"What you should do is stop looking at me like I'm a fucking porcelain doll. It's insulting."

"Insulting?" Alex sighs. "I don't think many others would be insulted."

"Isn't that why I got to this point in the company? Because I'm *me*. I work my ass off, sick or not." He touches his chest. "I've got to keep moving." He inhales. "I can't *stand* this."

"This is beyond work, Greg. You can't even see that, can you?"

"No, what I see is that my travel has been cut down to almost nothing, that you're giving all the good stuff to Franklin and Jean. What the hell do either of them know?"

"Greg."

"I hate Franklin. He doesn't win anyone over. Smug little wimp."

"Greg, this is your *life*."

"Is it?" He thinks of the double-M name for his disease. He thinks of his bad plasma cells, his defective bone marrow. He lets Alex's word *life* roll around in his head. Life. What is a life? Is this really his life? Has he used up most of the good times already? The effortless way he and Freddie would hold hands walking around downtown after dinner, Addie skipping in front of them. A Sunday where the three of them would climb into bed in the afternoon and watch a movie. A spring day where he'd soap up the Mercedes in the driveway and spray it off. All that traveling for work—the excitement of wheeling his bag behind him in the airport, the old clients who remembered him, the new ones he had to impress. He loved crashing at some hotel later those nights, ordering room service and spreading out in the middle of the bed, calling Freddie and Addie and saying I love you, I love you. God, this whole thing has been love: with Freddie. With Addie. And life, too. He loves his life.

He hates himself for not being better at this. He always figured if, God forbid, he got some disease, he'd be valiant and humble. Not this prickly thing who spits in the face of a wonderful wife, a caring boss, an excellent doctor. "Well, I want a *life* where I'm not sick."

He feels his limbs go weak, feels light-headed. He was never dainty like this. He forces himself to stand, and he walks

19

to the window, keeping his back to Alex. "I can't be sick," he says. "Alex, I can't be sick."

His throat aches, and a familiar feeling comes over him from when he was a boy, a sadness so deep he feels like it will never go away—the sadness when his grandmother died, the pain when he fell out of a tree and broke his collarbone. He feels like a little kid again. Scared. He starts to weep. He doesn't want to leave Freddie, Addie. He imagines Freddie will let Addie sleep in their bed at night, rubbing her back while she cries.

He doesn't want them to cry for him.

He doesn't want them to eat their dinners alone at the small kitchen table. He wants to be with them every part of the way— he wants to see Freddie get a book published, he wants to see Addie go to school dances. He wants to help her with an economics paper when she's in college someday, even if she calls him at two in the morning. He wants her to get married to a guy he can teach to play golf; he wants them to have children whom he and Freddie can invite over for sleepovers and cook waffles the next day. He has thought about all of this. He wants to be in this office until he's seventy. He wants to keep seeing the next season. He squeezes his eyes shut, but the tears come anyway.

He feels Alex's hand on his shoulder, and his head slumps forward like a resting marionette. There are pigeons on the roof of the building below them, and the guys are on their suspended platform squeegeeing the windows across the street. He sees a plane creep by in the empty blue sky, and he lifts his head and wipes his eyes with the side of his hand.

"People get better all the time. Every day, someone in a hospital is fixing something. Thousands of people go in sick and come out cured. Every day that's happening," Alex says. His voice is a low whisper, and Greg loves this man for saying this. He wishes Freddie would say this—that she wouldn't look so uncertain. He wishes the doctor would say, "We're going for a cure. Nothing less."

"But I don't feel lucky. I've won too much already." He thinks of Freddie, beautiful and perfect with the winks she gives him, the way he can look into her eyes and know exactly what she wants to say. He knows the patterns of her breathing, how she'll inhale sharply before she says something important, how she'll barely breathe at all if she's waiting for him to say something. He thinks of the Mercedes he feels so proud of, even years later, how he grins when he gets into it every morning, the familiar sag of the leather seat, the confident way it starts up. He thinks of this job in its old, classic, gray building. Their peaceful house with the light blue door. He thinks of Addie. How she looks into his eyes while she talks to him about planet names she invents. How she leaves misspelled notes on his bedside table (*Dady I mis you*). He shakes his head and sighs.

"You're always a winner. Why should this be any different, huh?"

Greg listens for false cheer in Alex's words, but hears only sincerity.

"Yeah," he says. "Maybe." He remembers pressing the elevator button in this same building all those years ago and shaking Alex's hand the first time. He remembers what he said when Alex asked his plans: to keep developing his skills and have his responsibilities grow. He was only twenty-two. He remembers how Alex trusted him with clients right from the start.

He remembers, too, how Addie saw his framed MBA degree from Yale (he did the executive program while he worked full-time), and she wanted to know what Yale was. A school, he told her. Not far from here. "Maybe I'll go to college there, too," she said, "and you and Mommy can drive over to see me whenever you want." He remembers showing her pictures of the campus on the computer, how he promised he'd take her on a tour there. Why hasn't he done it yet? How many promises has he made her that he hasn't made good on? Skiing in Vermont, visiting Disney World, Hawaii. He thought there would be so much time.

Will she even remember his voice? Will she tell people about him?

"Let me help you," Alex says. "Let *us* help you. Kay loves you guys. We can make dinners, watch Addie, walk the dog. I know you don't want charity and that you don't need help. It would just give us an excuse to be with our favorite family more."

"Thanks," Greg says. "Freddie tried to get me to stay home a couple of weeks ago."

"Listen to her then." Alex claps his shoulder the way he used to do after a round of golf, and Greg aches for that old feeling when nothing else was going on.

Nothing else.

Now there is nothing else besides this, he thinks.

He could call his life perfect if he weren't dying.

They stay in silence watching the cars on the street. He sees the fountain below, and in his head hears the splashing sound it must be making as the water cycles through one layer to the next. He sees the old St. Vincent's Church steeple and tries to make a wish on it. "Alex," he finally says.

"Yeah?"

"Thanks."

They walk toward the door together. Maybe after this, he'll go see Freddie. Maybe they can drive to Yale when Addie gets home from school. Yes, he will take her to Yale. He will make time. He will carry her if she gets tired of walking.

Addie and Yale. How many kids her age care about college? Does she already have some notion of what she wants in life? He did. He always did. She is a little force of nature. She seldom blinks. She is so precise when it comes to her drawings, her clothes, the way she situates her stuffed animals on the bed.

Could she feel like she's inevitable, too, the way he always did? For a second, he is proud. But then he doesn't want her to feel inevitable. Maybe he jinxed himself that way.

When he applied for the job, he was the best applicant. He felt it in his blood, in every cell. He had the firmest handshake, the best answers to the questions. He was so damn alive and on fire. He made sure his shoes gleamed when he walked into this building.

He doesn't want Addie to care about any of that. She should just be free. He wants to blurt that out like an epiphany. He wants her to keep skipping. He wants her to hold two halves of a peach in her hand the way she always does and keep staring at the fruit with wonder—as if it contains a secret. He wants her to jump rope, to keep giving a voice to the dog and cat. Hell, he wants the dog and cat to live forever, too. He wants her to know that he did all he did, that he tried so hard in everything—in school, in work, in being a husband and dad. He wants her to think that what he did—all this stuff—was enough. To know that she and Freddie were the most of all of that. The most he could ever ask for.

He grabs his bag and nods at Alex. His throat hurts so bad that he has to whisper. "I'll keep you posted," he says quietly.

"Yes," Alex says. Greg holds his car keys and walks past the picture of Freddie and Addie, past the round table where he usually sits for meetings, and he can feel something has changed—maybe the sun outside has gone behind clouds, maybe the music in the hallway has gotten quieter. He can feel his boss watching him—as if he's the applicant again and just had an interview—and he opens the door now and slips away.

3.

Care Is Costly

Darcy Crowley will scold them later. She will get on the phone when she is back behind her desk, the invoices stacked on the filing shelf, the door closed so the seamstress won't hear, so customers who come in won't hear, and she will *tear them down the strip*, as her husband, Von, used to say.

She will let them have it. This afternoon. After coffee, after the stuffed tomato she'll get for lunch. She will blot her face, she will take a breath, and they'll be sorry.

But for now she stands outside the row of garages. Somewhere she hears the unmistakable chirp of a cardinal. The Open sign for Mercury Storage blinks on and off. There are about twenty parking bays in the lot, and she sees where the window to hers has been broken. The hole is large enough to hoist a slim person through. Why hers, out of all the garages?

She stands in the empty lot, and it's so clean she could almost count the pebbles. It's that time of year, she thinks. That perfect sun of October, the sky that feels as if nothing can happen. Down the street, she sees a woman come out of Dairy

Land with two chocolate vanilla twist cones, and cars come by and then disappear around the sharp turn.

She shakes her head. Why didn't someone tell them that windows were silly on garage doors? Glass is so fragile. They were asking for this.

This is a business, she will say, and you have a responsibility not to let things like this happen. Don't people use cameras now? That's how burglars are caught. That's how her neighbors, the Ellersons, showed her a picture of a bear that visited in August. *A damn bear*, Von would have said. *Right across their front grass like he owned the place.*

She cannot not think of Von.

Ten years now. Ten years and that laugh—she can still hear its bounce, its echo.

His wavy hair, almost all gray, but with that trace of blond from when he was young—the hair they made him cut when he was in the service. His sloped back, his watch always ticking with its gold stretchy band. During that first year, how often she reached into the drawer to pull out his watch and wind it. How often she slid it around her small wrist (feeling selfish for not burying it with him). It would hang there and she would stare at the space between the watchband and her arm.

She can close her eyes and hear him talk. She often thinks of what he would have said. *Is this a garage or a playground for criminals?*

She had to be so tough. Taking over the dry cleaning place in her late fifties, when all her friends were retired or retiring, when she had hardly ever written a single check. The kids said she had enough money (the savings, Social Security, his pension), but she felt vulnerable. She got a business going she knew nothing about. She read for nights and nights about how dry cleaning worked, and how to outsource most of the cleaning and pressing services while still pulling in a nice profit.

She has had to stand up straight these ten years, pretend she has grit when she feels she has nothing.

She faces the keypad outside the garage and slowly punches in her code. The motor starts to hum, and the door lifts slowly. She feels as though she's in a horror film, about to see something terrible. She holds her purse and hugs it against her body.

Her eyes adjust to the darkness. Her foot kicks a small piece of glass—probably one the garage people missed when they swept up the mess.

First, there is just dust, as there always is: dust on the headlights, dust on the hood with the swirl she made with her fingers the last time she was here. Dust on the tires that have lost their air, dust particles in the sun that peeks through the broken window. On the wall is an old poster she didn't put there with a war bond slogan—Care Is Costly—featuring a soldier with a troubled expression, a bandage wrapped around his knee. She focuses on the car, and sees what they've done.

"Von," she says, and her lips are so dry. "Your car."

She walks over and touches the hood. Broken glass from the side window. *I could have fixed that*, she thinks. *Glass is glass*. But then she sees the gashes in the convertible top. Three gashes each at least six inches long. She walks closer. An empty

Doritos bag inside, a cigarette burned into the leather seat. "Hoodlums," she whispers.

She wants to promise Von she will fix it. She has learned from his dying that there is much she can do. She has also learned some things are unfixable. Which is this?

His 1964 Lancia. How he worshipped that car. It hardly left their own garage for twenty-five years. He would wash it weekly without fail, rub that special cream polish into its seats. He would get that flicker in his eye and say, "I think we're taking Betsy out tonight," and a Betsy night was always a better night. He would wear the aviator sunglasses he kept in the glove box, and he would smile when she'd take that scarf out of her purse and wrap it around her curls. "Ooh, the movie star's with me."

She never should have brought Betsy here. She failed Von by putting her into storage. She hiccups with guilt and makes a noise that sounds like a sob. She wants to find the people who did this. She wants to hold their shoulders, shake them and ask if they knew what kind of man her husband was.

In the trunk is a soft wool blanket. Do they know how many times Von took her to the overlook and they sat on that blanket and stared at stars? Do they know how he covered their children with that blanket at a drive-in picture?

She wants to kick something.

She thinks she could kick Betsy, even.

Darcy is ashamed. She always thought she'd come here one day and rescue the car. Wash it again the way he used to, or take it on a road by herself where the trees were high, and the breeze would blow through her hair, and she'd miss Von properly—finally—but she'd tell him she was okay. *Look at me doing this. Driving her for you.*

The truth is she couldn't stand looking at Betsy. Every time she'd come out to their garage to get into her own car, the sight of Betsy would give her a sudden leap of hope: just that second-long trick was too much. She had gotten rid of Von's truck when he was sick. "I ain't gonna be hauling concrete blocks anywhere anymore," he said. "But when I'm better, we'll take Betsy all the time."

She remembers first telling their son, Luke, about the rental garage. Sweet broken Luke—broken from his girlfriend, Ginger, leaving; broken from his father dying; broken from the pain of always being too sensitive and never being able to shake things off. She remembers his sullen face when she handed him the keys so they could put Betsy in storage, and she followed him the five miles in her car.

How she watched Betsy with regret that day, its navy blue body gleaming, its simple red taillights, its small rectangular window and cloth top. It was wrong to be putting the car in storage, wrong to have made Luke drive it with all his father's touches still inside—Von's sunglasses in the glove compartment, his plastic bag of quarters for the tolls.

She pauses now and thinks about Luke in the driver's seat. How defeated he must have felt putting his dad's car away for good. Maybe that's what led him further into that world: the pills, the drinking, the—whatever else.

Maybe she had asked too much of him by having him

help her do such a heartbreaking task. Wasn't that the person she always was—the woman who asked too much of everyone? Making their daughter, Mary Jane, practice and practice the scales on the piano when she was in junior high, shaking her head at Luke because he wore a shirt that was too wrinkled, getting the lawn service to come back because they left some grass clumps around her alstroemeria bed.

She clutches her purse and walks away from the garage. She will be relieved to get back in her own car. To run to the market for muffins, and to the bank with yesterday's deposit. She will relish being at the cleaners where she can sit in her small office for a few minutes and settle herself.

That day they brought Betsy here, Luke stepped out of the driver's seat. She can still see the scene as if it's a clip played on repeat. The car made that soft clicking sound it always did after it was driven. The interior light switched off when he gently closed the door. Luke put his hand to the windshield and glanced inside one last time. She remembers thinking how he looked like a young Von then: the light whiskers on his face, the way his shoulders slumped just a bit, his ears, his jaw.

"That's that, Mom," Luke said. He held the keys with the plastic Hula dancer on the key chain in his palm. He smelled vaguely of cigarettes. He looked at his feet, and Darcy said nothing. She was always too complicated a woman, too restrained. He worshipped his father. Those two hardly ever fought. Von would always be thumping him on the back or flicking his ear. "Hey, Lukey," he'd say.

The day they put Betsy away, she should have gotten out

of the car. She should have hugged Luke. She should have just given him the keys and let him take Betsy. What would that have meant to him?

She longs to have a do-over. She would go back to that day. She would stand beside her son, reach for his shoulder the way other mothers do. She would have said something smart like, "I know, dearie. I know."

Darcy opens the door of Crowley Cleaners. The stereo is not on, and the room seems odd without the usual sound of "Mainly News," an NPR segment she looks forward to. She hears the hammering sound of the sewing machine in the back.

Tabitha, the thin college girl who works the register two mornings a week, gives a shy wave. "Hey, Mrs. C," she says.

"Good afternoon, Tabby," Darcy says. "I brought mini pumpkin muffins for anyone who's interested."

"Definitely me," Tabitha says. She gently plucks a napkin from the pile Darcy places on the counter. Her fingers hover over the tiny brown muffins and she picks the smallest one.

The sewing machine whirrs behind them, and Darcy can see the seamstress Frederica in her cubicle, hunched over the green paisley bridesmaid dresses for that wedding. They look like a tapestry, not like wedding attire. She wonders what kind of wedding Luke would have had if he had married Ginger, that sweet girl who called the house all the time. The one who went on to become a veterinarian in Georgia.

Behind Frederica are spools of thread and a bright spotlight angled on the sewing machine. Darcy wonders if Frederica will be able to see the redness in her eyes, the tiredness of her face under the makeup, but when Frederica looks up, there is something parallel in her expression. Something so defeated or frightened that it almost makes Darcy gasp.

Darcy holds her hand to her heart, and the two women stare at each other—so equivalent, it seems. Frederica's eyes are devastated. What has happened? What has broken? She knows Frederica has a husband and daughter—a perfect family. Did he leave her? Is someone sick? Maybe one of her parents?

If Tabitha weren't here she would go to this woman, her seamstress, a few years older than Mary Jane and Luke, pretty and fragile with her blond wisps of hair in her face. She would hug her the way she should have hugged Luke those years ago. "Whatever has happened, dear?" she would say. She hears the words exactly as she would say them: *Tell me. It'll be okay. You'll see.*

She thinks she would send her home, to go fix what's broken. She surprises herself by feeling she would do anything to help mend this. Darcy wants to hold Frederica against her like she's her third child. She knows, she knows, what it's like to feel that type of pain.

"I can't believe it's fall," Tabitha says as she bites a muffin.

Frederica holds Darcy's gaze for a moment longer, and then there is the chime of the door and a burst of talking: the

Peruvian woman with her two small children who sometimes bring Darcy drawings to hang below the cash register.

Darcy shrugs and watches Frederica as she shakes her head as if clearing her mind. Frederica angles one of the dresses a different way, and the machine makes its reliable pounding sound.

Oh life. Oh broken glass.

4.

Hurts

Luke Crowley lies in bed, arm folded behind his head, and watches his new girlfriend, or whatever she is.

Hannah stands in the kitchen with his T-shirt over her body and pours herself a poor man's mimosa: Korbel champagne and Turkey Hill orange drink. "Cheers," she says, and holds it up to him.

He gives her a half smile. Her hair is mostly blond, but the ends are dipped in pink, and he likes the lines of her body: smooth long legs and the way the shirt stops just below her ass. She has two tattoos, but he likes that only he can see them and that they're covered when they go out. He likes the earrings she wears, large hoops or the silver ones that dangle like feathers.

His mother would size Hannah up and roll her eyes. "Next in line," she'd say, clicking her tongue. The pink hair would set her over the edge (*So we're into punk rock?*). Hannah says *gonna* and *wanna* and chews too loudly. His mother would probably disappear into the kitchen and whisper a prayer, and when she'd talk to Hannah, she'd use that awkward voice, the way someone talks to a foreigner or an old person.

Oh well.

He looks at Hannah and lifts the covers. "Want to come back?" he asks. His morning voice is hoarse from too many Camels, from shouting over the music last night at Rocco's and telling her the band sucked and he could have played better.

She winks at him. She sips her fluorescent mimosa and places it on his kitchen table—among the binder pages with his artwork, the scattered bills, the measly tips (mostly singles) from his shift Thursday night, the invitation to his niece Lizzie's party (so colorful and promising against his sad stuff). She tiptoes in his direction over the scuffed hardwood floor and lifts the shirt over her head. "You rang?" she says.

The party is at one.

He stands out on his small balcony overlooking the city, in frayed sweatpants and no shirt, even though it's on the chilly side, and smokes. He tried to keep a plant out here, but it died in the early frost a few weeks ago. Now it sits like a brown squid in the planter.

Another planter next to it is filled with cigarette butts, and there is a folding chair someone was throwing away. The city is gray today, and a couple walks by in J.Crew-style coats holding hands, gripping white coffee cups, making the most of the morning. A fit woman jogs by in a sports bra and leggings, and a father and little daughter come out of Let's Bagel with a large paper bag. The girl wears ladybug boots and marches ahead. Luke blows smoke out of his nose.

He has got to clear his head. The party is at one. He hates when things are at one. Too in the middle. Either be at ten in the morning or six in the evening. He hates the middle of the day.

It takes at least thirty minutes to get from Wharton to his sister's house in Middletown. His sister, Mary Jane, has probably been awake since 4 a.m., arranging the napkins in a perfect fan and trying out some alcohol-free punch recipe from Pinterest. He guesses the party will be circus-themed, since the invitation showed Lizzie in a lion tamer's costume. Why didn't he hide the invitation from Hannah? What if she asks to come? Should he bring her to stuff like this? He's not ready for that. *Keep that can of worms inside another bigger can*, his dad would have said.

Mary Jane will have made her husband, Alvin, wire up some complicated red-and-white tent and spotlights to the garage ceiling. There will be a tower of cupcakes and a clown walking around. She may even have enlisted their mother to pass out cotton candy and small bags of popcorn. He shakes his head.

He feels his back being touched. "What are you getting her?" Hannah asks.

He cringes. She knows. He turns to look at her. The sun is in her blond hair, and there is this girlishness about her he never noticed beneath all that eye makeup. Her eyes are light green, and he imagines his father saying, *She's a looker, Luke*, and doing that thing where he'd push up his eyebrows a few times. Luke lights another cigarette and keeps staring at her.

"Sorry," she says. "I saw the invitation."

"It's okay." He sighs. "Yeah, a day with the family," he says, hoping she won't ask to come. He touches her cheek, and he wants to love this girl. Why can't he? Because of the disapproval from his mother, his sister? Because she's not who he pictured he'd end up with? He sees two extra holes in her ear, and feels let down. By everything. By the day getting away, by the fact that he hasn't bought a present for Lizzie, by the fact that he's not showered yet and just wants to play his guitar and climb back into bed with a white pill or two. He wants to be better than this guy who stands around in the cold morning with his raspy voice. With his mistake tattoo on his rib cage, another mistake tattoo on his left shoulder.

He wants to bring Hannah to the party and not have his mother whisper to Mary Jane. For him and Hannah to be that couple he saw below with the expensive coats and coffee cups and good degrees and a Range Rover. He wants to wash that pink shit out of this girl's hair because she'd be so beautiful without it. He wants her to wear a sensible sweater and a piece of heirloom jewelry and stop blowing bubbles with her gum. Stop chewing gum, even. He wants his own hair to be cut better. His face to be clean-shaven. Has he been clean-shaven once in years? He wants his shirt to be tucked in and pressed.

He wants to put Lizzie on his shoulders and not have people wonder if he will fall over. He wants to be asked, just one time, to babysit his niece, his favorite little person. To make a blanket fort with her in the living room and watch a Disney movie and make her some kind of cool uncle specialty sundae.

At the party he wants to say something about circuses that doesn't sound drug fueled and foolish.

"I didn't get a gift yet," he says.

Hannah stoops and picks up a few stray cigarette butts and places them in the planter. "Let's get dressed," she says. "A kids' store just opened on Walnut Street that has old-fashioned toys like Lite-Brites and Barrel of Monkeys. We can go there." Her eyes are so hopeful, and he can imagine her as a younger girl. As the quiet C-plus student with clothes from Kmart whom teachers overlooked. He wonders if she had the opportunities he had (his father paying him twenty dollars to weed-whack the lawn, his mother proofreading his sixth-grade paper on Lyndon B. Johnson), and feels worse than before.

He wants to hold her hand. To tell her how some nights all he can see is his dad gasping in his hospital bed, that awful fucking tube in his throat. The way his dad lay there, pale with his muscles sagging, in that humiliating gown, loose around his neck, all those tubes and wires trailing from his arm.

He wants to tell her how his dad—the guy who lifted a slab of granite with one hand, the guy who told Luke's baseball coach who was twice his size he would flatten him if he ever talked to his son that way again—looked like he was drowning with that tube in his mouth. Luke's sister sobbed, and his mother was silent, and his dad was wasting away. How his dad scribbled on a piece of paper, "Hurts."

Hurts. How Luke has thought of that word every day for the last ten years. What do you do with hurt? All this hurt.

Luke wants to tell Hannah how it feels to disappoint your tough-bird mother (who has to say he looks tired every damn time she sees him) and your sister who is perfect and did all the right stuff with a cheerleading trophy and a graduate degree and an adorable child—and even disappoint a dead father who meant everything to you. How it feels to be the guy who can barely keep a waiter job, a gig in a band. He wants to tell her, but he doesn't see the point. She is his sad reflection in the lake, isn't she? She is just as hurt, drifting by in the same way. Both of them lost and broken for no apparent reason. What's the point of talking about it?

He realizes he hasn't responded to her suggestion about going to the toy store. "I'll figure something out," he finally says. "I need a shower." He shrugs, leaving her standing there in that T-shirt, the cars going by below, her pink-tipped hair lifting in the wind, the church bell ringing faintly (maybe a wedding, maybe a funeral) in the distance.

It is noon, and he stands in the toy shop holding a Bozo the Clown Bop Bag and a wind-up scuba diver toy Lizzie can play with in the bath. Hannah was right about this place. He should have brought her. Now he regrets ignoring her attempts to help him out. God, he regrets everything these days.

He hopes no one else got Lizzie these things; he hopes they're the type of stuff a four-year-old would play with. He hopes his credit card will go through. There is nothing worse than when that shit happens: the irritated look on the clerk's face, what he imagines the people behind him think. He looks like a guy whose credit card gets rejected, doesn't he? Even today in his green-and-navy-striped polo shirt and one pair of jeans that isn't ripped. This is as close to presentable as he can get. He thinks—*thinks*—he paid the minimum a week ago. Forty dollars or something. He got the rent in at least.

The store is busy this Saturday. One hippie mother with too-long wavy hair is letting her kids run around freely, pulling pink rubber balls out of the plastic bin and giggling madly as they bounce. A divorced dad (he thinks) is guilt-buying a mechanical robot for his small son who barely answers his questions. The cash register is an old-fashioned one, and the gears inside ring and the drawer thuds open. "Have a fun day," the cashier repeats over and over. She wears one of those multicolored propeller hats and a purple vest. Every so often she puts on an oversized foam hand to wave at kids and parents coming in.

It's too crowded. He feels hot in this six-person line, and he wishes the hippie's kids would stop screaming. He scratches the four-day scruff on his face and regrets not shaving. Why is everything so hard? Some days, he barely does two things and it's already four in the afternoon. He means to scribble song lyrics in the notebook he bought. He means to try to book some solo gigs. He has to get clean.

He sleeps too much, regrets it all the next day. He looks down at his shirt and jeans. He reaches into his pocket and puts a Lifesaver into his mouth.

When the door chimes again, he looks absently over to see what chaos is now coming through, and he recognizes the face right away. He is stunned, and his heart somersaults. Older but still as gorgeous: Ginger Lord, his girlfriend in his early twenties. Is he really seeing her? It feels surreal. It feels like he's not standing there and she won't see him. He wants her to see him. He has thought about her so many times. He has even looked at the online reviews of her vet clinic (*Dr. Lord is patient and sweet; The vet is the saving grace of this place; She held our old cockapoo and said he was a handsome fella, which made us feel instantly comforted*). Her light auburn hair is shorter, and she wears less makeup, dressed in a denim jacket, long sweater, and boots. She always looked Ivy League but never overdone. She notices him right away.

"Luke," she says, her eyes so wide, her face delighted.

He pretends to be surprised. "Oh, hey." She comes closer, and he doesn't know what to do. Should he hug her? His hands are full with the large Bozo box. Right away he can smell the familiar perfume: Chanel. He looks down at his boxes as though offering an explanation for not touching her, but she doesn't make any effort to come closer. "What are you doing in town?" he finally asks.

"Just here for the weekend." She smiles and tucks her hair behind her ears. "I'm actually going to be in Suzette's wedding next month—remember her? The bridal shower is tomorrow at The Manor House."

"Suzette," he says. "Yeah, I remember her. Didn't she move to Iceland or someplace?" This sense of being so familiar with a person feels like what he's been missing. He suddenly just wants to smile. He feels like he can tell Ginger anything. He stares into her round eyes, so sincere, and is proud of her. He knew, he knew, she was headed for good things. She was easily the best thing that ever happened to him, wasn't she? He has a flash of memory of the day they broke up before she left for Georgia. Late summer. Her dog lying lazily on her parents' porch. She kissed his forehead. *Be good to yourself, Luke*, she had said.

"Finland." She grins now. "She only stayed for four days."

"Huh," he says. He advances in line, and she stays near him. He likes that she doesn't try to leave just yet. "So what brings you to toy heaven?"

"Oh." She looks around. The cash register jingles again, and one of the hippie's children is on the floor in a full-blown tantrum. "One of the other girls in the wedding asked if I could get some kind of princess crown for Suzette to wear tomorrow when she opens her gifts." She rolls her eyes. "Always something, right? My mom told me about this place."

"Well, you'll find that here."

"Definitely." The man who's paying is writing a check, which makes almost everyone in line sigh and grumble. But Luke marvels at his luck. His body remembers her. At a time like this, waiting in line, their hands would reach absently for one another. He remembers the feeling of her standing behind him and resting her head on his shoulder. He remembers how she closed her eyes whenever they kissed. Now here they are, both in their thirties, but sensing her so close makes him feel like he's twenty-two again.

He and Ginger had been broken up six or seven months when his dad died—is it really ten years now?—and the night he came home from the hospital, when they left his dead father there in that quiet room with the nurses starting to take everything apart, when he held the small cactus someone had bought his father and the *Sports Illustrated* rolled up that he meant to read to his dad, and the stack of cards people had sent, that night when he came home from the hospital, he remembers how Ginger rang the doorbell. She was home for spring break in her first year of vet school.

He heard her soft footsteps coming up the stairs after Mary Jane let her in. She stepped into his room without knocking and hugged him and let him sob and sputter into her light blue turtleneck. She rubbed his soaked face and kissed his cheek, and kept saying, "I'm so sorry, Luke," and listened to him bawl and talk in a way he never could with any other person. At the funeral, he glanced back every so often, and there she was in a far-off row, smiling dutifully at him. And then she was gone.

"So how's work?" he says now. "How's Savannah?"

"I love it," she says. "But it's too hot sometimes." He notices an emerald ring on her finger and wonders if a guy gave it to her. Maybe she's married. Could she be? He feels a familiar wave of disappointment, but what does he expect? Who wouldn't be lucky to have Ginger? "It's so nice to be here in the fall. I caught the leaves at just the right time."

"You really did," he says. He looks down at his toys. "Do you know Mary Jane has a kid?"

"I did see that, yes. She and I exchange messages on Facebook every so often. Her daughter looks like you, I told her."

"I don't know about that," he says. Something about her keeping in touch with Mary Jane makes him feel grateful. As if they could get back together and it would be seamless. What a silly thought. He wonders if she and his sister ever had a heart-to-heart, if Mary Jane ever says things like, *If Luke hadn't been such an idiot . . .* The cashier motions him forward.

"All set, sir?" she says, and holds the scanning wand to his purchases. "Some cool stuff here." Luke's palms start to sweat. He pulls the credit card slowly from his pathetic-looking wallet with the worn leather. He wishes he had cash. Cash is so definitive.

"Twenty-four fifty," the cashier says.

He hands her the credit card, and she swipes it. He doesn't breathe until he hears the paper printing. She tears off the first receipt and hands him an oversized purple pen. "Sign here."

Thank God. Thank. God. He holds the shopping bag. Ginger waits for him by the door. "I guess I should go find that crown," she says, and shrugs. She reaches out and touches the side of his arm, such a familiar gesture, and he wants to freeze time, feeling her hand there in just that right way she always had with him.

He knows his mother thinks he ruined things with Ginger.

And he probably did. Of course he did. He had nothing going on when she graduated pre-vet from Fairfield. He could have told her he'd go anywhere with her when she was deciding which program she should attend—Cornell or Penn or Michigan State. She was accepted everywhere.

But his dad was sick, and things with Jimmy and Murph and Chucky were going great. Their band had a monopoly on all the local haunts—two gigs a weekend sometimes, and he was happy doing that. His hands on the guitar, the encouraging audience, the way he and Jimmy would lean in to each other on the songs they'd cowritten and belt out the words. He loved being onstage and in the moment, forgetting all the bad stuff: his dad's eyes when he would sit feebly on the back patio and stare at the trees, his mother's insistence he find "something stable." Looking back now, he wonders what he thought he wanted then. Did he just want to go on that way forever because nothing bad had happened yet, or did he have future plans—maybe a record deal, marriage? A home with Ginger where she could run her vet practice right out of a downstairs office? Had he ever gotten that far in his mind?

Yes, he remembers hoping all that would eventually happen. He remembers thinking they'd have a nice Connecticut home where he wrote lyrics or banged away on his drums in the basement, her coming downstairs with some injured animal in her arms. "I couldn't leave him in the cage for the night," she'd say. But he was so damn afraid of the future then. How could he wish their relationship were further along when he knew it meant his dad would be gone and Luke himself would be older with fewer and fewer chances of having made it (didn't you need to make it when you were young?), and, God, his mother's impatient prodding. Ginger's future was so bright, it was guaranteed to be bright because that's who she was, so where did that leave him? Her definite future made his feel scrawny. At times he was jealous, wondering what it felt like for everyone to know you'd end up well. For him, it was only if he stayed with Ginger that he'd be successful, and that slowly ate away at him.

Ginger stopped coming to their concerts, and one night he kissed that girl with the eyebrow ring behind the stage, and he drank more than he should have, slept more than he should have, started messing with pills Chucky gave him. "Are you okay?" Ginger kept asking. "Fine and dandy," he'd reply.

When Ginger said University of Georgia offered her a great scholarship package, he said, "Hey, go for it. Take the midnight train, right?"

He wanted to trick her with that pathetic statement. He wanted her to say she might go far away but he was worth waiting for. He wanted to feel good enough for her. He needed convincing, didn't he? He wanted her to ask him to visit whenever the band wasn't playing. Maybe he wanted more fight: them to fight for their love the way his father was fighting for his life. And he felt betrayed. Why in the world would she choose a school thirteen hours away?

He didn't know about the uncertainty of right then, but he had no doubt they would be together down the road. He wanted Ginger to say no place would be right without him.

She didn't. The girl with the eyebrow ring was the proof he needed. Their kiss was too dry, too foreign, and he bolted from her immediately afterward, saying, "Sorry. I'm sorry." He only loved Ginger. He wanted to know she loved him as fully and as achingly as he loved her. It was a childish want, but he needed to be sure. If she had said she needed him, he would have quit the band then, wouldn't he have? He likes to think yes. But her eyes looked so hurt after he said she should just go without him that he still tries to forget her expression. They were sitting in his car in her parents' driveway. She had just moved out of her apartment. Her eyes were red, and he saw the late-day sun hit the small diamond on her necklace. "Be good to yourself." She closed the car door gently, and he watched her walk inside the way he always did when he dropped her off.

He meant to fix it. He meant to call her in Georgia some night, have one of their epic long talks, and all of a sudden, he'd be buying a train ticket, or she'd be in town, and little by little they'd reclaim what they had. But as the months went by, he knew she was doing better and better, and there he was, right where she'd left him, sinking.

Now, at the toy store he tries to stand straighter (the way his mother would instruct). "Well, I hope you have fun at the shower," he says. "It was great bumping into you."

"You, too, Luke."

"If you're ever in town again, we should—"

"Yeah," she says. "Say hi to your mom and Mary Jane, and happy birthday to your niece." She starts to walk away.

"Um, do your parents still have Thunder?" He has no idea

why he asks this. It's been ten years, and ten years is an eternity for any pet. But in his head their border collie is still the puppy that used to love that red whistle ball Luke would throw. The happy dog that used to let out a certain bark when Luke's car would pull up, and Ginger would say, "We knew it was you. Thunder told us."

"They do. He's still kicking. He rides with my dad to the post office every day."

"That's awesome."

"You should come see him," she says. "He'd remember you."

"I should," Luke says, and waves to her as she heads toward the back of the store. She turns sideways past a little girl winding the handle to a jack-in-the-box, and she smiles and helps a young boy who dropped puzzle pieces on the floor.

"There you go," she says to the boy, and she glides behind the next rack, her shoulder bumping a set of chimes before she's finally gone.

5.

Yes to Love

The green paisley dresses are not a hit.

When Ginger agreed to be in the December wedding, she imagined velvet gowns. She imagined snow outside the reception hall, lanterns in the trees. She imagined a grand Christmas tree and poinsettias on the tables. She did not envision this scratchy green paisley with a small fur collar shawl that made her feel like an American Girl doll from the Victorian era.

The other bridesmaids are incredulous as the seamstress kneels at their feet to pin the hems. Cameron, who is tall and lithe, who does CrossFit and Pilates on alternating days, who in high school had two football players fight over who got to escort her out on the field during homecoming, doesn't even look good, and she'd look good with an army surplus blanket draped around her body. The cut of the dress is boxy and thick, and the waist is too high. "This is *not* what I pictured," she says. "I look like Oscar the Grouch."

"You don't like them either, do you?" Cecilia, Suzette's grad school roommate, whispers to the quiet seamstress who appears to stare at the lopsided faux fur shawl Cecilia wears. The seamstress in her V-neck orange shirt and fall boots, who looks good for forty or whatever she is, takes a moment to register the question.

"Well," the seamstress says. "They wouldn't have been my first choice." She scribbles a note on her small clipboard. "But I've gotten fairly used to them over the weeks, and they're definitely one of a kind. The bride seems to like them, no?"

"Tuh," Cameron says.

"She's just doing a psychology experiment on us," Cecilia says.

Ginger stands off to the side and tries to like herself in this dress. She squints and thinks about Luke Crowley with his messy hair and those complex eyes. What are the chances she'd run into him? She forgot how easily they could start talking, how sincere even his smallest words could be.

She wonders if he still sings. She can hear his voice at the concert at Woodsen Park singing "The Air That I Breathe" that Memorial Day when they were twenty-one. She remembers how the people in the audience stirred with the chorus of that song (*And to love you . . .*)—with Luke in the T-shirt she had bought him from Macy's—how the retirees, the teenagers, and the young kids on their mothers' laps stayed still and just watched him. He was young and charming, his voice smooth and gravelly all at once. The sky wasn't dark yet, and the pink magnolia trees were in full bloom. There were strings of lights crisscrossed above his head, and he hit every note. She remembers looking up at him, and the old woman who sat next to her, who saw her get to her feet as she listened, hands clasped with pride, tapped Ginger on the arm. "You're smitten," she said.

Now Mags, who is the most petite, steps out of the dressing room. She has it the worst, Ginger thinks. She looks a bit like a Weebles toy. Or a character who rolls out with a prophetic message in a Tim Burton movie.

The bell dings on the front door, and Suzette, the bride, comes in with her old Louis Vuitton bag over her shoulder, her hair light with beach waves, a car key dangling from her hand. She glances from girl to girl, and her eyes sparkle. "My crew." Ginger is always amazed how Suzette has this way of instantly disarming everyone she meets. Once you get past her nonnegotiable level of beauty—her sturdy cheekbones, her smooth, blemish-free skin with perfectly placed freckles, she is warm and sincere, with eyes that laugh and a powerful hug.

Suzette looks at you and makes you feel as beautiful as she is. Ginger has never heard her say a bad thing about another person. She remembers how quiet Suzette got when her older sister Lisa died, and as a counselor how many forgotten teenagers in the foster care system Suzette had given her own jackets and scarves to, stuffed twenties and fifties into their hands, told them to call her day or night. Ginger adores Suzette, regardless of these dresses. "Well?" Suzette says now.

There is a moment of stillness, five girls in green paisley stand before the trifold mirror, and the seamstress looks up at them and lifts her eyebrows. Ginger is the first to speak. "They are so elegant," she says. "I feel like a winter queen." The other girls quickly chime in with, "Love them!" and, "So original," and Suzette touches her heart and smiles.

"You all dazzle." Suzette stands behind Carrie, her younger sister, who came in with her and quickly got her dress on. "Wow. The pearl necklaces are going to be amazing, and the white pine branch bouquets . . ." She shakes her head and smiles. "It's all coming together."

Ginger glances down. She can't look at the other girls. Seven weeks to go. "She'll be in Vera Wang," Cameron said earlier, "and we'll be waddling in like my grandmother's curtains come to life."

Later, the seamstress at Mrs. Crowley's shop helps her out of the dress. Ginger stares at her own arms and quickly covers herself up. It feels glorious to get the itchy dress off her body. Couldn't they request a softer lining at least?

"Okay," the seamstress says, and slides the dress onto a hanger, holding the faux fur shawl over one arm. She jots down a few notes. "You're all gorgeous girls . . . don't worry." She pats Ginger's back before closing the curtain. Ginger is not worried, she wants to say to the departing seamstress. She was shocked initially, but she'll get over it. She's worn worse. Most days at work, she can't keep a shirt clean: cat vomit, bird blood, you name it. The wedding and dress and all this will come and go. She'll be back on a plane the next day. Just like tomorrow. After the bridal shower, she'll board her flight, making her way past the older couple holding hands or the fearful young parents with a baby on the seat between them, or the college-age couples who always seem like they're going to a beach somewhere, who lean in every so often to kiss.

Ginger pulls her hair back into a sloppy bun and slips her clothes back on. She hears Mags whispering loudly to Cecilia about the dress. Even the girls who didn't know each other have bonded over their hatred of paisley, but Ginger doesn't care. She cares that she will come to the wedding alone, without Johnny. That she will leave the wedding and sleep in her brass bed with the ruffled comforter at her parents' house and then fly home alone, her paisley dress still on the hanger in her old bedroom.

She is disappointed not to have seen Mrs. Crowley, Luke's mother, here, but of course right now she's at that birthday party probably holding a garbage bag to pick up stray napkins, maybe having a quick taste of cake. "My figure!" she always said when Luke tried to get her to eat pizza or have a scoop of rocky road.

Ginger wonders what she would have said to her. When Ginger first heard the fitting was here at Crowley's, she imagined coming in the front door, and Mrs. Crowley looking up from the register. "Heavens, Ginger! Is that you?" She imagined hugging her, that smell of Mary Kay moisturizer and hairspray from a fresh wash and set at the hairdresser's. Though Luke's mother put him down—she really did, hardly ever coming to see him sing, always telling him not to slouch or asking what dumpster he got his shirt from—Ginger felt nothing but love from the woman. "Darcy Crowley's so clenched," her mother said once, "she could make tree bark into paper."

"Not once you know her," Ginger had said. She looks around the dry cleaning shop, and it is all so her: neat and sterile with precise notes on the dressing room doors about garment fitting instructions, and a sign by the cash register about returned checks. Behind the counter, instructions for the employees about turning lights off and putting fifties and hundreds in the safe. Oh, Mrs. Crowley. Such a time capsule of a woman, but still so modern.

Ginger used to love to sit back and watch her in action: barking at Mr. Crowley about how long to leave the meat on the grill (he'd just raise his eyebrows and ignore her, chuckling); clearing the dining room table after a big meal in mere seconds, not letting anyone help, or ordering a new gadget from a home shopping channel and insisting it would improve their lives (a toothpaste dispenser, a cordless phone with an intercom, a posture perfect desk chair). Ginger looks at the sweater over one of the chairs in the back and knows it belongs to Mrs. Crowley: a lilac color. She can just see her slipping it on and off throughout the day. What a gutsy woman, starting up a business from scratch that she knew nothing about after her husband died. Where did she find the nerve? Ginger hugs her arms to herself and wishes Mrs. Crowley would drop by right now. She misses her as much as she misses Luke, doesn't she? The seamstress then comes back to the counter, smiles politely, scoops up all the dresses, and lays them together in a pile that looks like a green rowboat in front of her. "Back to work," she says.

"Thanks for your help," Ginger says, and waves.

Out in the parking lot, the girls hover around their cars. The sky is clear and blue, and the occasional leaf slowly zigzags to the ground. At the intersection only one or two cars get by before the light turns red. Ginger hands the toy crown to Cameron after Suzette and her sister drive off. "So about one o'clock tomorrow to set up?"

"I'll bring the champagne," Cameron says.

Cecilia buffs out a smudge on the door of her RAV4. "Have paisley dreams, ladies. And we've got to talk to Carrie about bachelorette weekend."

Ginger nods. She opens the door to her mother's van. After this she will pick up the heartworm pills for Thunder, a six-month supply with stickers her parents can put on the calendar. She should check in with Johnny. She should. But the idea makes her feel uneasy. She breathes. Being back in the old neighborhood, so near the park where Luke sang that summer night, with the small Italian restaurant where they would sit at the lopsided table and drink cheap wine, with Luke's parents' house just a few blocks away and the bike trail where they would ride their matching Trek bikes to the lake with a picnic in Luke's backpack, she can't think about Johnny.

She looks at the ring he gave her. The alternating emeralds and diamonds. "Must have cost a pretty penny," her mother said when she saw it.

"I guess," Ginger said (even though she knew exactly how much, which was more than she ever wanted a piece of jewelry she wore to cost).

She should call Johnny, but she turns the radio on as

she pulls out of the parking lot. Madonna is singing "Like a Prayer," and she gets lost in the words as she drives past the string of factories and then Woodsen Park. The stage is empty, and she can still imagine Luke standing there. Twelve years ago. Twelve. She remembers when she could subtract twelve years from her age, and it would take her back to being in elementary school. Now twelve years takes her to still being an adult. Luke onstage. Luke. His guys in the background on drums and bass, Luke's voice the great connector between them. She swore some women cried. Even the men mouthed the words. *Yes to looooove you.* And it wasn't just at the park. At the small clubs, at the backyard parties, when Luke sang, a stillness came over the crowd. He could switch from Sinatra to Elton John to Bon Jovi, and he made it his own. He was that good. Did he know he was that good? Did she ever tell him he was better than any guy on the radio? She loved him before he sang, but, God, the power of his voice made it impossible not to crumble.

It wasn't just his voice. His voice was rock solid. But he brought *soul* to every song. She hates the word *soul*, it makes her uncomfortable, but it is the only word for Luke's vulnerability, the understanding he seemed to give the sad lyrics, the happy ones.

Does he still sing? She hopes so. But wouldn't his sister post a picture of him at a concert every so often on Facebook? Wouldn't Ginger see his name anywhere when she searched it? Luke Crowley. Luke and the Killers. Nothing. If he doesn't sing, what does he do? What else could Luke do? She should have asked him, but she sensed something was off. She knew the question wouldn't make him happy. How did she still understand him so well?

She should think about Johnny. She is lucky to have him. He's probably in their apartment right now. Johnny, with his slight southern accent and dark, dark eyes, his tie loosened, his Burberry oxford shoes and Rolex. He says, "How goes it?" whenever he sees her, holds her hand when they're out, and will listen when she talks about a cat that bit her or an old dog that died from anesthesia on the operating table. Johnny, in his late thirties, has a son named Jeremy, eleven, who lives forty-five minutes away. He loves that kid, and seeing them together, seeing how Johnny would die for this boy, makes Ginger love him more. Johnny's got a deal in South America on the day of Suzette's wedding and can't come.

Leda, her neighbor who has been in the building the longest, sized him up. "Looks like a young Paul Newman. Charming," she said.

In the beginning of their relationship, Johnny would drop by her office to see what she did. To see her checking a kitten's throat or filing down the teeth of a pet bunny. The other ladies—the vet techs, the receptionists—would watch him the whole time. "*Where* in all of Georgia did you find him?" one said. "Holy hotness," another said, and the fact that he smiled at them, that he joked with them, too, just made him more popular. But Ginger finds there is a limit to his charm. She hates to say it, but she could sometimes take him or leave him—and she doesn't know why. When he goes on trips with

Jeremy, like the two-day skiing vacation they took last winter, she feels a thrill when he leaves, when she knows he'll be gone. As soon as the apartment door closes, she silently celebrates. She hates that she feels this way. He doesn't deserve that.

Maybe it's Luke's fault. Maybe she can't trust anything to be real—even something that appears to gleam with certainty and possibility—since her first major relationship dissolved the way it did. She should call Johnny right now. She should say she misses him. She does miss him. She does. She misses his sounds—his throat clearing, his burpees and push-ups in the apartment, his fingers hitting the laptop keys, his blender whirring with a protein shake. She misses the way he stands behind her and says, "How's my girl?"

She knows she shouldn't think about Luke. Ancient history. She just wonders why she saw him. Maybe the universe wanted her to. Is the way she felt when she watched him sing, when she would wake up next to him in her apartment and just study his silent lips, his long eyelashes, how she should always feel?

The day his dad died, she wanted to never leave him. She never felt a person just disintegrate the way he had: his face slick, his breath bad for the first time. She knew, knew he was using something at that point. She never knew what. He slept too much, he would be too punchy when he'd call her late at night. Was it terrible she didn't think badly of him for it? That she just thought he was sensitive, and sensitive people felt things so deeply, to the point where it could wound them. If he needed to take a pill or two, smoke a thing or two, even though she was never, ever that person, wouldn't she be able to get him back to where he should be? But she couldn't. The day she returned to Georgia, after his dad's funeral, it was March. It was still so cold. The ice hung on the power lines, the ground was frozen. She remembers thinking "Come find me, Luke" when her plane finally was cleared for takeoff.

But he didn't.

Two years now with Johnny, and he will probably propose soon. Why doesn't that make her happy? He makes her happy. He does. She loves his smile, his sense of humor, juggling apples and imitating Leda's voice perfectly. She loves to lie naked with him on a Friday night—to go away with him to Jamaica, a bed-and-breakfast in St. Simons. She thinks of a poem she read once: *This is what the living do.* Yes, this is it. If you're lucky enough to have someone like this, you never let them go. You love them back, fully. But at the end of the day, she can't ever see herself wanting to do what Suzette is doing; she doesn't want to walk down the aisle toward Johnny.

She forgets to stop at the vet's for the heartworm meds. She passes right by. She turns off the radio and knows she shouldn't drive over to Luke's old house. But it's so close, she feels like she needs to.

Mrs. Crowley's house—does she really live there all alone now?—sits on a charming street. There are rocking chairs on the front porch and electric candles in every window. The same stone swan sits at the top of the porch steps, and on the door is a rope wreath with an autumnal bow.

Ginger sees the basketball hoop in the driveway and re-members how she and Luke would stand out there in summer and he would guard her, but then back off so she could shoot. She sees the hydrangea bush and remembers the white one he picked for her. How it dried perfectly to a brown-pink and she kept a piece of it for years and years in her jewelry box. She may still even have one last petal in there.

She should call Johnny. She should say, "I miss you," to him. She should tell him that they should take Jeremy someplace fun soon—to Michigan fishing, or to one of those kid-friendly island resorts. Maybe you get out what you put in, and she has not put enough effort into Johnny. She wants him to be right. God, how she does. He really is a decent, lovely man. She thinks of him talking to Jeremy—that kind, kind voice he uses. The way he can't resist pulling his son to him and kissing the top of his head. She thinks of the way he holds the door open for her, how he reaches over when he's driving and puts his hand on her leg. She could marry him, couldn't she? Couldn't she?

She pulls over for a moment and dials his number, but she is on Luke's street, and it feels disrespectful. She hits *end* before it rings. Luke's neighborhood has not changed one bit. It makes her happy to know this: the trees, the driveways, the streetlights. Time has barely touched this area.

She wishes she had gotten Luke's number. Maybe she

would suggest drinks now. Tell him to drop by and see Thunder, who would certainly wag his tail and remember his old buddy. She stares at the clear road in front of her as she starts driving again and waves at the two little girls playing hopscotch on the sidewalk. What's done is done, she thinks. Luke looks okay—mostly. A little disheveled, his wallet a bit bare. How could she even think about getting wrapped up in that again? Who knows what his story is? Maybe more drugs. Maybe unemployed. Hell, he may even have a girlfriend. Five girlfriends. What does she know? Does she need all that? But that sad smile. Those eyes. God. Her heart is thumping fast, and she hasn't felt this nervous in years. She has never cared as much about anything as she did about him. That is what she is feeling now: the leftover particles of the care she once felt. What do you do with that?

Her phone rings in her lap, and she jumps. It's Johnny. Maybe he can sense that something is different, that she's gone to a place right now she won't be able to return from. She ignores the call.

When she came home this time, she'd hoped to see Luke. She wished for it, and *poof*, there he was, waiting in the toy shop like a gift. It has to mean something. Luke. Goddamned Luke. She imagines him onstage singing each word, holding each note, watching her, her always waiting for him out in the audience.

6.

Trying to Wake Up

Dear Mom,

I want to say I'm sorry for how I acted at Lizzie's party. I had a lot going on that day, and the thought of Betsy being ripped apart made me feel crappier. When you said I smelled like smoke, which you always have to say, it got under my skin, and then you said calm yourself, which I hate, and then you exchanged looks with M. J., so it was a triple whammy. But I shouldn't have snapped at you. I know it's your job to say stuff like that, and if I had a kid (which I don't don't don't, no panicking necessary), I wouldn't want him to smell like smoke either. My point is, I get it. I get why you worry.

I started this letter and thought I knew what to tell you, but I think the only thing I want to keep saying is I'm sorry. I'm sorry I'm a waiter. Sorry I don't have anything going on that you can tell Patty and Helen at Bridge Club about, or that I messed things up with Ginger, and that I quit playing Grandad's trumpet, and that I dropped French my junior year in high school, and that I didn't do that internship you wanted me to do at Garroway & Associates, and that I look like hell when you see me, and that I still haven't taken my drum set out of your basement. I'm sorry about all of that. I wish I was more like M. J. She is such a together person, and I watch her with Lizzie and wish I could have turned into something kind of the same.

Yesterday, I walked a few blocks to the Regent Theater because they are hiring a special events curator. For a second, I imagined myself there, more serious, working as part of the team, maybe even holding a clipboard and fountain pen, and it excited me. I didn't know how I'd convince them, but I wanted to. I stood up straight. I wore a wool coat. I held a folder with my résumé in it. But when I got to the main door, a woman in the lobby asked if she could help me. I froze. I couldn't do it. The ceilings were too high. The floor was too polished. The whole place seemed so big to me. I had to just reach for a brochure and leave. I don't know what that's about.

I'm trying to wake up. I'm trying, Mom. I wish something in me would snap, that I'd be closer. Closer to what HE was. Man, I still can hear his voice so clearly. Can you? I wish I could fix Betsy with my own hands, that you'd see me driving her *and you'd feel proud, and somewhere, wherever he is, he'd feel good about me, too. It hurts. It hurts that I'm like this.*

Maybe it's better if you and I don't see each other for a while. Maybe we should just write. I don't want to fight with you. Maybe I can be better soon.

Love,
Luke

7.

The Blue Bicycle

There are some things Alex Lionel can't accept, and one of them is that St. Vincent's switched to electric prayer candles a few years ago. As people shuffle out of five o'clock mass, he and Kay make their way to the front of the church. He rests his hand between Kay's shoulder blades on the peacock-blue coat she's had for years. She limps slightly from her broken ankle over the summer (she slipped on their wet deck steps) and his elbow has been bothering him (too much golf?). He wonders how they became an old couple all of a sudden, slowly making their way up the aisle.

He smiles at Theresa, the organist, who has just lit her own candle, and he nods to Will Garlin, who lost his wife last year. A boy in his twenties with longish dark hair and an old overcoat sits in a pew by himself in the middle of the sea of polished wood, looking up at the ceiling. He holds a book that Alex thinks for a second is a Bible, but then recognizes it as *A Separate Peace*, something Benny read once in school.

The priest is gone, the lights are dim. The electric candles flicker in their fake way, but there is still something touching and holy about the whole thing. The ceilings reach high, and in a few weeks, they will bring in the poinsettias stacked in a pyramid behind the altar, and place greenery along the aisle.

"Do you have money?" Kay asks, and Alex holds a ten-dollar bill in his hand and makes it dance for her.

"Silly." She stands in front of the candles. Her face is still young in the glow, and he cannot believe they have been together for fifty years. They met in college. He remembers asking her to lunch that day, how she turned her head to the side. "Lunch?"

"Yeah, in case you don't like me," he said. "Soup and a grilled cheese at the diner, and then I'll be out of your hair."

"I love diners," she said.

He remembers the jukebox playing "Tracks of My Tears," the way he felt grown-up all of a sudden when the waitress offered him coffee and he accepted, and then Kay accepted, and he whispered to her, "I hate coffee, by the way," and she giggled and said, "Me, too," and he knew, he knew he loved her. Right away. This girlish woman with her high ponytail and white blouse. The light pink polish on her bitten fingernails. The woman his friend Lawrence said looked like she could be Audrey Hepburn's little sister the first time he saw her at the college library.

Now Alex looks at Kay, her hands resting on the shelf in front of the candles, and he wishes she would put her hair up in a ponytail again. She doesn't look much different from that day at the diner—even with all that has happened. Lucky her. But he feels a hundred years older, even though he is healthy.

Once in a while, he still thinks he gets a glance here and there from a hostess at the country club or one of the middle-aged females in his office. He tries to keep his weight down. He still does the treadmill four times a week, and golfing keeps color on his face.

He notices the three rows of flickering candles. Only about half are lit. He doesn't remember the price per candle—how petty, he thinks, but shakes his head—maybe he will put in a twenty just to be safe. He has never minded giving the church a bit extra.

"How many are you doing?" Kay asks. She presses one button, and whispers something he can't hear as the square flame snaps on. He wishes there were still the stick matches in their small glass jar. He loved holding the match briefly, watching the vigil candles come to life as he and Kay tried in their own tiny way to change things over the years.

"Four." He knows she can only mentally account for three of these, and that's why she gives him the sideways confused glance as she lights her own. He doesn't offer any clues about his mystery candle. He wants to tell her about Iris. His stomach flips and he gets that crackling feeling in his neck.

The first he lights is for Lawrence, his good friend, the best man at their wedding. Alex can still see him in his tailcoat dancing with that bridesmaid, champagne in one hand, a cigarette in the other hand. Lawrence. Killed after only a week in Vietnam. *Always with me, pal*, he thinks. Kay will be lighting ones for their four dead parents, for her aunt Ginny who is ninety and in hospice now, and probably for their neighbor who just found out she has breast cancer. And then she will spend the most time on her last one.

He is surprised Kay hasn't bent down to take out her rosary. She believes so much in these candles, in her beads, in her words whispered to the stained glass above them. She has so much reason not to believe, but she still believes.

He'd like to think that Lawrence is smiling down on him, that both their parents are nodding solemnly somewhere as they wait to greet him and Kay, that they'll get to see who they want to see most when they die (What would that reunion look like? *Is it really, really you?* they'd say), but lately he wonders. He wonders about the reality of life and death. What if this is all there is?

He looks over at Kay. Behind her is the scene of Mary holding the dead body of Jesus. Kay has been just as brave and noble, hasn't she? The dark red carpet below their feet is so thick that it hushes his thoughts, and in the pews, he sees an old woman sit by herself and blot her face with a handkerchief. He wishes he could go to this woman, put his coat on her shoulders as some type of comfort, even though he's sure she has her own coat, but he has to stop this business of wanting to save everyone. He smiles meekly at his wife.

If he tells her right this moment about Iris, what will she do? Will she stare at him with that pitiful, crumbled face she can get and grab her purse and limp away from him? Will she wait by the car outside in the chilly November air and not talk to him? He breathes slowly and lights a candle for Greg Tyler, whom he can't stop thinking about. *Be good to this one*, he thinks—if there's someone who can hear him. *He needs you.*

His heart stings for Greg. The last of the good boys. Okay with only four hours of sleep. Never, ever said no. Greg the American Dream. Greg whom he could send anywhere: Mexico, China, the Middle East. A younger, better version of himself. That sweet wife. That outspoken little girl Kay buys Christmas gifts for. The Tylers have had them over for dinner a few times, and their home was one of those places you don't want to leave: the sun setting, golden on their hardwood floors, the cat in its bed, the old dog by the fireplace. "You did pretty well for yourself," Alex said, squeezing the back of Greg's neck. He had never done this to anyone, felt this fatherly to one of the company guys. *Fatherly.* That word makes him ache.

"Will you say something for Gregory?" he whispers to Kay, and she nods. He always feels Kay has a better line to the holy network.

Can Greg beat this? Of course he can, can't he? The guy can run a six-minute mile. People aren't dying the way they used to, but Alex knows better than anyone about tragedy. *We are guaranteed nothing.* Lawrence's words in the only letter he would write home.

Alex thinks of Benny then and the blue bicycle, how twisted and mangled it looked. He always tries not to think of that bike. His first instinct was to bend down and start untwisting with all his might. He wondered if they could loan him a pump for the deflated tires when they showed it to him in the back of the police car.

He closes his eyes and tries to cast that image away. *Greg.* Think about Greg. Greg who's still among the living.

Greg's eyes, his quietness: he knows it's bad. Will Greg be able to know what he knows and shake this? Alex hopes so. To stop working and do the treatments and listen when the doctors say to rest? He can't imagine Greg Tyler in a hospital bed. He can't imagine Greg in pajamas, lying still. He watches the candle he's lit for Greg, and can't help but feel powerless as the small lightbulb flickers its best. *You can do this*, he thinks. We are rooting for you.

Kay whispers a few more things, rosary beads now in hand. The heavy artillery. Good. He turns around and notices they are alone in the church. The long aisle, the gleaming wood of the pews. In the back is a framed corkboard with announcements and a box where people take the weekly news bulletin. Alex thinks of his third candle. He and Kay each always light their own for Benny.

Could Benny really be dead twenty-four years? He thinks of their son, their only child, the child they didn't have until their early thirties because "God was taking his time," Kay said. The kid who turned fourteen so fast, who only ate Kraft macaroni and cheese and Honey Smacks most of the time; the kid who made a sculpture out of old egg cartons that won an award in the junior high art show. Benny with his ribs always showing, with his cowlick. Benny trying to learn Spanish at the kitchen table, his accent so Connecticut.

Alex tries to imagine him in his late thirties now and can't. He can only see that bike, and for the millionth time, he tries to remember the last moment he had with him that Saturday, and has no idea. Benny was going to Ryan's, Alex knows. He was wearing that Vermont sweatshirt he loved. Alex only knew from seeing it on the floor in the hospital. So much blood. *Can Kay get the stains out?* he wondered as he stood there, hand over his mouth. What was the last thing he said to his son that day? What did Benny's voice sound like? Did he look up from his newspaper or whatever he was doing when Benny said good-bye? *Please, please*, he thinks. *Tell me I did.*

In the days that followed, how quiet their house was. He couldn't say anything to Kay because there was nothing, not one thing, to say. *Do you want him back, too? Do you hate the sound of our house, too? Do you wish you had died instead? Do you keep thinking we can't have dinner because we're waiting for Benny to come through the back door, head sweaty, clothes smelling like outside the way they always did when he played football?* He can see Benny's fine hair, his clear blue eyes. That scar on his hand from carving the pumpkin when he was seven.

He can go back to that time so easily, because he can pin-point that it was his worst year. Kay mostly ignored him those days. He remembers how she'd make herself a piece of toast with honey for dinner and stare out the window. He remembers how she just left the loaf of bread on the counter, as if a vague gesture to him. *This is what we need to eat to stay alive, even though we have no reason to stay alive.* He remembers want-ing visitors on those quiet days, but their friends avoided the house.

How did people survive these things? He wondered that all the time. He would go to work, and everyone would nod politely and look down. He would close his office door and put on the AM news station and listen to the traffic report and the weather and sob in his hands.

Some days at lunch, he'd leave his briefcase below his desk and drive and drive. He would let the cold air of late autumn hit his face and pretend Benny was out biking on the road beside him. Alex would keep driving until he escorted him everywhere safely. When a big truck would come by, Alex would give it the middle finger, a gesture he rarely used. He'd pretend to watch his boy cycle beside his car, beside the stretches of field. "Ride in the field," Alex would say. "Ride where no one can get you."

Then he'd sit at that family restaurant drinking black coffee and maybe have a cup of soup: pepper pot, beef barley, New England clam chowder. The waitress Melinda was always working, and she started saying, "There's my guy," when he walked in. Sometimes she'd touch his shoulder when she brought him the check. Sometimes she would put the coffeepot down and tell him about her day. About her mother who owned the antiques shop in Ohio, about the stray cat she fed. She was in her thirties, and when she smiled, her eyes were almost purple. Like Liz Taylor's.

One day he said, "Your eyes settle me," and when she gave him the bill, she drew a small heart by the total.

Driving to her house that first afternoon when her shift ended, following her old Chevy in his polished black Lincoln, he tried to talk himself out of it, but it was exciting. It was the first time he drove that he didn't imagine Benny biking beside him.

"You sure you want to?" she said, and he nodded.

He went there at least seven times, and she would take off her work clothes as soon as they walked in the door. Once, she convinced him to get in the shower with her, which he and Kay had never done. On his last day there, she poured them each a glass of cranberry juice and put out a plate with Triscuits and cheese. "You know I can't continue this," he said.

She sipped her juice and shrugged. "I figured—sooner or later."

"I shouldn't have." He looked down at his glass but couldn't drink. It was as though he was coming back to life and realizing what was happening. There was no room for her. Because of her, he was saved, and now he had to save Kay. He had to. *I got to the shore—some shore. I'm no longer drowning.* He had to get Kay there, too. The midwinter sun was reflecting brightly off the February snow outside Melinda's window, the icicles dripped with a hint of promise, and he wondered for a second why he never saw dishes outside for the stray cat. "Thank you for helping me," he said. He knew she would know what he meant.

"Don't mention it." She crossed her legs and looked up at the ceiling. "I'll see you around," she said.

He didn't hear anything from her until Iris was four. When the lawyer came to his office with a file folder and the picture of his child, who looked curly haired and serious in the Kmart portrait with the blue background. "What's this?" he said, and the lawyer had humorless eyes, as though he were some sick deadbeat pervert. "The mother of your child would like support for the day-to-day care of your child."

Every time she said *your child*, he thought she meant Benny, and the dizziness he was feeling from this unexpected news was replaced with a tug of sadness. "Tell her I would have liked to have known about this earlier, but I will meet these support requests."

"Does that mean you want to keep it quiet so your wife doesn't know?" the lawyer asked. Her eyes were so dark and stern.

"She knows already about my time with that woman." He lied. "So you may leave the paperwork here and remove yourself from my office." He made a shooing motion, which felt good. Which helped to relieve the rush of worry and sickness that was coming over him.

He told Kay that afternoon. She didn't shriek. She didn't say anything. She nodded as though she really did already know. Her cheeks looked so smooth and polished, and she sipped her tea.

"Well?" he finally said.

She pointed to the door. It was two o'clock, and the sun was steady and bold. The cuckoo clock ticked in the kitchen.

"Please get out," she said quietly. He didn't know where to go. He almost went back to work. He felt shame and guilt and fear about what would happen between him and Kay (he could not lose her—he would fail Benny if he did), but he also felt a faint new possibility. Maybe Kay would come around. Maybe Iris was a solution, not a problem. He went and saw two movies and fell asleep in the middle of the second one.

That night when he returned home, she ignored him. She put on her nightgown and rubbed lotion on her hands. She clicked off the bathroom light as he stood by their bed, not sure if she wanted him there, not sure if she'd tell him to leave again. "I don't want to ever hear a word about this child," she said.

"I'm so—"

She put up her hand. They were fifty then. Why did he do what he'd done? How could he have hurt the only woman he loved? "Pay the bill they send from your office, but never, ever mention this girl."

He nodded. She shook her head and went to her side of the bed. "Is this where you want to be, Alex?"

He nodded again. "Of course."

"Then that's that," she said, and turned off her light.

He lay awake that night listening to the clock over the white fireplace in their bedroom. He looked at her every so often to see if she was still awake. He wanted to tell her they should meet this girl. That it wasn't her fault. That maybe, maybe she could bring something to their lives. But he knew better.

So every other month or so, he met Iris in secret. She was beautiful. Always smiling. She had Benny's nose, he thought. Sometimes certain words she said (*hug, button*) reminded him of Benny's voice. It made him teary but also made him sing inside. He'd take her to the zoo like divorced dads did. He'd buy her new shoes and give her a fifty-dollar bill. "Hang on to this in case you need anything," he'd say. Her eyes would be so big holding the money.

His life seemed to be divided into Iris time and non–Iris time, and he counted the moments until he saw her again. Once in a while, he'd cut out of work a couple of hours early and call Melinda (they were always cordial—not warm but cordial) to tell her to cancel the babysitter, that he could meet the school bus, that he could take her somewhere for dinner. God, how thrilled he was by this girl. He loved to look in his rearview mirror and see her buckled in his back seat as he took her to the park, the miniature golf course, the café. How did the universe know she was just what his empty world needed? Why couldn't Kay give this a chance? He hated sneaking around, but to be honest, Iris was worth it. And he thought he brought something to Iris that benefited her, too: a lightheartedness as a parent, a patience her mother sometimes lacked, a sense of financial security most young parents could only wish for.

What a gift this lovely girl was, what medicine, for lack of a better word. She had a good vocabulary even at six or seven, and she had an earnest quality not many kids had. He watched her become a teenager, and he couldn't believe she still wanted to meet him regularly. "Sure," she'd say. "I could eat pizza."

Never, ever mention this girl. So he didn't.

He wondered if Kay had any clue. When he said he worked late and went to her chorus concert, sitting in the very back row but clapping the same as any parent. When he bought her those skis for Christmas or told Melinda he'd pay for her class trip to Disney. And then college came, and his money went to tuition, to textbooks (when the hell did they get so expensive?), to a meal plan. But he was happy to do it. *That's my girl*, he thought once when she made dean's list.

He felt so selfish delighting in this young person when Kay had nothing else. Over the years, she joined the garden club, a book club at the library, the country club holiday committee, but she still seemed to be languishing. He would find her lying on the sofa with her pots of violets behind her in the window. In her nightstand drawer he found a journal in which she regularly wrote letters to Benny. He couldn't bring himself to read them.

He thought about Iris (his daughter, his daughter) at night when he couldn't sleep. He whispered prayers to watch over her as Kay slept beside him, once in a while reaching over to hold his hand. "You're missing out," he wanted to say. "You'd love her," he wanted to say. Kay had always wanted a daughter. God, how she would have loved to pick out prom dresses or go to the cosmetics counter at a department store with Iris or listen to her talk about boys. Kay was still so girlish at heart, Iris would rejuvenate her.

A few times he tried to mention her, but he stopped when Kay scrunched her eyebrows in that angry way. "Never mind," he'd say.

Now twenty-three and in graduate school for occupational therapy, Iris told him about the baby yesterday. "You're going to be a grandpa," she said. She hardly ever called him Dad— maybe she sensed how complicated that word was for him.

Of course it's too soon, he thinks. Of course she should have waited longer. Of course she barely knows this guy in her program—who she says stays over at her apartment most nights. Maybe, he thinks, she should have considered other options here, but Iris has a good head on her shoulders. A baby. *Grandpa*. He can't help but feel ecstatic.

Now in the church, he watches Kay put her rosary away. He wants her to be a part of this. He thinks of Benny and what they missed out on. He wants to hold her hand, tell her he's sorry for the thing with Melinda, for the shame he brought with Iris, his child that no one knows about. But on the other hand, they could gain something. They could be grandparents. Wouldn't Kay love that? Wouldn't she be as good as she is with the Tyler girl? Couldn't she forget where this baby came from? He wants to say: *She renewed me. She almost, almost fixed me. Let Iris help you, too.*

He rests his hand on her back again and they walk slowly up the aisle. "I have news," he tells her and she looks at him in that way.

"I don't like news," she says, and shakes her head. She can tell from his look. She always can. "It's about the girl?"

He nods. "We need to talk about her."

"You know better," she whispers.

"Hear me out."

"No." She pulls away from him, and he holds back. She trembles as she slowly marches toward the door, barely limping now, her ankle and foot cooperating. "No," she says again.

Alone, he touches each row of wooden pew after wooden pew. He looks at the soft carpet below his feet, and the holy statues in the back. He knows all the fake candles they've lit behind them are flickering, and it makes him happy they will burn through the night. He feels relieved already, but he doesn't know why. He hums some recessional hymn in his head as he leaves. He has to tell her. Outside in the car, he will tell her about Iris and pray she will listen.

8.

Until You Do

The Cul-De-Sac is a new restaurant outside of Wharton on Route 23, about a mile past Crowley Cleaners. Out front are pots of boxwood around the benches, and the dumpsters are off in the corner surrounded by a lattice screen. They designed the interior of the place, for some reason, to look like a dive bar. Bowls of peanuts on the tables (with a peanut allergy warning on the double glass doors), cluttered pictures on the walls, red leather booths, and a cement floor that looks aged but is so clean it almost shines. Freddie holds her daughter's hand as they wait for a table with Mr. and Mrs. Lionel by the hostess station. Servers in black T-shirts and jeans hustle by, and the podium with the menus and pagers is draped in a pine swag. Freddie wouldn't have picked this restaurant, but what can she do?

Her husband pleaded to get out of the house. A round of chemo later, almost two months since the follow-up diagnosis, Greg has gotten so tired of the walls of their home, of her hovering. He sits on the long bench to their left, next to an old woman who keeps leaning over to talk to him. Greg sitting while they all are standing, who would rather die than sit because he never sits. How many times, she thinks, did this man give up his seat for an elderly woman on a bus, on a train, and now there he sits right beside one.

Freddie is surprised she convinced Greg to sit. "I'm fine," he said. She glared at him, hoping the Lionels wouldn't notice. She gave him that *please just do it* expression, and she sees how resigned he looks now as he slumps and converses with the strangers near him. Greg in a blue ski cap because his hair is gone. The woman keeps blotting at her nose with a crumpled tissue, and Freddie wants to rush over there and pump hand sanitizer into Greg's palm. Now she wishes she had let him stand. A cold could be his end.

He looks over at Freddie with his wide eyes, so much more clear since some of his eyelashes have fallen out that she can see hints of blue to their hazel. "Look," he said one day. "Confetti." He held some of the small dark hairs in his hand and blew them into the air. "I hope you made a wish," he said quietly, his voice only half joking.

She tries to make small talk with Alex and Kay, but she can't take her eyes off Greg. Addie twists against her. "I'm going over to see Daddy," she says. Freddie watches her safe passage to her father, and when he says, "Puppy dog!" and scoops her up, something wilts inside her. "Please Come Home for Christmas" plays on the speakers amid the background noise of pagers going off and a group of smiling servers singing "Happy Birthday" to a woman in the distance whose face is illuminated by a brownie with a candle in it.

This place breaks at least four of her personal health rules, rules Freddie never had before. She hates rules. She wants to eat ice cream for breakfast and drive her car for weeks after the *change oil* alert dings at her. She wants them to take Addie out of school for a month and go to Hawaii, to Greece, to a cozy cabin in Maine where the smoke trails out of the chimney.

She has no business doing it, but she has been secretly filling out the application for the Iowa Writers' Workshop (December 15 deadline) for next fall. Why? There couldn't be a worse time for her to start something so many states away. But she realizes she loves the way it is so far-fetched and absurd that it makes her keep wanting to creep toward it. What woman with a sick husband even thinks of something like this? But she will send in her application, she will cross that bridge when it comes. She is sick of rules.

Greg, on the other hand, always loved rules, and he needs her to have them now.

The first rule is no germs. Absolutely no germs, and what are they doing at this place with the old woman and her snotty tissue and God-knows-who has sat where Greg is sitting, and even Addie's hands on his face—did she swing on the monkey bars today without washing them? No germs. She changes their sheets every other day. She keeps Wizard off the bed, out of the bedroom, and the cat in the basement mostly. She hasn't kissed Greg since when? She can't remember. Will she regret not kissing him if something should happen? This thought makes her feel pressure in the back of her eyes. Will she say she should have kissed him? No, no, no. These are necessary measures. If he gets better—*when* he's better—this will have been worth it. *This is how people get better*, she thinks. By wanting it enough to make a thousand sacrifices.

Second rule: she cooks every meal for him. Why did she agree to come here? She washes her hands at least two times as she prepares chicken in a clean pan or lets beef and onion soup simmer on the stove. For the last three weeks, she has cooked everything. That is what the brochure that the nurse gave her said—it eliminates the unknown preparation germs, or chemicals a restaurant might use, so Freddie listens. His compromised immune system needs her to listen.

Now that she has opened her eyes to all of this, she has found out how dirty restaurant ice is, how easily a restaurant can get roaches, how many people might handle their food without washing their hands or wearing gloves. She should have packed a drink for him—a sugar-free soda (sugar is the enemy) with the can wiped off. Maybe she could have brought him a sandwich. "Am I a toddler?" he would have said.

She hardly uses salt these days, too. For Thanksgiving, just the three of them, Addie told her something was wrong with the mashed potatoes. "They taste too quiet," she said, her description summing up the bland potatoes perfectly. Freddie never tastes what she's cooking with her spoon. She wonders if her spit could kill him.

She cooks every meal for him, but Greg couldn't say no to Alex, his boss. He never could. She watches Greg sit there, and the woman next to him in her sweater with the snowman coughs into her tissue. *No, no*, she thinks. She is so close to going over, but Addie is rubbing her hands on his smooth cheeks and he's doing that thing where he says, "Spaghetti . . . Sauce . . ." Then he puffs out his cheeks, and she hits the air out of them while he says, "Meatballs!" He is too far away and the restaurant is too damn noisy, with an office Christmas party in one corner and people crowded around the horseshoe-shaped bar, looking up at the flat-screen televisions. Dive bar. Sure. What dive bar makes "Ho Ho Ho" margaritas?

She shakes her head. Why try to be a dive bar? Why call it Cul-De-Sac? A *dead* end. She winces. She hates how that word creeps into her normal thoughts.

When she met Greg, he was finishing up at Boston University, and she spent most weekends there. They slept in his beat-up twin bed against the wall in the small apartment. He took her to a real dive bar nearby, and they ordered wings and waffle fries and clinked Heineken bottles together. "If we get married," she said then, "we have to go to a place like this once a year at least."

"To remember where we came from," he said.

God. How strong his arm was as he picked up the beer then and lifted it to his mouth, tilting his elbow high so he could drink every last drop. "Two more, buddy," he said to the bartender, and looked at her and kissed the air, making her love him so much that she never wanted to leave that place.

Alex Lionel gives Freddie the *just a second* sign and ushers Kay over to a seat in the waiting area. Freddie loves how Alex holds Kay's arm, and how easily she settles into his support. She always loved old couples—her parents, the ones she sees at the mall, at doctors' appointments. She loves their endurance, the familiarity in their gestures: the hand on the arm, the finishing of each other's sentences, the knowledge in their eyes, knowledge that comes from knowing another person over years and across circumstances. She sighs. She takes a sanitizing wipe out of her purse and quickly wipes off the pager she holds and then her hand before anyone can see. Kay smiles as she sits down, her posture regal, and then leans over and waves to Greg, who is three people away on the long bench. Kay is in a pink mohair sweater, and she wears her brown hair in a pearl clip. She holds her white coat between her knees and takes a small bag from her purse and motions to Addie. "Santa left this in my mailbox for you," Freddie can faintly hear her say.

Alex looks both ways before he crosses the crowded walkway where the servers come through with trays and pitchers of beer and returns to Freddie at the hostess stand. He crosses his arms. "Christmas is right around the corner," he says. His cologne smells like a country club. Like brandy and good soap.

A hostess squeezes by Freddie and calls a table of twelve. "Yeah. I feel like I have nothing ready." She holds the pager in her hand and wonders when it will buzz. Her heart thumps as she starts to panic. Greg shouldn't be here. He shouldn't eat this food. At home, he only drinks distilled water.

"How's he doing?" Alex asks, gesturing toward Greg. As though she could think of any other *he* right now.

"Okay." She wonders how many people have touched this pager. She never used to be a germaphobe. She used to wipe her hands on her jeans after pulling weeds. She never worried about anything then. Dirt. Poison ivy. A kiss from the dog. She drank out of the milk container once in a while. "At least he's listening to what they tell him . . . he doesn't want to stay in the hospital again."

"I miss him at the office." Alex smiles at a woman who comes in with two baby carriers. "Hands full," he says, and holds the door for her. "Twins—can you imagine?" he whispers to Freddie after the woman passes. Alex has nice lines around his eyes. He is seasoned. A later-years Michael Douglas or James Caan. Will Greg ever be his age?

She looks across the people, holding their coats over their arms, some carrying holiday gift bags. Addie is lying on Greg now, her head against the arm where all the bruises are. He doesn't flinch. He holds her there and closes his eyes.

The third rule is that she will not cry. Her role model in not crying is Mrs. Crowley, who always keeps herself composed. She can try to be Darcy, can't she? When she sat in Darcy's office at the dry cleaner's that day in October after the big appointment when their whole world seemed to collapse, Darcy stayed calm and took in every word Freddie told her. She sat at her desk with her hands folded, and Freddie sat in one of the chairs opposite her, slumped over, sharing the news in a low voice.

Darcy's steely eyes watched Freddie carefully. She nodded as Freddie spoke, voice cracking, saying it was bad, saying she might have to miss some days, saying she might have to leave the seamstress job altogether, saying she couldn't even look at

Addie. Darcy stood up then from her desk chair, and it rolled backward and bumped the wall, and she shocked Freddie by rushing over to the seat beside her. She patted her shoulder. "I have no idea what's next," Freddie said, and she started to cry.

"I will do anything, anything to help you, my dear. And I mean that." The blazer she wore was scratchy against Freddie's neck, but the hint of her perfume felt like a blanket. Darcy put her hand under Freddie's chin. "Look at me," she said, and her voice was unwavering. "You will get through this, and you will help him. And I will be with you." Freddie didn't want Darcy to move away from her. She never imagined sharing something like this with her boss, but now she felt like they could never know each other in another way. Something about Darcy's steadfastness inspired her to push forward and confront the disease head-on.

"Thank you," Freddie whispered.

"Anything you need, you say the word," Darcy said. "I'll even send those paisley dresses down the river if you want." She raised her eyebrows.

For a moment, they laughed.

Freddie hasn't been great about not crying.

She cried in the bathroom once, her hands on the white pedestal sink. She cried in the car when the doctor first told them on October 17 that it was much more serious than they'd initially thought. Greg laughed and said, "Should we swing by the gas station so I can start smoking?" She sobbed and slapped his chest and then felt awful.

Now she sees her daughter lying against the father she

loves so much, and Freddie hears in her head a thousand things she could write to chronicle all this. She presses her teeth together. She cannot cry anymore. Even though Greg looks so young and vulnerable with that hat on. *What a shame*, she thinks for a second. What a goddamned waste. A perfectly good person wasted. She shakes her head. She will not think like this. She will not cry. Even though "Have Yourself a Merry Little Christmas" (Rosemary Clooney) plays, and that song always gets her. Something about the longing in the words, the hope and vulnerability: *if the fates allow.* She hears everything differently now.

She could almost start writing. She thinks the words could explode out of her everywhere, like steam through a cracked pipe. For her application, she has been touching up some of her old writing—nothing new. She promises herself she will write again if Greg gets better. What if he doesn't? Will she write anyway?

But she will not cry, not in front of Greg, and certainly not in front of Alex Lionel, who has probably never cried once in his life. Alex who no doubt smiled a stoic businessman's smile at people on the day of his son's funeral and told them he appreciated the fact that they came. How did he and Kay bear all of that? How did they assemble themselves back together like this?

The table next to the partition has a man and a woman with their heads bowed, and that brings up the next rule: she will not pray. She will not say, *Please don't take him from us.* Or, *I will give up my own life for him.* She will not sit in church like a hypocrite and beg for a favor and strike a deal the way some people do, even though she heard Greg whisper, "Please," once. Such a loud, forceful whisper. He still had his hair that day—charcoal gray and thick. He was looking out the window of the den, and Freddie saw all the leaves gone from the trees but a bright and trustworthy sun, a sheet of diamond frost across the grass.

She will not pray because people pray every day, and often the answer is no. She will not ask a yes/no question because she doesn't like one of the answers. But her mother and father at the farm pray. Her mother even mailed her their church bulletin that had Greg's name in it. She imagines all these parishioners praying for a man they've never met.

Her rule for all of this is that she play a part: the strong wife in a movie. Maybe a Meryl Streep role. Something Sally Field could do. She can be this woman who doesn't flinch. Who says *I will not let him die.*

So when the pager starts vibrating, the circles of red lighting up, she holds it in the air as though she has won something. "That's us," she says.

Greg drinks ginger ale at the table (no ice) and Kay leans over to Addie and asks if she can help her color the holiday scene on the place mat.

"The branch of holly? You'll let me do that?" She clasps

her hands together, and her green-blue eyes sparkle. Addie nods. "Why thank you, Miss Addie."

"You're welcome," Addie says. She pulls her top lip up. "See my tooth?"

Alex leans in. "Goody good," he says. "What's the tooth fairy's going rate these days? I used to just get a note that said, 'Maybe next time.'"

Greg and Kay chuckle, and Addie says, "Five dollars."

Alex looks at Greg and Freddie, eyes wide. "That tooth fairy should come to my house." He smiles, and then pulls out a five-dollar bill from his pocket. "Here. For when the other one comes out, in case the tooth fairy oversleeps."

Addie smiles.

"What do you say?" Freddie says.

"Thank you." Addie hands the money to Greg, who has always been the money keeper. Freddie wonders for a second about money. They have plenty, and she does okay at Crowley's with her in-high-demand alterations. But she realizes she would miss this terribly—the way Greg takes care of everything. The bills, the online accounts, the check at the restaurant when they're out together. He always has his credit card ready, always smiling in his charming way, flagging down the server. She imagines a quiet table in a place like this, her and Addie alone. No. She wishes she had a button in her brain that could reset bad thoughts like this.

God, she could write now so easily. She'd have a thousand things to say. This new urgency gnaws at her, as though the words are crackling inside and need to come out; as if she's one of those writers who needs to scribble ideas on a napkin, something she always found ostentatious. She hears phrases (*unashamed sky*). She could write all day and skip lunch. She could write about her rules.

Next rule: only positive thoughts. The dark ones breed and gallop through her mind. She has to steer clear. She has thought too many bad ones already: her holding his limp fingers as he takes his last breath in a hospital, in a flannel shirt at his gravestone. Her alone in their bed the way she was when he spent ten and a half days at the hospital for the first round of treatment. Her holding her sobbing daughter. Her having to answer her daughter's questions. No, no, no. Happy happy thoughts.

"So where did you say you're going next week?" she asks the Lionels.

Kay glances at Alex. "To, um, it's north of Hartford. Just two nights."

Greg sips his ginger ale and smiles as the waitress sets his soup in front of him. "And they made it extra hot?" Freddie asks.

The waitress nods.

Freddie sees Greg roll his eyes. *I didn't make these rules*, she wants to say to him.

When the waitress brings drink refills, Freddie doesn't want Greg to touch his. One glass is enough. She takes a bottle of water out of her purse and tries to nudge it toward him. He pushes it away and takes the new drink from the waitress's hand.

"Perfect," he says, and sips. Freddie glares for a second but then smiles at Kay.

"That sounds like a fun trip."

Kay nods. "Oh, we'll see. It's just a little inn."

"We're going to catch up with friends," Alex says.

Kay starts to say something. She colors a red holly berry, checks on Addie, who is immersed in her coloring, and says quietly, "To be honest, they're not exactly friends."

Freddie and Greg look up. Addie tries to trace her green crayon through a maze shaped like Santa's hat.

Alex looks nervously at his wife. "You should tell them," Kay says. "It's okay." Her expression is calm, her face is relaxed.

"Tell us what?" Greg asks.

Freddie is imagining Alex's retirement. Maybe a house they're buying. She racks her brain, trying to figure out what news they'd have. An illness? Something bad? She thinks for a moment she doesn't want their news. She doesn't want another ounce of change. She wants to hold her hand up in a *halt* signal. She has enough news to weigh her down forever.

Alex looks at Kay, his face worried. His gold watch catches one of the restaurant's recessed lights. Is he trying to read her expression? But Kay nods at him, and he looks relieved. "I have a daughter," he says.

"Oh my," Freddie says. She and Greg exchange a silent glance. They push their knees together. *What do we say?* she mentally asks him. She wonders if her eyes are ten times their normal size. What the hell is going on? Where could a daughter come from? The Lionels have been together since they were in college.

"You do?" Greg holds a pack of crackers in his fingers.

Kay gives them a controlled smile. "Isn't that a shock? She's in her twenties."

Greg puts his crackers down. He looks crestfallen. Freddie worries for him. He shouldn't be under any type of stress. Damn them and their announcement. Freddie guesses he thinks Alex would have shared something like this years ago—during a golf game, during a lunch together, and maybe he feels betrayed or disappointed. But beyond this, she thinks how nice it is to have a true distraction, a real conversation about something besides cancer and treatment and germs. She looks at the Lionels. They don't seem devastated or bothered. It feels okay, it feels good to be lifted away into whatever this is. "What a surprise," Freddie finally says.

"Ta-da," Kay says. She keeps her voice low because Addie hasn't looked up yet. Fortunately, the news seems to go over her head as she slowly plays connect the dots on the next activity.

"Yes." Alex unwraps his napkin and stares at the silverware. "We've, um, been working some things out." He looks over at Kay and they lock eyes for a moment.

Kay nods as the waitress places her salad in front of her. She lets her crack some black pepper over it and then picks up her fork. She frowns and then leans in. "It feels good to just say what you don't want to say sometimes." She shrugs. "Secrets do you no good, do they?"

Alex looks over at her, and Freddie can see relief on his face. "I, of course, made a big mistake." He clears his throat. "But Kay has been so, so wonderful." He touches the space between her shoulders. Freddie can see his posture soften. "We've gotten to a good place with this."

"All it took was some screaming and shouting." Kay

laughs. Her voice is so smooth, but her expression is nothing but earnest.

Good for them, Freddie thinks. *Good for them.* She could write an essay about forgiving Greg for anything if it meant they could get to Alex and Kay's age. She could get over any single thing—an affair, a gambling problem. Two affairs even. She never felt that way before, but now she knows, without hesitation, she could get past anything. She could forgive Greg for a whole list of things, except dying.

Greg just nods. He sits back and Freddie can see his eyes—the distracted look he gets when he digests something unexpected. Alex his hero. Alex with feet made of gold. Freddie thinks about Alex and Kay, about the thousand journeys you make when you've been married many years. All the stuff you survive. All the wounds that heal over. She wonders if one day she and Greg will be old and think back to this horrifying, confusing time and shrug. *Remember when we thought you might be dying?* How lucky Alex and Kay are that they have the power to just *decide* to heal something.

But where the hell did this daughter come from? Did they just find out about her?

Addie tugs Freddie's shirt, asking for her iPhone, and Freddie slides it over to her without taking her eyes off Kay. "Oh, well, it happens. I mean, it happens, right?"

"Yeah," Greg says quietly. He puts his spoon into his soup.

"I made a mistake," Alex says again, and shakes his head. He looks at Greg as if sensing he might have lost his confidence. "Years and years ago—after Benny." Greg nods as he listens. His face seems to soften. Alex: his idol, his father figure, his boss. Freddie bets Greg is over it already. He is too busy trying to live. He doesn't seem to care about details the way he used to. She notices his expression now, and he seems checked out. No, that's not the right word. He's something. A look she hasn't seen much before.

"I feel better about things," Kay says. "My God, it's easier to be happy, isn't it? And the girl, Iris. I just met her last week. She is quite lovely."

Alex smiles. He looks younger all of a sudden. Proud, too. His smooth shave, his crisp blue shirt. Kay puts her hand on top of his. "She's a great kid," Alex says.

"And a baby on the way," Kay whispers.

"A baby?" Greg says.

"Wow," Freddie says.

"Who's having a baby?" Addie says.

"Their daughter," Greg says, and then stops.

"Oh," Addie says, and shrugs in her adult way. "Neat."

"Yes," Kay says. "I'm excited to meet this baby." She looks up at the ceiling. "Who would've thought," she says. "My mother always said don't say what you'll do until you do."

Alex and Kay who lost their son, Benny, all those years ago before Greg even started at Garroway & Associates. Hit by a tractor trailer on his bike. Someone said Kay screamed when the police told her. People at the office told them that Alex's voice was so much quieter for months afterward. Now this girl out of nowhere with a grandchild on the way.

Another rule. A rule Freddie likes: *you never know*. You never know what can break you. What you can fix, what you can stand up to. You never know what time will do, what will defeat or surprise you. You never know. Freddie feels a hopeful possibility ticking inside her—like her body's typewriter is working on something. She even feels hopeful about Iowa and her application. She will definitely send it in. She needs to. You never know.

"How wonderful for you two." Freddie stands to hug Kay. "And congratulations. A grandbaby!"

Kay reaches up and says, "Thanks, my dear. We appreciate that."

Alex winks at her. Freddie rests her palms on the table. When Addie places her small hand on top of Freddie's, Freddie slides hers out and they start playing the stacking hand game.

Addie looks at Greg, and her blue eyes light up. Her bangs are swooped to the side, and she looks at him like she has just remembered something. "My Daddy taught me this," she announces.

Greg puts down his spoon. Freddie knows he feels his illness most when he thinks about Addie, these small crumbs of life he might have given her in the whole scheme of things. He tries to smile at Addie, who looks to him for approval, but his face crumbles. Freddie's face burns; she feels like she's been kicked. Greg is the tragic hero. He has done nothing but try, try, try to beat this. Freddie watches him dissolve.

For a second, Freddie tries to remember holding Greg's hand. She tries to remember a time when she and Addie and Greg were at a restaurant putting their hands in a pile. Just like this with nothing else but the fun of it. How Greg would always be so fast to rip his hand out, how eventually he'd flick his hands like windmills and upset the pile. How he'd dart his hands down to tickle Addie when the game was over.

As the four people at the table look at this tired man in his ski cap, his eyes so injured, his iceless soda in front of him, he pushes back his chair and stands up. He looks at Addie and at Freddie with the sorriest eyes she's ever seen. "I need to get out of here," he says, and the waitress stands over them now carrying a giant tray with all their entrées. "I'll wait in the car."

"Say, Addie," Alex whispers. "Show me that music game on that phone. Can an old guy like me learn it?"

"I'm sorry," Greg says to the waitress, backing away.

Freddie can see how his black sweater hangs on his frail body. She can see how pale his skin is in this dim light. She can see what her husband has become, feeble hands at his sides.

At that circular table with their laminated menus stacked next to the napkin dispenser, in the corner of the restaurant next to the Christmas tree whose lights blink on and off, Freddie breaks her rules. She looks at him leaving, and the tears come spilling out, even though she doesn't want Addie to see, even though she wants to keep it together for the confused waitress and the Lionels, and she whispers, "Please, God, please." She uses her hand to cover her face as she watches her tired husband walk away.

9.

The Star in the Box

Lucas,

I do look forward to your letters.

However, as you know, letters do not take the place of seeing people, and I wish you would remove that restriction you've placed on us. Thanksgiving was not the same without your jokes about my oyster stuffing. I sometimes have to remind myself that you are not oceans away but merely a quick drive.

Anyway, I hope you like this Christmas card. The kid on the front reminded me of you when you used to put on your mittens and boots to play in the snow. Remember those red boots you had? I hope you put this check to good use—may I suggest starting a small retirement account as you are still young but the years will fly by, to which I can well attest? Or, just ignore me and use it for groceries or parking or anything you want. Maybe buy yourself a nice sweater at least (not acrylic please). You look handsome in navy blue, but I will stop meddling.

Betsy has been restored, and I would like to talk with you about her. I'd love if you'd stop by the house. Just stay a few minutes, and I guarantee I won't be critical or say anything remotely impolite. Bring your new gal, if you'd like.

I put up the tree in the living room, and it would be nice if you came to see it with the lights on. I kept the star in the box because I remember that used to be your favorite part.

Love and peace,
Your mother

10.

How We Love Them

She is famous for Finland.

Suzette Campbell knows this. Knows they are all waiting to see if she can go through with this wedding. Knows they think the paisley dresses are ridiculous. Who picks paisley? And green paisley. She loved the fabric when she saw the dresses at the bridal show in Boston. She swears she didn't pick paisley to be quirky.

She resents that she is famous for Finland. No matter what else she does, how many kids and teenagers she helps as a dual-certified social worker/counselor.

Suzette has done at least a hundred things to prove herself as stable and responsible—got engaged, bought a house and renovated it this past year, gotten countless people's power turned back on when they couldn't afford their electricity bills, worked with schools so kids' lunches could be covered, drove her mother everywhere after her knee surgery. But she is still the girl who went to Finland and came back less than a week later. She hates that reputation.

And hates that right now, with her wedding coming, she feels the way she did when her plane landed in Helsinki.

Trees and lakes. She remembers how dense they were in Finland. The snow and frozen land. She remembers the overnight flight, and how the sun was just coming up when the plane descended, the sky orange and pink behind buildings still black with darkness. She remembers the feeling, like the first day of kindergarten—her mother's writing on the inside of her jacket, heavy lunchbox in her fingers, the world seeming overwhelming and vast. She remembers her older sister Lisa walked her to Mrs. Tussle's kindergarten room, holding her hand the whole time, and then patted her when it was time to part. "See you on the bus," Lisa said. "Bus number six, okay?" And Suzette felt nervous and empty as she watched Lisa walk away.

Suzette remembers waiting to step off that plane in Finland. Her hand shaking as she held her small carry-on and the local woman next to her still sleeping, her head almost on Suzette's shoulder. Suzette looked at the woman, her open mouth so peaceful, and thought, *What will we all do here?* Which was really an absurd thought, because this woman spoke no English, so she probably belonged there already. Maybe she slept peacefully and felt, "Ah, home."

Now Suzette looks at Damon's text, then puts the phone down on her lap while she drives through Wharton. Damon is a good man. She cannot have another Finland. Her parents have spent almost forty thousand dollars on this wedding. She overheard her mother say to her grandmother on the phone in a low voice, "I haven't ever seen her like this. This guy has brought Suze so much serenity." As if Damon were a Buddhist garden.

His text says, *I'm worried. You okay?*

She imagines the feeling of his hand holding hers, and starts to bite her fingernails.

Today Connecticut looks like Finland: cold ground, green trees. And she feels like she did in Finland: uncertain, slightly sweaty.

She puts both hands on the steering wheel and finds a spot at Crowley Cleaners where she has her last fitting with Freddie Tyler, the seamstress. She knew Freddie through her parents' good friends Alex and Kay Lionel. Freddie's husband worked for Alex. Suzette had seen Freddie at several events before she learned she was a seamstress.

The sign says Open, but just one car is in the lot today: a shiny Buick that's at least five years old. On the glass door of the cleaners is a plastic elf holding a sign that says Season's Greetings, and in the window box are fake poinsettias and white lights. Her wedding is eight days away. Eight days, and she refuses to let it be another failure that will be held against her for years.

She walks up to the door and sees Mrs. Crowley at the counter replacing register tape.

Did Finland really happen? How odd that a person can have such things belong to them. She had been right out of college. She remembers her roommate in Finland—Helmi—a kind girl her age with large trusting eyes and a birthmark on her left cheek. Helmi had very fine hair, dishwater blond, and could patch together some decent English.

Already we go dinner for you?

The school where Suzette would be teaching matched her up with Helmi. Helmi made Suzette a strong cup of coffee that day she arrived, which is still the best cup of coffee she has ever had. They sat at a small wooden table in the kitchen of the apartment, and Helmi shrugged as she sipped and asked about Suzette's flight. Then she stood in Suzette's small bedroom with the plain bed that looked like a cot and brass lamp and tiny window and helped her unpack each item of clothing. *This I put here?* She remembers how suffocated she felt as Helmi laid her sweaters on the closet shelf and used one of the three hangers to hang Suzette's black Stella McCartney dress. *Very beautiful,* Helmi said.

Suzette remembers how she talked faster than usual because she was nervous, and Helmi smiled politely, not knowing how to respond to her rapid sentences.

Then, a day later, the director of the English immersion school in Espoo showed Suzette to her tiny classroom, just a couple of days before the nine- and ten-year-olds would arrive. She remembers the cracks in the walls as she walked the hallway of the school, not seeing locks anywhere. She remembers the odd smell—like pinecones—and how paralyzed she felt. How this teaching and this life were right there, right in front of her, but she felt buried, bubble-wrapped.

How had she thought it would go? Did she not know moving to another country was not like in the movies: the satisfied stare out the plane window, the plucky heroine rolling her suitcase behind her?

She should have known better, but once there she felt like

vomiting. What would she teach those kids on their first day? She had applied to the program and never thought she'd get in. She majored in social work in college. She never took an education class. "Paper clip your picture to the packet," her father had said. "Guaranteed they'll hire you." She did. And they did.

A week later, when she was back home, when her parents and younger sister, Carrie, whispered about her downstairs, she sat in the picture window of her bedroom and held a throw pillow against her chest, chewing absently on the corner. "It wasn't a good fit," she had said calmly, but she didn't tell anyone about how she left the school administrator a note (a note!) on her desk (in clearly printed words because she wasn't sure if her cursive was legible to someone whose first language was Finnish). She didn't say how she told Helmi she could keep the black dress, how she gave her a stack of euros (probably way too much) to cover the rent, how before she went to the airport she bought a pack of cigarettes in a bar and drank mulled wine and smoked and hiccuped and cried.

She cried because she couldn't give this beautiful city a chance. She cried because she broke Helmi's polite heart and because they'd never stayed up late to talk about boyfriends or watch a movie together the way Suzette had envisioned. She cried because she felt so alone, and no one in the bar even noticed her crying. It was one o'clock in the afternoon, and she didn't even know if her *I'm sorry, but I can't do this* note was received yet. She cried because she never even sat in her teacher's desk chair and because maybe they were relieved that she'd quit. Because the students wouldn't have been able to learn from her anyway.

She cried because her older sister, Lisa, had gotten leukemia two years before that, and nothing, nothing had been right since she died. She felt so far away from Lisa in Finland, and she cried because returning home wouldn't fix anything.

She wasn't programmed to lose her sister. Never. She could still easily see Lisa walking her to her kindergarten classroom—Lisa's curls, her dark eyes and knowing smile, Lisa's small plaid book bag she held like a briefcase. Her parents had adopted Lisa when they thought they couldn't have children, and she was given everything in a way that didn't spoil her but made her generous and confident. In a couple of years, her parents ended up being able to have Suzette, and then Carrie, and for a few years, the three girls slept in one room like *The Brady Bunch* kids.

At the bar that day so long ago, Suzette lit another cigarette, stronger than an unfiltered Camel. She cried because Finland could have changed her life, and she wouldn't stay long enough to let it.

Now when the door opens with that subtle ding, Mrs. Crowley snaps the plastic guard of the register in place and runs the paper through it. "Hello there," she says. Her curls are perfect. There are so many spools of thread behind her, and the radio quietly delivers a news segment from a BBC reporter. "Chilly one, isn't it?" She glides over to the seamstress's empty chair and takes a sweater off the back of it. "The air just stabs you when it hits, doesn't it?"

Suzette nods. "I forgot to wear a coat."

"You mustn't . . . the bride can't have a cold." Mrs. Crowley laces her fingers together. "Ms. Tyler knows you have an appointment? Shall I ring her?"

"No, no. We talked yesterday. I think I'm a few minutes early."

"You must be tickled that all this planning is coming to the end." The woman adjusts her Christmas tree pin on her sweater. She wears a cream-colored satin blouse under the sweater, and pants that are so pressed they could hang without a hanger. "Want a candy cane?" She holds out a small ceramic gingerbread house with holes in the roof for miniature candy canes to sit in.

"Yes, please."

"I love Christmas weddings . . . if Mother Nature cooperates for you."

"Yes," Suzette says. Did she eat today? She feels like she didn't.

"My daughter, of course, was bound and determined to be married in July. I said, *Mary Jane, you're going to be hot the whole day. Your face will be shiny in pictures. You might not even want to take pictures outside.*" She shakes her head and sighs. "And then she asked her friend's toddler to be a flower girl . . . a two-year-old who wants her mommy, a sweltering day. Need I say more?" She looks up to the ceiling and smiles. "But it was lovely, all of that aside. A lush green golf course in the background." Her smile comes and goes like lightning.

Suzette smiles. "I always wanted a Christmas wedding."

"And your fiancé? Does he like a Christmas wedding, too?"

"Oh yes. Yes. He loved the idea."

"Good."

"Yeah."

"I can't imagine Ms. Tyler being late." She looks at the seamstress's empty work station. "I always tell her she has an atomic clock wired to her brain."

"Traffic probably."

"Probably."

Suzette sees her dress hanging in its thick white bag on a rack by itself and she feels her shoulders sag. Her sister Lisa had just picked out her wedding dress before her diagnosis. She never even went for a fitting. When the boutique phoned one day inquiring about the dress, her mother told the man to keep the damn thing. Suzette coughs now. "Did your daughter—"

Mrs. Crowley looks from the parking lot back to Suzette. "Did she what, dear?"

"Feel weird?"

"Weird? About getting married, you mean?"

"I guess."

"Oh. Well, maybe." She pulls out her own candy cane and holds it as if she's never tried one. She unwraps it carefully and tastes it for a second. "If she did, she didn't tell me. But I did. If an old lady matters." She chuckles. "Do you?"

"What? Feel weird? Um, a little. Well, not weird. I just feel, I just feel . . . vacant." The word surprises her. It is perfectly chosen, and she just chose it. Yes, that is the feeling. Her cheeks burn. Why did she say anything? People always gossip, and no one needs to hear this. It's Finland all over again. *Oh, and with everything her poor parents have been through.* "I kind of don't want to put that dress on again." When did this feeling start? She can't say. She wants the wedding to be over, and she wants to never put on the dress.

"Maybe you're just tired of the preparation." Mrs. Crowley's eyes dart back and forth between Suzette and the parking lot. Suzette looks. Not a car in the lot besides theirs. A moving van charges by on Route 23, and way down the street she can see the traffic light for Gatehill Mall, a cluster of cars with people going Christmas shopping. In the other direction is The Dock, the restaurant where Damon proposed. (Damon's sweet face that night, so hopeful.) The sky outside is crisp blue with threads of clouds. "Maybe you want to just be married, without all the fuss?"

This brings Suzette a moment of quick relief. Is that it? "I don't feel like I know. I know that Damon's a terribly nice guy. I know he has a smile that makes babies smile back at him when we walk downtown. I know if we had kids, they would be loved and valued—by him, by me. I know it all seems to fit. That I could set up an office in our home. I know he will go with me to chop down the best Christmas tree every year, and I know he will pour me wine if I have a bad day, and we can sit on the porch and I can put my feet on his lap. I know all this. I know it can be great. But I don't want to pull the trigger. That's what I don't want to do."

Mrs. Crowley nods. Her glasses reflect the overhead lights.

"I'm not stupid, Mrs. Crowley. I mean, I'm not crazy. I hear people say maybe they just don't want to be happy, and I don't think that's me. I really want to be happy. I am pretty happy. I just feel, well, crushed by this. I keep fighting the urge to call Damon and say we need to cancel right now.

"Why would I want to do that? How twisted would I be to do that to the best man I will probably ever meet? I sound crazy. I'm sorry. I'll be fine. We'll have the wedding, and I'll be fine, and you'll see me one day at The Greenhorn or at Mateo's sitting across from Damon, and you'll think, wow, all that moaning for nothing. I mean, I'm in my thirties. I know what I'm doing. I said yes because I knew? Didn't I know?"

Mrs. Crowley rests her elbows on the counter. She clicks her tongue as if she's about to speak, but the words don't come. Her face looks concerned, serious.

"I'm sorry," Suzette says. "I—I still don't see her. Maybe we should call her? I'm sorry. I really don't know why I'm telling you all this. I think I'm just tired. It's been dress fittings and paint colors for the new house and passport renewals and my parents. My parents think I'm like this mustang that Damon finally broke—only because I was kind of, I guess, trying out who I wanted to be. And they didn't get to, you know, with my sister—they didn't get to see her become an adult and all that. But I'm not wild. I just think, maybe I could do without all this? Is it bad to think that?" Suzette takes a deep breath. She feels mostly relieved. She has gotten out what she wanted to say for so long.

"No, dear, not at all. We feel what we feel, and we

shouldn't apologize for ourselves. There's nothing wrong with you. Nothing." Mrs. Crowley picks up her cordless phone and dials Freddie Tyler's number slowly, her eyes looking at a laminated sheet of paper with all the important numbers written on it. "No answer," she says.

"Hmm," says Suzette.

"I believe that's her home number. I thought I had her cell phone number, too, but it's not on this list." She shakes her head.

"I have it." Suzette reaches into her purse. She sees Damon's text again. She rereads his words. *I'm worried. You okay?* Poor Damon. She should write back right now. *Yes. Of course. I love you.* She finds Freddie's number under recent calls and dials it. "Right to voice mail."

"I don't know what to tell you, dear."

"She'll come."

"No, I mean about your problem."

"Oh, well. It's not really a problem. I'm making it a problem."

The radio mumbles. The door chimes, but it's the UPS man. Mrs. Crowley smiles at him and signs for a small package. The deliveryman nods at Suzette and leaves. When he closes the door, the tinsel garland that's draped across the store sways under the fluorescent lights.

"I think you should talk to your betrothed. I know what sadness is, my dear, and you look sad."

"Oh. Well, I'm not . . . Maybe, yeah. A little." Yes, she is. Is that what this all has been about? A need for something she can't find? Why has no one else noticed this besides the woman who owns this dry cleaning place? But Damon notices. That's what his text is about. He notices. He cares.

"Does something about the wedding make you sad?" Mrs. Crowley puts a dollop of Avon lotion on her hands and rubs them together.

"Kind of." She takes off her vest. "It's warm in here."

"I'm always cold, as you can see." She gestures to her sweater and smiles again.

Suzette is in full nail-biting mode. She shreds her thumb nail with her top tooth. "She makes me sad," she finally says.

"Ms. Tyler?"

"No. My sister."

"Oh."

"You remember her, don't you?"

"If I recall, there were three girls in your family, no?"

"Good memory. My older sister, I mean."

"Of course. Beautiful, beautiful girl." She frowns and looks down. She shakes her head. For some reason, Suzette wishes she'd say her name. *Lisa.* "You don't ever get over that loss. It leaves a scratch in you like a record that never plays right again." Mrs. Crowley reaches her hand out and waves it at her. "Now, don't bite your nails, dear. Let's not make things worse."

Suzette smiles. "I haven't bitten my nails this much since she was dying. It's awful for someone to know they're dying, isn't it?"

Mrs. Crowley's stare is far away. "Yes, yes. It is."

"I didn't know what to say to her." She takes a deep breath.

"I tried to act like she would still wear that dress . . . that this was like a broken leg, and she'd be out and about when it healed." She looks at her other hand and realizes she hasn't eaten the candy cane. The wrapper comes off so easily, and she wonders if they plan it that way in the factory. The thought comforts her—that someone in a far-off place cares.

"Tell me her name again?"

"Lisa." It feels so good to hear it in the air. The two syllables echo for a second. *Lisa. Lisa.* She whispers it sometimes when she's in the car by herself. Sometimes she writes the name over and over on a notebook page or a dry-erase board. She just wants her name to stay current. She loves when someone sends a Christmas card to the family and still puts Lisa's name on it.

"Lisa, yes. Well, we do the things they weren't able to," Mrs. Crowley says. "We vote because they can no longer vote. We look at the ocean because they can't. We think about them when we put up a Christmas tree, and later when we sit there and gaze at the lights. We do all the things they can't. That is how we love them when they're gone."

Suzette swallows. She hopes her eye makeup isn't running. She wipes her face and checks her hand. "I just wanted her to wear a wedding dress first."

"I know."

She snorts. "I think I picked these green dresses so she wouldn't feel bad. Maybe in the back of my mind, I didn't want my wedding to be nicer than hers, even though hers didn't happen."

"Oh, darling."

"I moved to Finland because I was so sad. Because I wanted to try to be happy. But I couldn't stay there. I couldn't make it work."

"It's good to try as many things as you can. Who knows what will stick." Mrs. Crowley comes around and holds out her arms. The woman never seemed like the hugging type. Suzette holds the candy cane in her fist and laughs through tears as the older woman wraps her arms around her.

"Thank you."

"I think you should give this a try. This guy. This future that might be happy. You might like it."

Suzette digs a tissue out of her vest pocket and blots her eyes. "Thanks."

The door dings then, and Mrs. Crowley ducks away and heads back behind the counter. "Ms. Tyler."

"Sorry," Freddie says. "Dead cell phone, and a dead car battery. Both on the same day." Her eyes water from the cold, and her fine hair in a ponytail bounces as she hurries to her station.

"Oh no," Mrs. Crowley says.

"How horrible," Suzette says.

The three women look for a moment at each other, and then Suzette walks toward the bag with her dress in it. Freddie Tyler takes off her coat and grabs her materials from her station. Mrs. Crowley puts two new candy canes into the ceramic gingerbread house. The radio plays a holiday jingle.

Suzette holds the dress bag over her arm, and as she slides the curtain closed, she imagines Lisa standing outside the dressing room, smiling, hands clasped, waiting to see her. Wouldn't she tug the curtain open before Suzette was ready? *Lisa! Wait!* Wouldn't Lisa sigh as she saw her little sister, grown now, holding the layers of tulle on the skirt as she tiptoed out into the light?

Suzette slips the dress on, and it doesn't feel as heavy as she remembered. She wants to see Damon at the end of the aisle, beaming as she walks toward him. She wants to walk toward him. This isn't Finland. This isn't Finland. She wants what's next.

11.

Homesick

The dresses aren't all that bad. Ginger lines up with the other bridesmaids in the high-ceilinged reception hall at Oak Gate Country Club. Maybe she can see what Suzette was going for. The seamstress did a good job. All their dresses fit well, the fur capes on their shoulders look almost regal, and with her hair up and the pearl necklace, Ginger feels elegant. The other girls smile for the camera in a comfortable way, in a way that says they feel what she's feeling.

"One more," the photographer commands. "Stay close together." The groomsman assigned to Ginger is named Ahmed, Damon's best friend since nursery school. He keeps his hand on Ginger's hip and smiles mechanically. "Death by flashbulbs," he whispers. Ginger laughs. The band has started playing, and she sees the lead singer out of the corner of her eye and for a second convinces herself it's Luke Crowley, her ex-boyfriend. Maybe the one who got away, if she believed such things.

Only he didn't get away. They veered directly away from

each other ten years ago. She won't look at the singer full-on because his build is similar, his hair the same color. Luke. What would he say to see her there in this dress, listening to the music?

After the pictures are through, she sips a Mistletoe Martini and goes to find Suzette's parents. People linger around tables in the large banquet room as the band plays in front of the dance floor. This room with its twinkling Christmas lights leads into a lounge area with a long polished slate bar. She finds Suzette's parents near a raw bar of shrimp and oysters on ice. "Ginger's the veterinarian," Suzette's mother says to an elderly aunt.

Ginger nods and half laughs. "Does anyone have a cat or dog in their purse that needs checking?"

"No, dear, I'm allergic," the aunt says seriously. "But you look the nicest in your dress."

"Oh, thanks."

The aunt is wearing a gardenia corsage. Ginger can tell she had her hair done today because it's perfectly in place. The woman touches the top of her hand. "Some of the other girls are too skinny."

Ginger smiles and moves on. Does that make her fat? No, that's not what the woman meant. She is fine.

Ginger thinks about how she will return to Johnny in a few days. How he'll probably give her a belated Christmas gift, maybe some chocolate from his stops in Argentina and Peru, and she'll give him that brown attaché bag she got from the Coach Men's store: not wrapped, maybe just a bow around it. Why can't she wrap a gift for him? Does she love him that little?

She wishes Martin, her cat, weren't alone in the apartment in Savannah. She hopes their neighbor will check in often. She wonders if everyone her age feels this unsettled.

Since she set up practice in Georgia, she has felt like she's at an extended sleepover at a friend's house. Sure, she knows where everything is (it was she who found the apartment, who bought the flatware, the plates, the small sofa from Crate and Barrel), but she still wants to be home. Home. That apartment with Johnny isn't it. But what is? Not her parents' house. She's homesick for something that isn't anywhere. Thirty-three and homesick.

Damon, the groom, has requested Sinatra, and "Strangers in the Night" plays as he beckons Suzette. She puts her bouquet on the head table and walks coyly to him while everyone watches. She kisses his cheek and rests her head on his shoulder as they slow dance. A stunning bride and groom. They look otherworldly, classic, like something from the fifties. The windows at the country club are high, and outside Ginger can see stars and the black sky. There is a tall Christmas tree by the French doors, and on the large fireplace is a garland with red ornaments the size of grapefruits. Each table has an ivory tablecloth and ten flickering votives.

The band plays, and Suzette and Damon sway, and Ginger wants to ask her if this is everything she wanted, and how did she know? How did she know it would all work?

How does anyone know? How do you not just sail through your twenties and thirties, only making the next step? All through high school and college and then vet school, all those good grades, and what she wanted was just a cozy place to call home. She wanted love. She wanted that feeling of "ah, yes" when she pulled into her driveway after work. She wanted to stand side by side with someone every night, washing dishes. She wanted long drives heading nowhere, picnics by the Naugatuck River.

She thinks of how settled she used to feel when Luke would stay at her little apartment in college. How one year they had that small Christmas tree with the multicolored lights in her bedroom. How she bought them matching flannel snowflake pajamas and he came out of the bathroom with them on, his top unbuttoned in a way she found adorable, and they lay there and watched *White Christmas*. He had made popcorn balls that didn't stay together, but they sipped cold eggnog and pulled pieces of popcorn and marshmallow out of the bowl, and she wanted that night to last forever.

When she started to fall asleep, he got up to unplug the tree, and she whispered, "Wait, can you leave it on?" and he stood there and smiled at her. All through the night, she would wake every so often to see the glow of the tree, and she felt something inside her that was as close to fullness as she's ever felt. In the morning, he woke her by slipping a silver ring on her finger, and she remembers how the sun came into the apartment that day. How her mother had always said Christmas day sun is the best sun, and Ginger knew she was right. It lit up the leaves of the poinsettia on the kitchen table, it made patterns on the wall. It shone on Luke's back as he sat on a barstool and ate the silver dollar pancakes she'd made.

He had gotten the ring at an antiques store. She wondered how he afforded it. It was from the 1930s with scrollwork on it. A bit scratched, but she loved it. Did it mean anything? Was he asking her something? She didn't care. It fit perfectly. It turned out he just liked it. He wanted her to have it. He wasn't thinking about marriage. Nor was he not thinking about it. He loved her and gave her a ring he couldn't afford. She still has it.

Ginger waves to Cameron, who is dancing with two teenage boys, and thinks of Suzette's house, of the counseling office she will set up there. She admires Suzette so much—all those teens that Suzette gives as much as she can, buys them milkshakes or Happy Meals. Ginger imagines Suzette and Damon's beautiful future children and the holidays and the Pottery Barn bed they will probably sleep in and feels an incredible ache. She is standing alone at this wedding. This is where she has ended up.

She should stop daydreaming. She needs to deal with reality, with what's really here. If this were a movie, she thinks, a song would come on. A song that Luke sang once, and she'd think of him, and decide finally that she only wants Luke Crowley. That's it, isn't it? Isn't Luke what this is all about? In her green paisley dress, the camera would film her backing away from the wedding, and taking a cab or some other classic form of transportation, and arriving at Luke's place. He'd crank open his apartment window, which she imagines would be street front, and look down. "Ginger?"

Stop doing this, she thinks. She rests her chin on her hand at one of the high tops and sips her drink. Luke . . .

He would see her there in her green dress. Her pearl necklace, the gold of her earrings, and she'd have tears in her eyes. He'd know she came all that way, and she'd deliver some long speech. She'd be breathless, and maybe it would be snowing lightly, maybe winter rain, and he'd duck his head inside and she'd see a light come on below, and wouldn't he run down to her, wouldn't he agree with everything she was saying? Wouldn't he kiss her under a lone streetlamp as her cab pulled away and she'd stay there with him? Wouldn't this Christmas be the best Christmas?

She doesn't know where his apartment is. Or Luke. He might have a girlfriend.

And is she the type of person to cheat on her boyfriend?

Ginger shakes her head and sips her drink. She is irritated with herself. She cannot live in a fantasy world. Someone taps her on the shoulder then.

"Miss me?" Ahmed says. His eyes are playful. He has a faint five o'clock shadow on his face.

She smiles. "Of course." She sips the last of her drink. "Please don't tell me we're being called back for more pictures."

He raises his eyebrows in mock surprise. "If they do, let's just agree we're escaping."

She offers her hand. "Deal." He holds it and they shake.

"You know what this wedding is missing?" He clears his throat. "Reindeer."

"I'll tell Suzette."

"I'm serious. Wouldn't a pen of reindeer on the lawn that we could go out and visit, maybe feed them some oats or something, be just the thing?" His green tie is loose, the top button of his shirt is undone.

"I would feed a reindeer if given the opportunity."

"Hell, you could check its vitals, too, couldn't you, Doc?"

"I probably could." She shakes her head.

"I like Doc. That's what I'm going to call you."

She'll probably never see this guy again after tonight, but she lets him think they'll keep whatever this is going. When she met him last night at the rehearsal dinner, he fist-bumped her. He said, "You hit the jackpot. I'm the most fun guy here, even though I'm an accountant." She says now: "I've been called Doc before, but you say it in the most charming way."

"It's cool that you're a big doctor and you don't act like it," he says.

She smiles.

"Anyway, I think they want us to sit and eat now." The band is finishing up "Someone to Watch over Me," and she looks at the long table reserved for the wedding party where Suzette, Damon, and the others have gathered.

"Ah," she says. "Lobster time." She realizes how hungry she is.

"Want me to escort you . . . for old time's sake?" He puts out his arm. "After tonight, who knows when we'll be paired together again?"

"I hadn't thought of that," she says, and laces her arm through his. "It would be my pleasure."

"So what are you going to do with the dress after this?" he asks as he leads her across the room. The band has switched over to prerecorded music. Something instrumental. Along the table, there is a salad at every place, and the goblets are filled with water.

She looks down at her feet, how they walk in tune with his. "Maybe every year I'll have a fancy Christmas party to go to, and it'll be just the thing to wear. Maybe I'll still wear it at seventy and they'll think I've gone off the deep end."

"Doc, you say some funny shit." He pulls out her chair for her, his face close to hers. He looks at her, and she looks at him. She doesn't know what she feels. Something light. Something that makes her nervous. Maybe it's the martini. Maybe it's the piano music. But whatever this is, she smiles as he reaches for her hand. She blushes as he bends, like an old-fashioned gentleman, and kisses the tops of her knuckles.

Later they take a walk outside. The frozen grass crunches as they stroll across the expansive grounds. There are tall pine trees and a row of blue spruces in the distance. It is cold, but a still, windless cold. A cold you don't mind. Men stand by the French doors and smoke cigars, and a little girl, maybe Suzette's cousin, sings "Jingle Bell Rock" amid a circle of delighted adults. Ginger can still hear the band from inside. They walk by lit trees, and there is a huge sleigh with a spotlight on it in the grass by a stable. "Shit," Ahmed says, "this is right where the reindeer pen could go." She sees his breath in the air. Her heels dig into the cold ground every so often. He slips off his coat, and offers it to her, a gesture that seems clichéd, but she doesn't care. The coat is warm. He never stops moving, she has noticed. Maybe he is never cold.

"Thanks," she says.

"Nah, I was just hot," he says. He kicks a piece of ice in the grass with his polished shoes. "So what are you doing after this?"

"Staying at my parents' house . . . and then I fly back to Savannah after Christmas." She knows she doesn't sound excited. So matter-of-fact.

"No, I mean . . ." He gestures toward the wedding. "Does this shit scare you? Do you feel like you have to change your life after events like this?" He puts his hands into his pockets. "I do. I mean, now that Damon's out to pasture, there aren't too many of us who aren't married. And people keep saying to him, *finally*. Like, you finally did it. *Finally* makes me think it's way past time. It scares me. I guess I should be doing something different." She can't believe this guy is expressing exactly what she feels, and is being so honest and real. Yes, real. He is a real person. His smooth face has a glow to it.

"I don't think it is way past time," she lies. It is, at least for her.

She wonders when she'll finally arrive where she wants to

be. What will it feel like? She imagines Suzette and Damon coming home from their honeymoon in Greece and Croatia. That relieved and settled feeling they will have. "You seem like a pretty young guy," she says.

He keeps his head straight, but his eyes move to the side. He smiles. "Thanks. But it's just an act. I have fucking retirement savings, man. I go for yearly physicals, I fall asleep when I drink red wine."

"I hate New Year's Eve," she says. "Too late for me."

"I have a club card at Giant."

She grins. "I have a cat. Like an old lady."

"I go to happy hour some nights after work . . . not for the drinks, but for the appetizers."

She shakes her head. "My checkbook has those boring yellow checks my dad used to have. I used to always think I'd special order a beach scene or something."

"Okay, that wins. My checks are at least green. I paid two dollars more for green."

"See? You're young."

"Okay, I'm young, Doc." He puts his arms up in a victory pose. "Woot!"

"I'm too old to know what *woot* means."

"Damn, Doc. Woot. Like you just won. Woot woot!" He shakes his head. "But twenty-year-olds probably don't even say that anymore."

She looks at the long, dark stretches of quiet golf course. The tall trees. The lit ballroom of the reception a football field's length away from them, where people are dancing in the illuminated windows. They can still hear the band playing faintly. "I'm having fun with you," she says. She doesn't know why she has to confess this. She is no longer cold at all. She feels like she could stay out here all night.

He smiles again. "Me, too."

"You asked me what I'll do after this. I think I'm going to break up with my boyfriend in Georgia." She shrugs. "God, I hope he doesn't care. I hate disappointing people."

"That's rough." He clicks his tongue. "I would care. Shit, I would care a hell of a lot if a girl like you ditched me."

"Thanks."

"But you gotta do what's right."

"I think so."

"If it makes you feel better, you know, more straightened out, then go for it . . . just try to keep the cat."

She smiles. "I will." She puts her hands into the jacket pocket and feels a pack of Lifesavers. "I'll need him when I'm a lonely old cat lady."

"You're lucky though."

"I am?"

"I wish I had someone to break up with."

"You're crazy."

"No, then I'd know that it might fix something in some way. You have a chance after this breakup, don't you? Otherwise you wouldn't do it."

"Maybe." She loves what he says. It lifts her. Maybe this will open up some opportunity. She wants to tell him about Luke. About her small hope that she could run to him in her paisley dress and everything would be fixed. She wants to say she loved Luke in this whole way that she never loved anything. She wants to say running into him that day almost two months ago in the toy store felt like the most terrific coincidence, and she wishes she had put something in place then—given him her number, made plans with him. "But the nice thing about chances, I think, is that we don't know the chances that are coming. There are obvious chances, and hidden chances."

"The only chance I have is that after you figure things out, Doc, you'll remember the groomsman who talked about reindeer and gave you his coat." He looks away from her. "And you'll call me." He grins.

Ginger's stomach flips. She feels something she hasn't felt in forever, a rush of something familiar. But she stops.

Joni Mitchell's "River" plays faintly from inside. *It's coming on Christmas. They're cutting down trees.* Ginger forgets Ahmed and stares straight ahead at the reception. She sees the slow-dancing shadows of people inside. She can see occasional flickers of candles. The song seems to get louder. Why would they play this at a wedding? A song about regret.

A memory of Luke singing this at a piano. Luke onstage. How he broke every person's heart in that small club with this song. How she loved him even more with those words. *I wish I had a river . . . I could skate away on.* She feels the cold air in her chest. "I'm sorry," she says. "This song." She slips off the coat and notices his bewildered eyes. "I'm sorry," she says again, and hands it to him.

And then she is running across the frozen grass, hopping

lightly so her heels don't sink in. She is squeezing past the cigar smokers, the women looking at the ornaments on the large tree. And then she's back at the table, looking for her purse. She sees it a few places down, and Cecilia stops her. "Is this yours? The phone's been ringing nonstop."

"Oh, thanks." Her heart jumps. She digs through her purse as she walks. A patient emergency? She hopes the animals are okay. She hopes they called the on-call vet. She holds her faux fur shawl over her arm and walks toward the front door. She was supposed to drive home with Cameron. Maybe the valet can call her a cab? Maybe she can call her own? Her stomach is in knots about what to do, how she will find Luke, her mind half worried about the missed calls. Maybe just Johnny. She sees a handful of missed calls, and a text message.

Her mother, who never sends texts. Ginger holds her phone in front of her. She squints to see the words.

She holds her hand to her mouth. The doorman opens the front door for her, but she stays where she is. "Oh God," she says, and it hurts to breathe.

She rushes inside St. Margaret's after Ahmed drops her off at the curb. A mother holds a screaming boy with a bandage pressed to his head. She looks for the sign that says ER and follows the arrow. She could vomit. She sees Mrs. Crowley first, slumped over, her hands clasped in half prayer. She wears a white angora cardigan and a wrinkled blouse. Her daughter, Mary Jane, is talking to a nurse with her arms crossed. A police officer is nearby. "Mrs. Crowley," Ginger says, and kneels at her side.

The old woman looks up, her eyes the eyes of the worst disappointment. "Ginger?" She looks at her. "You're wearing the dress." She touches Ginger's shoulder. Her hands are cold. "It's good of you to come," she says meekly.

Mary Jane sinks beside her mother. "That's it," she says.

"That's what?" Mrs. Crowley says.

"Hi, Mary Jane," Ginger says awkwardly.

Mary Jane starts to sob. "He won't. He won't." She shakes her head. "It's too bad." Ginger notices her red cheeks. Mary Jane puts her hand absently on Ginger, and they huddle there. Three women in the emergency room. "We have to say good-bye," she whispers. "They said now." She starts to bend over. She looks as though she might faint.

Mary Jane shakes her head and stands limply. Her hands are shaking. Ginger stares straight ahead. The metal from a wheelchair gleams in the corner. The chairs, all in their careful rows, look high-end, not what you'd expect in a waiting room. A man in a flannel shirt holds a towel wrapped around a bloody arm. A baby in a carrier babbles at its mother, who doesn't look down. On the big-screen television, Kelly Ripa is standing in front of Cinderella's castle at Magic Kingdom. What the hell is Ginger doing here? What happened to the wedding? What happened to taking a cab to Luke's apartment?

Luke, she thinks. *I have to tell Luke about the accident.*

But then she realizes this *is* Luke. Isn't that odd to forget? It is Luke. He is inside that room, where the battalion of doctors and nurses just came from. It's like the movies in that way, Ginger thinks. Did someone say, "We've done all we could"? Did they?

Mrs. Crowley puts her hands on her knees and stands. She looks so tall as she marches. "I have to talk to them," she says. She squares her shoulders and heads toward the nurses' station.

Ginger saw her do this once before. At a restaurant on Cape Cod during a family vacation. The service was poor. The food was cold. Mrs. Crowley approached the manager. Luke's dad shook his head. "It's only supper," he said, and shrugged, but she walked toward the manager, who stood by the hostess. She walked in a way that said she meant business, and in no time at all, their drinks were refilled, they were offered free desserts. They were attended to, and Mrs. Crowley sipped her black coffee and smiled in a satisfied way.

Now, the old woman stands under the Exit sign, her finger pointed at some young resident, her glasses slipping down lower on her nose. Poor Mrs. Crowley. Mrs. Crowley with her quivering chin. She thinks she can get them to fix this.

Then Ginger notices the blond girl who comes running in. She wears a long sweater coat, her hair dipped in hot pink at the ends. She looks like a pretty waif, so many earrings in one ear, shining lip gloss. The girl searches from face to face for someone who will help her. "I'm here about Luke," Ginger hears her say. Ginger watches her look around frantically.

She doesn't see Mrs. Crowley or Mary Jane, whom she might recognize. She is so pale, so frightened. Ginger wants to hug her, to motion to her, but she stays still and watches her like this really is a movie and she cannot affect its outcome.

Hovering there beside Mary Jane, Ginger has the oddest feeling. Looking at the girl feels as though she is looking at herself. She feels exactly as the girl looks: confused, helpless, frantic. They are the same person, she feels for that second. Both of them in love with someone they could never really have.

"Can someone tell me about Luke Crowley?" the girl calls, and her words linger in the air like the sound of glass breaking.

A few days later, Ginger walks Thunder, her parents' dog, around the block. He is old and takes his time, and she feels selfish because the walk is more for her. He looks up at her every so often, his eyes earnest with the cloud of cataracts, as if he's asking, *Can we finish up now?* Christmas is in three days, and the houses have lights wrapped around posts and lit trees in the windows. The neighborhood is quiet, almost lifeless. She then hears the sound of hammering in the distance, at a house being built a block away. It is cool but not cold, and there is no wind. She wants wind. She wants the wind to blow her face hard enough to bring tears.

There was always a part to Luke she couldn't touch, and now he is at Lucatelli's Funeral Home in a closed casket. Viewing tonight, funeral tomorrow. "Couldn't they wait until after the holiday?" her mother said. "Jesus, what's the rush?"

At the hospital, his dying face was bloodied and broken. She remembers looking down at his fingers, and his right hand was still so perfect. Untouched by what had happened. The right hand he had used to scramble eggs for her. The right hand that touched her face. The hand that slid the ring on her finger. She wanted to kiss his fingertips the way she'd always done, but she stayed in the background while Mrs. Crowley and Mary Jane said goodbye and then the girl named Hannah placed her head on his chest and sobbed. "I love you," she said. Ginger wondered how long they had known each other, and if Luke loved her back.

Ginger had stayed behind, her eyes red, hand over her heart. Their group was led away before she could have any time with him. Did she imagine someone would leave her alone with Luke? She had no role, and she didn't want to ask for one. True, the Crowleys had called her to come, but someone had also called Hannah. Why hadn't she run to him earlier that night?

He wouldn't have been home anyway.

But she had run to him in a different way. She ran to the hospital as fast as she could, leaving poor Ahmed behind in the car. Ahmed who nodded solemnly and waved goodbye.

The funeral home smells like carnations and floral ferns. Ginger hears music playing dimly in the background and realizes it's old tapes of Luke and his band. Mary Jane's idea, no doubt. She will have to ask Mary Jane for a copy. In the lobby there are poster boards with pictures of Luke as a baby, a boy, a teenager, and a man. Luke in a high chair looking at a piece of birthday cake, his hair so light and sandy; Luke young and in his karate outfit; teenage Luke in his basketball uniform shooting a basket; the four Crowleys at the Jersey Shore posing in front of a roller coaster. A recent one of Luke holding his niece in a backyard. She realizes she is looking for a picture of her with Luke. She doesn't see herself anywhere in his story.

Mrs. Crowley's grip is strong when Ginger approaches her. "Oh, Ginger," she says, and pulls her down to sit. Mary Jane and her husband are on the other side talking to a group of kids Luke went to college with. Mrs. Crowley slides an arm around Ginger's back and it feels good to be next to her. "Ginger, Ginger. What are we going to do?" Now Ginger stares straight ahead at the dark coffin. A spray of yellow roses and snapdragons on top. Yellow. His favorite color. Ginger remembers a faded yellow sweater he had: a rip in the sleeve, a bleach stain near the bottom. How good of his mother and sister to remember yellow.

"I'm so sorry," Ginger whispers to Mrs. Crowley.

"You're a dear girl." Mrs. Crowley's face is washed out. Still so pale even under the makeup. She wears a starched dark jacket and skirt. A ruby brooch. Ginger thinks she should stand, more people are coming. A husband and wife in black wool coats, the wife clutching a folded handkerchief. She looks at them and starts to rise. "Stay, please," Mrs. Crowley whispers. Ginger stays next to the woman who was never her mother-in-law. The woman who shook her head at Luke so many times. But Luke could lighten any dark mood of hers. He could poke holes in her seriousness. *Mom, you look like Annie Oakley.* And no matter how stony-faced she was, she would start laughing.

Ginger can see the cost of love on her tired face, and something about this brings her relief and joy. Did Luke know?

When people pass through, Mrs. Crowley says, "And you remember our Ginger, don't you?" and no one says no even though many probably have no idea who she is.

Ginger keeps her hands in her lap. "I thought about him so many times. I saw him at the toy shop before your granddaughter's birthday."

Mrs. Crowley nods. "He said he was going to take a ride over to your house to visit the dog."

"Really?"

"But he chickened out. I said, *Go. Go.* I kind of wanted to drag him over there. He never felt worthy, of so many things." She shakes her head.

Ginger imagines Luke pulling up to her parents' house, and she feels warm and relaxed all of a sudden. Thunder barking his familiar bark, wagging his thick tail and running toward Luke, smelling his hand. He would remember Luke. What would Luke say? "Hey, buddy. Been a while." She would stand on the porch. Maybe the late fall sun would be glowing through the trees. She would invite him inside. Why couldn't they fix what they lost? What does she do with all this now?

She holds Mrs. Crowley's hand. "Can I visit you when I'm home again?"

"I would adore that, darling." More mourners are walking up to the casket. Their hands leave fingerprints on the dark wood as they touch it respectfully. One woman bends down to smell the yellow flowers, and Ginger imagines Luke's expression. The way he would lift his eyebrows. The way he'd shake his head.

She stays next to Mrs. Crowley and keeps thinking of him coming over to her house that day in October. What if he had? What if he hadn't chickened out, what if *she* hadn't? What if she watched him from their porch, and he walked across the grass and smiled at her, and she smiled back, and right in that second, in that second that never happened, they would fix all this.

Wouldn't she have been able to help him? Wouldn't she give anything to have that day? She can picture the scene so easily: the bare trees, the excited dog. Her mother and father inside watching the news. Luke's ripped jeans and ragged sweater. His easy smile, his carefree laugh. His straight teeth, occasional freckle, the mole on his neck.

Right now, next to this woman with her perfect posture, her carefully worded responses to every person who bends down, Ginger is glad she came. Her parents sit in the back talking to a retired teacher her mother knows. There is a line out the door. Customers of the dry cleaning place, friends of the family, that seamstress lady, musicians Luke knew: Murph, Chucky, Jimmy—their faces shocked and frowning, all sweetly wearing their old Luke and the Killers shirts. Neighbors, aunts and uncles. She wonders about his last concert. What was the last song he sang?

Mrs. Crowley holds her hand, and Ginger's mind keeps slipping back to that imaginary day, Luke pulling up to her house. It seems so simple now. Why didn't he?

Why didn't she call him earlier from the wedding? Before he got into the car, before he took whatever route he took and swerved along the long, black road, those patches of ice, those oncoming cars. Poor Betsy never stood a chance, did she? Why didn't he know better? She wonders when the autopsy report will come out. She already knows what it will say: alcohol and probably more. She wonders if this information will destroy Mrs. Crowley and Mary Jane, but they must already imagine the worst.

Her mother asked her when it happened if Ginger thought Luke had wanted to die, but Ginger shook her head. She knew he'd never do that—she would bet her life on it. At his lowest point, Luke always had hope. He must have been in over his head with some bad stuff, trying to seem normal under the fierce grip of something terrible. Did he know he could have told her anything? Did he know she would have done anything to help him?

I should. That was what he said to her that day in the toy store when she said he should come by. Almost two months ago. His hand holding the white shopping bag with the gifts for his niece inside. His hopeful stare as she made her way to the back of the store. Did she wave to him?

Ginger smiles politely while Darcy talks to the seamstress,

Freddie Tyler. Both women cry a little together, Freddie touching Darcy's shoulder, patting her hand. "Call me even if you just want someone to watch television with," Freddie says, and Darcy nods.

"You're a gem," Darcy says. "And the carrot cake was lovely." Ginger turns to the side and sees Hannah a few rows back. Her thin face is drained, and her friends sit beside her, trying to make her smile. Hannah stares straight ahead, her eyes swollen. She wears a skirt that's too big, and a white silk blouse. Ginger can see what Luke saw in her. She's a pretty girl. She has kindness to her—Ginger can feel it. Then Hannah turns her way, and they are caught in a stare. Hannah's expression doesn't change, and Ginger doesn't look away. She wants to say she knows what this girl knows, she fought for him the same way. She wants to go talk with her, to say he was wonderful, wasn't he? Wasn't he as good as they come? Wasn't he just a tragic soul, stumbling around in an ill-fitting costume?

Hannah turns away then. Ginger thinks of Luke, of holding his young-forever face one last time. She hears someone say, "All our sympathies," and she feels so sorry, especially for Luke. Sorry that he couldn't make his way. Sorry that he couldn't live this out. Living is fixing, living is working on everything that's wrong—or at least trying your hardest to. And she feels free in that second with the line of people waiting for the Crowleys, with the priest getting ready to say a few words. She looks at the twenty or thirty arrangements of flowers, green and yellow and white and pink, at the mass cards placed on the side table, and Ginger Lord decides then she will fix all this for Luke. She will live for him.

12.

A Single Question

A Saturday in mid-February, Damon Savio freezes his ass off on the front porch waiting for his friend's truck to come down the driveway.

He sits on one of the green Adirondack chairs that his wife, Suzette, ordered from L.L.Bean two weeks ago. They came in these massive boxes—all slabs and bolts and packing foam. "Three-hundred-dollar chairs, you'd think they'd come assembled," he said. But she looked at him hopefully with those sparkling gray-blue eyes, wavy hair pulled up in a ponytail, and there he was minutes later with his drill while she held the chair parts in place. In a few hours, they had four green chairs on the big porch of their white clapboard house. The honeymoon cottage, as Suzette's mother, Marie, calls it.

He imagines how grown up he'll seem when his buddy turns onto their private road, the bare birch trees, the sturdy pine and holly, the long driveway twisting from St. John's Street to their secluded property with the old barn in the back. He has nothing to put in the barn, so it only holds a lawnmower, two bikes, and a rake. He blows warmth into his hands. His ears sting from the cold. He sits on the Adirondack chair and feels something that seems like embarrassment. What right does he have to this wife, this honey-I'm-home house, all this land, when his friend he's known since he was four is still a bachelor? Ahmed would make a great husband, a great dad. Damon grips the sides of the chair and waits. He notices the smell of woodsmoke in the air, and hears the sound of a twig snapping in the distance.

After a few minutes, he sees Ahmed rambling toward him in the truck he's borrowed: a four-wheeler in the pickup bed and another four-wheeler hitched to a small trailer on the back. When he sees Ahmed's expression, always excited, he starts to feel better. Ahmed gives him the finger, a loving gesture they use to greet each other. It seems to take a long time for him to reach the end of the driveway, and Damon wonders what Ahmed thinks of him sitting there on his damn preppy chair, the house with its new brass mailbox and topiaries on either side of the door. The sign above the window that says Pine Place because Suzette always wanted to name a house.

The wide front yard is faded green, and somewhere in the distance, a neighbor's dog barks. Ahmed kills the engine, and it's quiet again.

"Hey, Romeo," Ahmed says. "What are you daydreaming about?"

Damon stands. "Just waiting for your sorry ass. Since when does noon become twelve twenty-five?"

Ahmed smiles and shakes his head as he walks toward the porch. "Since I had to haul these heavy beasts. I couldn't drive more than thirty. When I went around the circle, I thought the one on the back was going to snap off. Tell Suzie I don't have a third, so we'll have to take turns." Ahmed holds a pair of gloves and reaches for Damon's hand, then pulls him into a hug. At some point during their friendship, they moved from handshakes to hugs. Damon can't remember when that started. Ahmed looks around. The wind blows the chimes they got as a housewarming gift from Mr. and Mrs. Lionel, friends of Suzette's parents.

"Suzette's not here." The sun is high above the trees, hidden by clouds. The air has a heaviness to it, a damp chill like snow might be coming. "She took her mom to a matinee."

"Shit, who's gonna call the ambulance then?" Ahmed grins.

They started four-wheeling in high school. Ahmed's uncle had a fleet of four-wheelers he always let them ride at his farm a half hour from Wharton. When Damon told Ahmed that they had bought this place, Ahmed said, "Dude, what I need to know is, how much land?"

"Five acres."

"You know what that means."

"I do."

"Poppin' wheelies left and right on Red and Blue." Now Red and Blue wait in the back like two Transformers, dried mud on their wheels. Damon cannot wait to hear the noise of the engines, see the rush of trees and grass, that reckless trajectory of every bump as the cold air blasts his face and he breathes through the ski mask he will wear under his helmet.

"You're a prince to bring these out here," Damon says.

"Dude, stop kissing my ass." Ahmed stands on the porch steps and seems to stare at the welcome mat by the front door. It is outlined in black with their monogram on it. Damon wants him to look away. He wants to tell him something he can't say. About Suzette. About this house. Something ticks inside him.

"But before Red and Blue . . ." Damon takes two cigars from his coat pocket and holds them like a game show model would. "Tradition."

Ahmed takes a flask from the inside pocket of his coat. "Cheers, buddy."

"I'll go get some glasses," Damon says. He wipes his feet on the doormat out of habit, enters the house, and closes the door without thinking. Why did he leave Ahmed outside? He doesn't know. But he sees the table in the foyer with a small lamp and framed black-and-white picture from their wedding day. The white couches across from one another, the brick fireplace. The throw pillows everywhere. He shakes his head. She stayed up so late, so many nights getting this house ready. The week before the wedding, she had the floors refinished, and now they are glossy. Damon can still smell the varnish. He can still smell the factory scent of the new furniture, the paint (Dew or Mist or some name like that), the fresh carpet up in the bedrooms. He stands there in the middle of the kitchen, looks at this museum of hers, and the room echoes.

He opens the cupboard, and the glasses are crystal—from somewhere like Nordstrom, with small anchors etched in them—and he imagines knocking one over as he's smoking his cigar with Ahmed on the porch and Suzette's disappointed face. She is wonderful, but he just found this out about her: she's the type to frown over a broken glass. Neither of his parents were like this. Most of his previous girlfriends weren't fussy, drinking beer from bottles, letting him smear their lipstick when they kissed. Suzette is different.

But he loves her. He does.

He loves the way she holds a book and sketches sometimes, that strand of hair by her eye. He loves at night when her contact lenses are out and she has her glasses on, sweet-smelling lotion on her face. Yes yes yes. He loves the worn pair of slippers she keeps by the bed and the glass of water she sets on the bathroom sink every night. He likes her body, her hand on his chest. He likes lying under the paisley sheets with her. He likes the texts she sends him: the winky face, the "C u soon i hope." He likes her work. The kids she cares so much about. She would do anything for them. She works with battered women, too, getting them new clothes, new apartments. She is a good human, and he loves that. She is tough, scrappy in a way you don't expect a rich girl to be.

He hears the furnace kick on. The heat crackles through the baseboards. On the kitchen table is the section of white scarf she was knitting. Through the front window, he sees Ahmed pacing back and forth.

He reaches to the back of the cupboard and finds two small glasses from his old apartment. They have a red and blue Phillies design, chipped and faded. He runs his finger over the small Liberty Bell in the center. They were his, before Suzette. Before Amanda even. He holds these glasses, *his* glasses that he picked out, and walks to the door, passing a porcelain umbrella stand with two new navy blue golf umbrellas standing at attention.

Outside, Ahmed has his back to Damon, hands in his pockets. Damon can see his breath in the air, and it makes him feel lonely. "Pour whatever you got in here."

"Nothing but the finest Scotch, Romeo." Ahmed has called him this since fifth grade, when Mrs. Waverly, their language arts teacher, made Damon read the part of Romeo. He can't remember who played Juliet, but he remembers her standing on the teacher's desk as a makeshift balcony, a sheet of cardboard around her like a railing. Did she have glasses? He thinks she did. He can remember the glare of them as he spoke to her. Damon was so embarrassed that he mumbled his lines, and the kids laughed. Ahmed should have been Romeo. He would have loved every second.

They hold their cigars and look out at the yard. They each have an inch of liquor at the bottom of the glass. "So who you been seeing these days, A-Team?"

"Oh man, nobody and nobody. My apartment must be like the house on *The Munsters*. Every chick that comes close just runs away screaming." Ahmed sips his Scotch.

"Bullshit. You're probably banging models. You just don't want me to feel bad."

"Yeah, like I wouldn't broadcast that." Ahmed shakes his head. "Damn, I'd let C-SPAN set up cameras if that was the case."

They hear snow geese over their heads in the gray sky, and they both look up to watch. The birds seem to avoid the clouds, keeping the sun on their wings. "Where the hell are they going?" Damon says.

"Away from here. I'm in the first stage of frostbite. My balls are going to shatter."

"Dramatic."

The Scotch burns Damon's throat in a good way. He loves the smell of the cigars, the heavy air. He loves how sturdy his feet feel against the boards of the porch. He looks out at all this land. Even though the acreage is mostly behind the house, you still can't see the neighbors' homes through the trees. Their neighbor Albert Fitch used to own all the land around here. He had a small airplane and a landing strip on his property. You could hear the loud engine in town and the buzzing whine of the aircraft creeping above the trees and fields. And then it would zip in for a landing. Damon wonders what happened to that plane. Did it just rust somewhere in Albert's yard? Albert is in his seventies now. Little by little, he divided off his property and sold some acres here and there. Now he is down to about ten acres of a mostly wooded lot, his house a redwood A-frame. Someone told Damon there is a small lake on the edge of Albert's property, and now Damon fantasizes about taking the four-wheelers out to look for it.

They are quiet for a minute, and a deer tiptoes past.

"Holy shit," Ahmed whispers.

"It's a buck." Damon doesn't sip his Scotch. He holds his cigar perfectly still. The deer has a sizable rack, and he steps over the fallen leaves in the wooded part of the yard to their right. It looks around every so often, sniffs the air, and then sees them. Damon doesn't blink, but the deer immediately turns and bolts away, its muscles rippling as it runs, its white tail bouncing.

"That was awesome."

"Man, every time I see one, it feels like a miracle." Damon instantly feels stupid for saying that—men don't say shit like that, but Ahmed never judges. He could tell him anything. Ahmed's family moved to Connecticut from Philadelphia when Ahmed was a baby. His brother is fourteen years older, so Ahmed essentially grew up an only child. Damon likes to think they filled in as brothers for each other. He never felt as close to his twin sister as he felt to Ahmed. They always just *got* each other. One night years ago, Ahmed got off the phone with his dad. They had had an argument, and Ahmed's eyes were red. "I fucking hate that guy," Ahmed said, and he banged his fist on the wall of his apartment.

When Damon broke up with Amanda, his girlfriend for a few years after college, he downplayed it to his parents, to his twin, Lara. "Plenty of fish in the big ocean," he said to them, but he had this lump in the back of his throat that wouldn't go away. He would sometimes not shower for a few days because he hurt so bad. He would put off paying his bills for weeks because he didn't have the energy to write checks. Screw it, he thought. Pay the late fee. He remembers going for a walk at four in the morning outside his apartment because he felt so awful and couldn't sleep and didn't know where to put himself. He'd walked the dark streets, shielding his eyes from passing cars. It started to rain, and he just wanted to lie down. What was he doing out here in the middle of the night? Why couldn't he forget her?

Amanda. One night she was sitting up in bed. Amanda with her smooth neck, her long dark hair. He rubbed her shoulders. He shouldn't have said it, he shouldn't have because it seemed to pull the cork from whatever this was, and she just erupted in tears. He shouldn't have said, "What's wrong, Mands? What's the matter?" Because she shook her head, and soon the sheets were wet from her crying.

"I have to leave," she said. "I don't want this anymore."

Why did he ask? How devastating that a single question could pull everything apart. In minutes, she was climbing from bed, dressed in her polka-dot sleep shirt he'd gotten her a year before for Valentine's Day, and it was almost as if she was relieved he'd asked. Like if he hadn't, she would have just gone back to sleep and stayed forever in that apartment with him, sitting on his parents' brown couch they used to keep down in the finished basement, eating at the dinette set his aunt Rosie let him have, stocking the old green refrigerator. And he was half asleep, so foolish in his Star Wars pajama pants, watching her stuff bras and blouses and her makeup into a garbage bag.

"We're breaking up?" he asked, and she glared at him. The same girl who once made him steak, who poured champagne for the two of them into glasses from the dollar store. He used to kiss her freckles. She used to cut his hair sometimes, and he loved it, even if she missed a spot at the top, even if his sister said his neckline was crooked. Are we programmed this way? he wondered. Can we not know we're unhappy sometimes until someone asks the right question?

Those months that followed after Amanda left turned him into a pile of nothing. He hated everything on TV. His heart jumped every time his cell phone rang. *Is this the price of love?* he thought one day when he started to dial her number, then hung up because he knew he'd seem pathetic. He tried to remember what his father said about if the train doesn't stop at the station, then it's not your train.

But over and over, he hated himself for asking her. Why did he invite that pain into his life? Ahmed was the only person he talked to about Amanda, the only one who seemed to understand. And after that time in his life passed, Ahmed was kind enough to never remind him of it.

Damon finishes his Scotch and looks over at his friend, who is also deep in thought, a trail of smoke coming from his cigar. What question could Suzette ask, or Ahmed ask that would unknot him? Does he have one? Is it strange he never told Suzette about the breakup with Amanda? Is it strange that he's kept that inside him, that he still doesn't know how he got over that sadness? Once in a while he catches himself thinking about her leaving that night, dragging her garbage bag behind her, and he still feels wronged, still feels like if he were back in that apartment those years ago and she knocked, he would open the door for her. He would shake his head and pull her into his arms.

What is he doing in this nice house, in his mid-thirties,

thinking about Amanda, who was nothing in the long run? He will have kids with Suzette, most likely, and she will be the one he sees every night. They will grow old together, and that's all that matters. *Thank God you left me.* He should call Amanda and tell her that. *Thank God you did me that favor. Look what I have because of that. Look.*

Why did he never tell Suzette though? Why hasn't he told her about what a failure he felt like that year? His other secrets are smaller. He cheated on a Latin test once in ninth grade because his friend found the same test in an old folder of his brother's and they memorized every question. When he was fifteen he was picked up at the mall for stealing a CD at the record store because Jason, the quarterback in school, told him he didn't have the balls to do it. He almost threw up when he sat in the mall security office. They didn't call his parents, only the cops, and the cop who came took him in her car to the station. He imagined his parents coming to get him there. He could feel the color leave him. As he sat answering a few questions, his hands shook, and the officer must have felt bad for him, because she got him a Dr Pepper from the vending machine, cold and syrupy as he drank it, and she sighed and touched his shoulder. She said, "Don't be stupid anymore," and told him the store wouldn't press charges. She didn't call his parents. She just drove him back to the mall and waved to him from the brown cop car as he walked away.

Why hasn't he said anything about any of this? Why hasn't anyone asked?

Ahmed finishes his Scotch and holds his cigar in his mouth. He zips up his coat. "Well, Romes, ready to hit the open farm?"

"Yeah." He looks down at the drink in his lap. He tastes the cigar, the liquor. He wants a mint.

"What's got you?"

Damon looks up. "Nothing."

Ahmed lifts his eyebrows. "Don't play."

"I'm not."

"Shit, I can feel it. What's eating you?"

He drops the cigar. He stomps the tip of it with his boot. He doesn't care if it leaves a mark. "I'm lonely, man." He clears his throat. "Nah, not lonely. That's the wrong word. I just feel fucking out of it."

He expects Ahmed to laugh. To punch him in the arm. He expects him to say something like *Time to change your tampon*, but Ahmed nods. "I feel you," he says. "I was putting myself in your shoes this whole time and thinking this must be awesome but weird, too."

How odd that Ahmed sees all sides—the good, the troubling. No, not troubling. That is not the right word. He assumed Ahmed envied his life, but he saw through the facade. "You could feel that?"

"Of course." He knows things are serious when Ahmed doesn't joke, but this is when Damon feels the best about their friendship, that they have this authentic thing, too.

Damon thinks of Suzette then. How on one of their first dates five years ago, she looked at him over her glass of beer and told him about moving to Finland. How she couldn't stay. How she wept for her sister who died, and left some of her stuff there and got back on the plane after a few days. How she never taught at the school where she had been hired. "It could have been such a blessing, a once-in-a-lifetime thing, and there I was, chain smoking and dragging my suitcase through that quiet airport." He remembers how he reached over and touched her hand, how she felt so warm, so full of life, and he thought *God, please don't let this go wrong. Please let this all be real*, because that's how it felt with her. Real and wonderful. Her vulnerability in confessing this touched him. She was such a full person, made up of perfections and flaws and kindness and sadness.

And after all that time of being sick over Amanda, he didn't care about her anymore. He didn't even think about her because there was this lovely blonde who laughed as she dipped her nacho into the sour cream. She was so open to tell him this. Maybe he thought then that she would make him more open, too.

He thinks now he fell in love with her the second he met her. But why has he been so guarded? Why couldn't he confess his stuff to her that night, or even months later? He trusts her. He does. If he doesn't tell her everything he is, isn't he no better than Amanda, who kept all that inside, who stayed when she didn't want to, until he asked her that question? He needs to tell Suzette: he has his own Finland. She will listen. She will touch his face. He doesn't want her to feel sorry for him though. He has been afraid of that part of himself, the part that couldn't get over what Amanda did. That part that walked and walked. He wants Suzette to know this was worth it. She was worth the difficult wait. "I'm just whiny, right?" he says as they slip on their hats and gloves and clomp over the frozen grass to Red and Blue.

"Nah," Ahmed says. "I'm lonely, too." He hands Damon a beat-up helmet.

"Yeah?"

Ahmed nods. "But I'll find my queen. I'm not even playing around with princesses anymore. Going right for a queen."

"She's out there, man."

"We'll see." Ahmed looks over at him. "Did that bridesmaid, the vet, did she, uh, ever visit or anything?"

"Ginger?" Damon remembers seeing them take a walk together at the wedding. Then she got word her ex-boyfriend died and had to leave. Leave it to Ahmed to fall for her: the best of the best. Smart, sensitive, beautiful. "Good pick, buddy . . . but I think she's, um, otherwise engaged."

"Yeah, she seemed it." Ahmed looks straight ahead and starts up Red. The engine is loud and confident. "Let's do this!" he shouts over the noise.

"Right behind you." Damon turns the key. The green light appears. He puts it in neutral and hits the start button. The engine growls. Ahmed gives him the thumbs-up and rumbles ahead of him, past the house, past the barn.

They zigzag through the grass, crouching over their seats. He feels the energy of the quad, the good wind, the tires as they bounce over the uneven land, and his friend is there, like a fellow soldier on a horse, like they're in the Crusades or something, riding toward destiny.

"Hell yeah," Ahmed shouts at the same time Damon hollers, "Yes! Yes!" and they drive and yell like this, their lungs burning, the engines roaring. Small flurries of wet snow start to fall. They stick to Damon's boots. They glisten on the sides of the vehicle, and he and Ahmed drive and drive, over all this land that is somehow his. Damon wonders how he found himself here, how his train stopped at this good station.

13.

The Winter Puzzle

Greg Tyler doesn't look at himself anymore when he brushes his teeth.

He notices this. He notices a lot of things. That a man's face needs eyebrows and even eyelashes to look right. That he probably can't do a pull-up these days (he hasn't tried). That the day drags by so slowly when you don't have budget meetings to attend, or board reports to write. That the taste of metal from chemo, even chemo that's been finished for weeks, ruins everything.

He looks at his wife as she steps into the shower, her blondish hair touching her shoulders, and he envies her healthy skin, the way she can stand so straight, the way the water doesn't wilt her at all. He squirts out a blob of Colgate original and closes his eyes while he tastes more metal and runs the toothbrush over his molars.

He wonders if he can survive this.

Of course he would have raised his hand and volunteered to take cancer so no one else would have to, and he's glad Freddie and Addie are spared. That means something somehow, that because he has this, they are spared. Aren't they? Yes, he thinks so. He always felt the world doled things out this way, like a game of duck, duck, goose. He is glad they won't feel sick, lose their hair, see the shock on people's faces. But even still he wishes someone could feel the way he feels for a second, to slip it on like a smock in art class in elementary school, so they'd know what he knows: that there is no God at a time like this, that there is nothing really. That you can't come this close to seeing darkness without it altering you. He realizes how ineffective it is when someone says, "You're in my prayers," or, "Let me know if I can do anything." You should regard someone who has cancer with silence because it is so heavy, so burdensome, that even when the patient is tough like Greg is, silence is the only thing you should offer. He wishes someone could feel how heavy and cruel this is. Then they could slip it off and shake their heads and say, *Oh, Greg. I had no idea.*

He blows Freddie a kiss and says goodbye. She must make it a point not to stare at him. She must work on it, because she waves and winks at him, her body glistening with shower water, her hair slicked back, and he slips on his track pants, his Columbia fleece pullover, and heads out the door. The one good thing about all this: it is so easy to get ready. No hair to pat down. No need to shave that often, although sometimes a faint crop of five o'clock shadow creeps across his face like hope.

He wears a ski hat and gloves. It is only one mile to the treatment center, and he uses what strength is left in him—somewhere in some compartment of his body—to walk. Freddie has stopped offering to drive him, knowing he needs to do this. And he can. Damn if he'll be driven like a junior high kid to band practice. Damn if he'll not make these legs continue to work for him. He is holding on to his independence because he needs to. Because almost everything else—his work, his ability to be the leader in the house, his energy—has been taken from him. He will walk. He will whip his feet like unruly horses.

He likes his sneakers bouncing on the sidewalk, the hills and slopes of the neighborhood, and then the way he weaves through parking lots like Hamilton's (where he used to take clients for cocktails) until he gets to the treatment center. Some of the houses have paper hearts in the window and red sparkling lights. There are small mounds of snow every so often from the storm a week ago, but mostly the yards and sidewalks are clear. He notices so much more now that he goes slower, now that he's not always rushing from the gym to work to a dinner with Alex or clients. On foot he notices everything, and he likes taking it all in. One of the houses has a snow shovel on the front porch propped by the door with a big shaker of ice melt beside it. Seeing this makes him feel weak. He misses shoveling snow. He hopes he can mow the lawn this summer. He is not meant to be a patient.

His mother was from a German family, and they prized cold air and honest work and not feeling sorry for yourself. He remembers how after his great-grandmother had a stroke she insisted they keep the lights off in her hospital room. "No television, no noise," she said. "I am willing myself to get better." Now, thirty years later he is doing the same. He feels there must be a benefit to the February air passing through his lungs, that the sun on his face must help in some way. He imagines his body is a factory, and good practices will make it produce what it needs—strong antibodies spilling out on a conveyor belt—to keep fighting this.

Even if he has to stop every so often. Even if his legs ache, and the site on his hip itches from the radiation, and he feels queasy sometimes. Through his pants, he thinks he can feel the tattoo where they marked him for the beams of radiation. He feels so sensitive lately—as though his brain notices everything wrong in his uncooperative body. He hears his own breathing, his blood coursing under his skin, his heart beating.

How many years did he just ignore his whole body as though it was machinery with a lifetime guarantee? He took it all for granted and assumed it could keep going and going. He wishes he had lain in a hammock more, resting his hand on his heart. He wishes he had enjoyed the freedom he had when he was well. He could have called in sick whenever he wanted and just sat in a café with Freddie and Addie, eating ice cream or french fries. Now everything is hard. Now the only thing he can do is walk to a doctor's office. That is his outing. What was he thinking before?

With his hat on, with the sunglasses protecting his eyes, he almost feels normal. Just another guy turning forty next week, out for some exercise. "Hey there," he says to the old man getting his paper three houses down. He looks at the sidewalk because there are uneven parts, and he doesn't want to stumble. With the blood thinners, a fall would be a mess. Freddie would go crazy. She would wrap him up like a baby.

He also is happy not to meet the man's eyes. Bob something or other, owner of the theater in town. A complete grump. Yet he seems healthy as a horse. Bob nods and mumbles, "Good day."

Marcia Peters walks her big Saint Bernard down Maple Street by Woodsen Park, and he notices that she pulls the dog closer. "Hey, Oliver," he says, and purposely goes over to pet his head. I am not fragile, he thinks.

"You're looking well," Marcia says.

"Yup. Thanks." He pats the dog's side and keeps moving. No time to think that everything hurts—his knees, his joints, even his bones. He grits his teeth. That is probably why his jaw hurts now. He's been doing that too much. But he's alive. And it's still worth it. Will there come a time where it won't be worth it? He chases that thought away. He is a fighter. He will keep fighting. That's what he knows.

Pain is nothing. If handling pain is all it takes, he will win this. He promised Freddie he would.

"I'm not going to die," he said one night a few days ago as he lay awake an hour after they'd gone to bed. He wasn't sure if she was still up. He said the words, and they echoed in the dark bedroom. She didn't say anything at first, and he watched the slow movement of the ceiling fan. He saw the way their front porch light made glowing lines above their curtain. He shifted his legs, and the dog jumped off the bed. He heard the heat kick on and the rush of air to the vent on the floor. He figured she was asleep, but then he heard the small gasps, the sobbing she was trying to choke back. "Stop," he said, nudging her leg with his knee. "I'm not."

"Greg." She whispered his name, and he could feel her body tremble as she tried to fight the tears. When he reached to touch her face, her pillow was damp, and he felt like a failure. For making her cry. For being this close to dying. He smoothed his thumb under her eyes, and tried to wipe her tears. He couldn't undo what he'd started, and now that he'd said the words, the businessman in him couldn't let them go.

"I promise I'm not."

His pride had always done this to him. Made him grab that drunk guy at the Yankees game a few years ago who told him to hurry the fuck up at the urinal. Made him drive two and a half hours back to Boston after he'd just gotten home from a meeting there because a client had emailed him and was unhappy. His pride once had him take apart a clubhouse he'd built for Addie the day before—hours of unbuilding and rebuilding most of its parts (in the dark, so she wouldn't see) because he didn't like the way the floor buckled. Freddie said he was crazy, ridiculous. "Get to sleep," she said. "Addie won't even notice. She will love it because you made it and because you sit in it with her. She's not putting a level on the floor!" But there he was sawing and measuring and setting it right. Where did this come from? Because he was an only child? Wanting, always, to be perfect, be a hero? His parents were lovely people. They never pushed him. But he always reached further than he should, always wanted more. Instead of running a 5K, he'd sign up for a marathon; instead of turning in a requested five-page report to Alex, he'd deliver fifteen pages with pie charts and color-coded data. Now, with cancer, one of the deadliest kinds, he can't roll over. He can't just try to survive. He has to promise he will. In some weird, competitive way, he is even happy his type of cancer is one of the most aggressive. When he survives, he will have survived the worst. What *is* that in him? Who did this to him?

He did it to himself.

And these days he couldn't feel more imperfect, more inferior than he does now. He wants to unzip his skin and crawl out. Did that lead him to up the ante and make that promise?

Now he has made a vow he may or may not be able to keep. She squeezed his hand that night like she was going to twist it off, and he listened to her get quieter and quieter until her hand felt still, and she sighed as she went to sleep. And then he lay there for another two hours, her body silent against his. His mind raced with guilt, with worry.

Why would he say this? He heard his father's voice. *When are you going to learn enough is enough?* His father had said that often—after Greg had signed up for two spring sports in high school, or after he'd stayed up all night working on his speech for student government, or even in college when Greg was doing double shifts in his bar runner job at Sidecar. He lay there that night with Freddie and wished his parents were alive again, for Freddie to forget this promise even though he suspected this had helped her fall asleep. But did she even believe him? She knows he can't know for sure. But still. She has trusted him all these years. What hubris, what haughtiness, to say that. Everything felt unbearable, even their comfortable bed. He finally brought sleep on by trying to remember all the kids in his third-grade class; then trying to revisit every hotel room he'd ever stayed in. He finally reconciled this ridiculous promise by remembering that most of the promises he has made have been challenging, nearly impossible, mostly out of reach, too. And he has fulfilled all of them. Wasn't this more of the same?

Now he is at the treatment center. One of those hospital satellite places with imaging and therapy and new signs with crisp logos and doctors' names. And beyond the sliding doors, standing there in the vestibule is his cancer gang. Rosco holding on to his walker and waving; thin Imogene with her small green hat and drooping earrings, holding a bag of something she probably baked for them; and Brandon in his thrift store overcoat, black nail polish on some of his fingers.

"What a motley bunch," Greg says. He thinks he's used that line a few times.

They wave to each other (hugging is too germy, too risky). They tell Greg he looks cold. "Brrr," Imogene says. They set up camp where they always do in the lounge for the patients receiving radiation. Imogene doesn't have any treatments prescribed for her (her numbers are good at the moment), and Brandon, whose dark hair is longish because he never had chemo, only has a week to go until he can ring the bell, a celebratory gesture patients do at the end of their treatment. Rosco, a spunky old man who reminds Greg of his grandfather, and Greg have the longest sentences of radiation: five days a week for six more weeks, give or take. This is a breeze compared to chemo, compared to the stem cell transplant the doctors are telling him they might try down the road if the numbers look good and they find a match. Greg's job now is to stay healthy.

They open the ginger ale Rosco has brought, and Imogene puts out small chocolate cupcakes with cream cheese frosting. They are not supposed to eat anything unhealthy these days, but Fifi, the nurse they all love, said small treats are fine. The group breaks off pieces of cupcakes and says they're like heaven and wow and thanks. Greg tastes only metal.

They have a good forty-five minutes until Brandon's appointment, and then Greg and Rosco go in later. Greg always looks at the toys in the corner of the room—one of those abacus-looking things with sliding balls, and Dr. Seuss books, and a small kitchen with plastic dishes and pots and pans. He is grateful every time that the toys seem undisturbed. He hopes they stay that way. He thinks of Addie and what she would do if she were here waiting with him. He imagines her sliding the wooden abacus balls back and forth. He imagines her sitting at the table next to him and resting her face in her hands patiently.

The group makes small talk about the Super Bowl commercials and the snow (just three inches) the other night. How fast it melted, they say. They shake their heads about the bombing on the news, and no one can believe it's been that many years since Peter Jennings died, and then Fifi pokes her head out to see what Imogene baked. "I might steal the whole tin," she says, and they smile and sigh and look at each other. What is it about this crowd that Greg so enjoys? He wants to get up and hug each of them. Even Brandon, who is sometimes a little whiny.

"How's our Addie?" Imogene says to Greg. She dabs her mouth with a Valentine's cocktail napkin she brought with the cupcakes.

"Good, good," Greg says. "Getting big." *She likes to rub my bald head*, he wants to say. *She started writing in a diary*, he wants to say. Greg can't bring himself to read it. He wants to say: *What if, despite all we do to distract her, she's scared and worried that I'll die?* It was always his number-one goal to never have her worry about anything. His parents worked hard to let him be a worry-free kid, and maybe that is what gave him this determination, this unshakable confidence. But Addie stares at him longer than she used to. She hugs him tighter, he thinks. Once he saw her close her eyes in the mirror when she hugged him, and he wondered what that meant—if she was trying to memorize him or something. He silently says a prayer for her—a quick one—and turns back to Imogene. "She joined the glee club at school."

"Cute," Rosco says. He coughs, and they can all hear the wetness in his lungs.

Brandon looks out the window and says something about the girl he's seeing. Selena. He says her name with a touch of an accent, which annoys Greg. Brandon likes drama. He is still young enough to want drama.

Imogene thinks her daughter is up to something. She keeps asking Imogene to write down her medication, the pension information, the stocks. She shakes her head. "Does she think I'm losing my marbles?"

"We'll straighten her out," Greg says. He only ate what

amounts to a large crumb of cupcake. He sips the ginger ale. Metal fizz. He wants something extra sweet—so sweet it will eat through the metal—like purple Kool-Aid or Cherry Coke. He keeps feeling guilt over his promise to Freddie. Days later, and it still burns him. What business did he have saying those words?

Once a week they make it a point to get together like this—though he ends up bumping into Rosco many other days, and sometimes Brandon. He met Imogene in chemo after the holidays. They would sit side by side in their chairs, with the tubes and the beeping monitors, and look over at each other and roll their eyes. "I'd rather be doing my taxes," Imogene said to him that first day.

He laughed. He got a dizzy spell at that moment, and she waited and watched him. "Sorry," he said.

"You okay? Should I call the nurse?" And just like that, he had a cancer buddy. This new friend who started to phone the house, who bought a ballerina music box for Addie once. Freddie started to pick them both up (it was impossible to walk home after chemo) and would drive Imogene to her small apartment in the retirement home. When the phone would ring, Freddie would hand it to him. "It's your girl-friend," she'd say.

When he was prescribed the weeks of radiation after his numbers were still sketchy, Imogene asked for the details. "Mind some company?" she said.

"Actually, no, I wouldn't mind." He didn't. He had gotten used to her at those chemo appointments. The way they stared at the tubes together. The way she never cried—only shrugged, only sighed. And he liked her jokes. "Just put it in this pincushion," she'd say, holding out her thin arm. Or, "You better stick a few extra doses in there, baby doll. Fill 'er up."

In no time at all, she had ingratiated herself with Rosco when Greg started at the radiation place. Rosco's wife died two years ago, and his grandson drives him for treatment and picks him up. Greg and Imogene collected Rosco to join them, and then Brandon, whom Imogene found outside with his hands in his pockets, wearing his headphones. "We're all on the same team," she said to them that day.

Now he tells them what he's wanted to say, about his promise to Freddie. Imogene looks up at him. Rosco shakes his head. A deliveryman comes through the doors with boxes stacked on a hand truck. Brandon laces his fingers together. "That's a shitty promise, man," Brandon says.

Greg glares at Brandon. What did he expect from his group? That they'd say an outrageous promise was okay, that it's fine for sick people to enter into risky contracts? Yes, he wants them to say this. He wants them to say they understand. That maybe they have made similar promises. In fact, he wants them to all promise right now that they will get through this. Sometimes a voice screams in his head that maybe half of them or most of them or all of them will die, and sitting here like this will not have meant anything.

"You thought you needed to," Imogene says. She pats Greg's hunched shoulder blades. It hurts, he wants to say. When you pat my back, it hurts like hell. It shouldn't hurt. He wonders the way he always does if his cancer has spread—he imagines an X-ray or scan with every part lit up, showing disease. But they've been monitoring him closely and he would know.

Rosco declares, "We got no business messing with God."

Greg groans and looks up at the ceiling. *What God?* he wants to say. It's just each of us alone. Each of us trying to hold on to who we love before we're ripped into the abyss. Greg frowns. He picks up his ginger ale can and what's left of the cupcake, stands, and walks over to the garbage. He is not pissed at Brandon or Rosco. He is ashamed. Haunted by what he said. He wanted their forgiveness, their understanding, a benediction of sorts. Can't he at least have this? He's lost so much. Can't he at least make a fucking long shot of a promise?

He glances over at the toys. He never noticed the jigsaw puzzle among the stacks: a winter scene with cardinals and squirrels. He stands there and looks at it. He imagines for a second spilling it out on a table in the corner by himself and how good it would feel to hold each piece and study where it belongs.

Brandon and Imogene and Rosco are staring at him. Imogene is so brittle. She must weigh ninety pounds, and Rosco wheezes as he shakes his head slowly. Brandon doesn't look sick at all. Greg never noticed how tall he was. How broad his shoulders are. Fucker. No one would look at them in a lineup and say Brandon has cancer. He will probably waltz in and out of cancer, and that will be that. He has a mild kind of lymphoma or something. They don't ask the specifics.

Greg sees Fifi and the other nurses march back and forth with files behind the glass window. He sees the clipboard by the window and wonders if he signed in. There are still Christmas cards taped to the ledge of the reception area. He thinks of cards he used to write Freddie when he was in college. *I'll be home soon. The weeks will fly by.* Or postcards he would send her and Addie from business trips to New York. Or Los Angeles. Or London. *I miss my two girls. Be back in a jiffy (with gifts!).* He has been solid with his promises. He has done what he's said, and now Brandon and Rosco are right—this is a promise out of his hands. He wonders what his mom and dad would say about all this. *Easy does it, honey. Let's just wait and see before we get carried away.*

He sees the bell by the door that people ring when they are finished with treatment. He can't wait to ring that damn bell. A shiny brass bell on a plaque with a small rope hanging from it. He wants his cancer gang to cheer. Brandon will ring the bell in a week. In college, Greg was on the rowing team, and in one match, his crew got off to a terrible start. They had no way of catching up to the other crews, but they paddled anyway. He feels as far behind as that. So many more weeks and days of this. He remembers being in that boat, how cold and black the water looked, how the sun seemed small behind clouds.

"Come sit, buddy," Rosco calls to him. Rosco holds a tissue in his hands, and his brown sweater vest has lint balls. He unwraps a cough drop and puts it on his tongue.

"I sounded like a dick," Brandon says to Greg. "Sorry."

Imogene bristles for a minute at Brandon's language, but then smiles at him.

Greg pulls out his chair. He takes his hat off and the air feels good on his head. He rubs his smooth scalp and looks down. "I had no right . . . I wanted to have a right to say it, and I don't."

He stares ahead and purses his lips as he watches the nurses laugh about something behind the glass. He doesn't feel insulted by their laughter the way some might. He is glad life is going on as usual for much of the world. "I just want to know I've done everything in my power to stop this," he says, his voice far away.

Imogene pats his hand. "None of us knows what works, do we?"

Over in the rows of chairs, a woman with a scarf on her head is clipping coupons and filing them into a binder. A man with glasses is turning the pages of *Vanity Fair*. Fifi calls Brandon in and he moans and plods toward her. "See you when I see you," he says. The hood on his sweatshirt bobs as he walks, and for a second, Greg thinks of him as a younger brother even though he doesn't know what having a sibling feels like. They wave to their friend as he disappears behind the door.

The three of them don't say much. Something about more snow on the way. Something about how the groundhog in Pennsylvania didn't know what he was talking about. Outside the big window, the trees are bare but sturdy. A cluster of birds lands on the branches. They are small and gray with orange beaks. They hop around and fly off again.

Greg feels for his cell phone to make sure it's there. He might have to call Freddie for a ride if he doesn't feel better. He holds his teeth together for a moment and the pain seems to stop. The door opens for him, Fifi smiling and waving him in, and he slips his hat on, stands tall like he has an important meeting, like inside there are new clients to impress, and he is about to walk toward her.

But then the idea comes to him. He gives Fifi the *just a minute* signal with his finger. He feels the other patients watching as he rushes toward the door. He tugs the rope on the bell that no one told him he could ring, and he stands there and listens to the clanging, the victorious loud metal sound like a race has begun or the stock market is open, or a war is over, and it feels good to hear it whether he deserves this ringing or not. It feels good.

14.

Watercolor

Hannah wakes up on the morning of her twenty-fifth birthday to the sound of her neighbors fighting again. She peels the sleeping mask off her eyes. She turns to look at the clock: 9 a.m.

She never hears the exact words the couple says, but loud mumbles vibrate through the walls of her studio apartment, the high tone of the woman who shrieks when she's apparently making a point, and the man who replies in grunts that sound like, "Chamomile, chamomile." She isn't even sure if they speak English or not, but they fight often. Sometimes they just scream all day. They must work at odd times, because for hours the silence is so dull against her beige walls that she thinks they've moved.

She flips the covers back, and today marks a slight difference for her. How did this happen? She feels relieved. A long-carried weight of disappointment is gone. She isn't expecting Luke to be next to her. Lucas Jefferson Crowley. Not in bed. Not fumbling with the coffeemaker. Not on the phone in a hoarse morning voice trying to straighten out a late credit card payment. She doesn't expect him to be anywhere today, her birthday, and she is not wrong.

Birthdays. On her twelfth birthday, the cop took her mother, barefoot, away in his car for writing bad checks. They were living outside Las Vegas then. Hannah remembers running after them with her mother's shoes in her hand. The dry air. The two stray cats that lived outside their small house. "Get the hell inside," her mother yelled, mascara smeared around her eyes. On her twentieth birthday, her friend Sammi, who is not her friend anymore, took her to a clinic for an abortion. Two years ago, on another birthday, she woke up and thought of jumping out her mother's twelfth-floor apartment window in New Haven. Splat. Or writing a long note and getting drunk and letting the bathtub fill up over her head. But she got dressed and went to work her shift at the restaurant, and that day, she met Luke.

The new waiter with messy brown hair had scribbled song lyrics on the cardboard back of his order pad. He looked at her when the manager was training him on the POS system and said, "Smile. You'll get more tips, won't you?" He was older, but looked adorable in his white shirt and black tie, the small apron around his waist. And though it was probably a year and a half until he held her hand when they left their shift together, and she walked home with him and the moon was a thin sliver and the stars were so bright and steady and she stayed the night at his place, there was something about meeting him that first day that propelled her along. That made her forget about jumping, about letting the bathwater finish her. She didn't want to be forgotten anymore. Did that make sense?

His jokes at work, his eye rolls at customers, his whispers of "Don't trip" when she was carrying a big tray—it all made her like the world better.

There are seven cracks in the apartment ceiling, and a hole in the wall where the cable was ripped out (she stuffed a bandanna inside this in case a mouse could poke through). The apartment has a hint of garlic smell that never goes away, and she has a small kitchenette with a dish drainer that came with the place that she is never able to clear because there isn't enough room in the three cupboards for her mismatched mugs and pots and pans. Now the yelling next door has died down. Or the woman might be crying. There is silence, then an occasional sob-like noise—as if someone is saying their last words through a gag. But she is proud to be here.

She found the apartment in early November. Luke went with her. The rooms echoed as they walked through it. "I like the high windows," he said, and she started to imagine how the place could look like Carrie Bradshaw's in *Sex and the City* with a little imagination. She pictured holding a coffee cup as the sun warmed her shoulders. She thought the far corner would be a good spot to set up an easel for the watercolor painting she was never great at, and maybe Luke would read the paper on a chair with an ottoman she imagined would fit perfectly in the carved-out nook by the small bookcase. She'd walk by him and kiss his head and that would be the start of her adult life. He would stay over more and more, wouldn't he? He would play songs on the guitar while she made them pasta and poured wine.

She didn't imagine the clutter she has now: the mismatched sofa and chairs that sag, the cheap coffee table with the split wood on the leg, the TV stand that serves as a catch-all for mail and her bracelets and hair things, the clothes she has draped over the coat rack in the middle of the room because her closet is too small. And the bed in the corner, with its rumpled blankets and shabby pillows. She didn't imagine it this way.

She didn't imagine waking up alone like this four months later.

Happy birthday.

She washes her face and fills a big glass of water, cracking ice cubes out of the plastic tray.

Is it odd she didn't expect Luke today? Almost like she went to bed sad and broken but woke up with some of that washed out of her? She feels guilty for beginning to be over him.

Is that what the brain is programmed to do? Wait and wait and then finally give up—like the story of the dog she saw once on the news that would wait under the tree for its owner who died?

She looks in the freezer where she keeps the coffee (the fair trade kind that Luke always bought) and then remembers she used the last of it yesterday. *Fuck my life*, she thinks. Her grandfather hated when she didn't plan. She closes her eyes and sees him—dead, like Luke. His pressed flannel shirts. His red suspenders he loved wearing. Her Pappy. She could use him now. She would love to be at his house while he put out a plate of those butter cookies he bought in a big blue tin. "You didn't eat nothin'," he'd say, and push a few more her way. She'd lick the sugar off the pretzel-shaped cookie and smile. He saved her so many times from her rotten mother. From all the times she'd fallen. "You'll see it the right way one day, and it will all come together," he said as he poured her coffee from a thermos and smiled.

She has eighty-three dollars and twenty-eight cents in her checking account. She is barely making enough money processing loan paperwork at the Kia dealership during the day, taking odd shifts at the restaurant to keep afloat. God forbid her car needs tires or the pain in her tooth gets any worse.

She shouldn't have gotten this place. She was overreaching. She wanted Luke to be impressed. Was he? She thought the apartment could seal this deal, that she could keep him with a respectable home. She never had a respectable home before. With this apartment, she wanted to be someone he could admire and fully love, the one who could save him.

She wants coffee so badly. The space between her eyes starts to hurt, which seems ridiculous. But it does. Her body needs it. She closes her eyes and thinks of the smell, the hot dribble and slurp the coffeemaker makes. Maybe she has transferred everything, every craving over to coffee. She barely eats these days. And no funny stuff. She has a glass of wine here or there, but not a joint, nothing, nothing since Luke's accident three months ago. She promised him that, but beyond that promise, she has no desire for any of it anymore. It ruins you. She doesn't want to be ruined.

Three months with no Luke. It is March, and she is ready for spring and summer. She needs them to come.

She stands at the kitchen counter in her flimsy T-shirt and the scrub pants her mother found for her at a thrift store.

Scrub pants. The young doctor in his scrub pants in December who put a hand on each of her shoulders and explained carefully what had happened to Luke. "Do you understand what I'm saying?" he said.

Yes, yes, she understood.

Understood that she had hoped for too much. The knowledge of this makes her numb, makes her half angry. When he died, the chances of her rising above who she was seemed over: the girl who the other girls called a *skank* in high school. The girl who got C's and D's and never thought of going to college. She always felt discounted, cheap. Yes, she was a cheap-purse, cheap-lipstick, forgettable girl. Worse when she dyed the edges of her hair pink, when she put in more than one earring and got that tattoo of her grandfather's signature across her wrist.

Once she had shown Luke a brochure for an evening college program where you could get credit for life experiences and start to earn your bachelor's degree. "Cool," he'd said. "Go for it." College was no big deal to him. He had a degree. His sister had a degree. They were from a good family. Upper middle class: a basketball hoop in the driveway, a green lawn. She imagined taking classes at night, holding a book to her chest in the apartment as she quizzed herself on art history or botany terms. She imagined furiously punching numbers into a calculator and saying something like, *I'm just double-checking my stats*. She imagined learning, finally, what the hell a sonnet was. Or getting further with her watercolor painting. She was relieved that Luke thought she could take on college, but at the same time, she wanted more credit for even thinking about it. Was he impressed, or didn't he even care?

She brushes her teeth, twists her hair into a bun, and slips into a long sweater with tights. Her boots are imitation Uggs. *Fuggs*, Luke called them. She will buy herself a hot cup of coffee for her birthday, from the good shop down the street: Annabelle's Brew House. She will even splurge on a pastry or croissant. She wishes she could go to a place like that every day. To stop being meager. She hates being meager. Did Luke think she was meager? This makes her heart hurt again for a moment. She knows she's meager. Whenever she has pretended she isn't, she feels like an imposter.

She moves things around on the TV stand and finds the apartment key. She slings her purse over her shoulder and opens the door.

"Oh, hello."

She jumps back. She is surprised to find Mrs. Crowley standing there. Luke's mom. A woman with high cheekbones and tinted eyeglasses. She holds a drink carrier with two cups from Dunkin' Donuts and a large shopping bag. "I hope this isn't a bad time, dear," she says.

"Oh no. Not at all." Coffee? Is this really for her? From this woman? She can't believe Mrs. Crowley is bringing her a treat. Has anyone ever done this? And on her birthday, no less.

Maybe this year will *be different*, she thinks. Maybe this is the start of something.

But Mrs. Crowley has always made her nervous. She feels every centimeter of not measuring up to this woman's high standards. In the time she and Luke dated, she never ate a meal with his mom. Luke brought her home just once in December: a clean house in that perfect neighborhood, the type of street she never, ever set foot on when she was younger, with a polished dining room table and stiff curtains. Mrs. Crowley was polite but didn't offer her anything. Didn't ask her any questions. At the funeral, Mrs. Crowley sat close to Luke's ex-girlfriend, a veterinarian. A goddamned veterinarian. Really?

"May I come inside?"

"Yeah, I was just going to get coffee."

"Lucky timing." She holds up the twin Dunkin' Donuts cups.

"You're a lifesaver," Hannah says. She melts for a moment. This is a big deal. *Happy birthday*, she thinks. When they step inside, she feels nervous as she closes the door. Something makes her terrified of being alone with Luke's mom. She is like the scariest teacher from high school, or a head nurse at a hospital who bosses everyone around. She speaks slowly and precisely. She emphasizes each word as though she will refuse to repeat herself later. Hannah looks at her sloppy apartment. Cheap. Unmade bed, all that clutter on the TV stand. This woman must be disgusted. *I am not a veterinarian, as you can guess*, she wants to say. *I don't have the clean face and honest eyes and good posture that that girl has*, she wants to say. *I was brought up on SpaghettiOs and Hi-C.*

"I should have phoned you. I apologize." Mrs. Crowley looks around, lifts her eyebrows for a second, and then puts her stuff (the coffee, the shopping bag) down on the small drop-leaf table. Hannah notices the lint on the floor. Mrs. Crowley wiggles a coffee free from the holder and hands it to Hannah. "I guessed cream and sugar."

"Works for me." She sips the coffee gratefully. Does she look like a beggar who just took a handout? She doesn't care. She loves Luke's mom now just for this. Maybe she will start having her coffee this way instead of black. It tastes like a cozy house, like care. She starts to wonder what has brought this woman here, and nervousness fills her body. I am meager, she thinks. This woman knows it. Why am I so meager? And how did she even know where I live?

Mrs. Crowley sips her own coffee. She gets lipstick on the cup. She breathes. Even her breaths are strong and confident. She gestures toward the shopping bag she brought. "I have some things of, of his."

"Oh." She stops being nervous. This feels nice, like she has, finally, been noticed. She sees Luke's face so clearly then. He is laughing. He is waltzing by her at the restaurant carrying a tray with mozzarella sticks and dipping sauce. The couple next door makes one sound, and Mrs. Crowley turns her head.

"I thought you'd like to have them. Mary Jane and I have been getting the apartment cleaned out. Not much there in the way of big stuff, but you know: a thousand little things. I told him once he was a pack rat." She laughs, but then there is a glimpse, a flash of hurt on her face even the blush can't hide. Hannah starts to like his mother fully in this moment. Poor woman.

Hannah loves the coffee against her throat. She loves the perfect sweetness and cream. She is almost finished. She doesn't know the etiquette. Should she take the stuff out of the bag now or wait until the woman leaves? "He kept a lot of stuff, yeah. Movie tickets, notes, fliers. Yeah." She scolds herself. *Stop saying yeah.*

Mrs. Crowley walks around and looks out the window. "My goodness, I think about him a lot." She puts her coffee down by the sofa. "You have a nice view here. I like the high windows."

"Thanks. And, uh, he said that exact same thing. About the windows." She lets out a polite laugh.

"He did?" Mrs. Crowley smiles gratefully. "Oh, that boy." She sighs. "Anyway, I won't keep you. I just wanted a quick visit."

Hannah feels honored. She can't believe she has even crossed this woman's mind. "That was nice. Especially the coffee."

"If you don't want the stuff, don't keep it for my sake. It's a sweatshirt, a few pictures of the two of you. A mug with his name on it . . . just silly stuff, really." Mrs. Crowley shrugs. She picks up her purse and starts to walk toward the door.

Hannah watches her. She glances at the stuff in the bag. Junk mostly, the stuff that probably avoided the garbage by a hair. *Silly stuff.* Did she give the important stuff—his guitar, the Navajo rug, the carved walking stick of his grandfather's—to the veterinarian with her expensive purse and straight perfect teeth? Probably. It starts to hit her. Why didn't they invite her to see his apartment one last time? To help them clean it out? She was there more than either of them ever were. She slept beside him in his bed. She bought bananas and oranges and put them on his counter. Was everything she left there—her makeup, a pair of flip-flops, the blanket she bought for their bed—assumed to be trash? She feels goose bumps. Jittery. She feels the way she felt in high school when she wanted to answer a teacher's question. "I didn't like it," she spits out.

"What?" Mrs. Crowley turns. Her eyes are so focused, intense. She looks half frightened, bracing for something. Hannah's heart races.

"I didn't like how you sat with *her* the whole time at the funeral. How you touched her shoulder to comfort *her*. How you introduced her to everyone." She starts to cry. "I was his girlfriend."

Mrs. Crowley doesn't answer at first. Hannah's words echo in the quiet apartment. "I'm sorry you feel this way, dear. I was not trying to make you feel bad."

"You did! You did." How did she turn the conversation into this? It had been perfectly polite. The woman was leaving. What made her do this?

But she can't stop. She swallows, chooses her words carefully. "My friends kept saying, *Isn't that his mother? Isn't that his sister? Go sit with them.* I couldn't sit with you. I couldn't even hug you in the hospital. I had no one to cry with. My mom is a . . . she doesn't care. I lost him that night and I had no one. And I know I'm not good enough for you, I'm not the girl a nice guy like Luke brings home. You probably wanted to keep him from girls like me. I know this." She holds the empty coffee cup, and her knees shake.

"You're fine, dear." Mrs. Crowley clears her throat. Her arms are folded tightly across her abdomen. "I just don't know you. That's what put us at a disadvantage. I met you only that one time at the house. When we watched him put the star on top of the tree? We never had a chance to get acquainted better."

"Because he was ashamed. I bet he had no problem bringing *her* home. She probably came to Thanksgiving, to Sunday dinners."

"Please, dear. I am certainly in no position to explain why I knew Ginger better and longer, but that's the only defense I can make. I knew her when they were young for a long time. We have history. That is all." Her purse hangs from her thin shoulder, and she keeps one toe pointed toward the door. "And I am very sorry you felt alone. I don't think any of us were in the right frame of mind, were we?"

"I was trying to help him. Did you know he was writing songs again that last month? Beautiful ones. He would sing them to me. I feel so lucky to have been there for that." She shakes her head. One was about swans he saw on a lake as a child. It broke her heart. "He saved me. When I met him, I wanted to die, and knowing Luke, just knowing him, saved me."

"I didn't know any of this." Mrs. Crowley compresses her lips. She reaches for a handkerchief and blots her nose. She points to the bag she brought. "I just wanted you to have these things."

"He was on his way to see *me* that night. I loved him." She stops. "You called her first, didn't you? To come to the hospital?" She doesn't stop to register the reaction on Mrs. Crowley's face, but her mouth is agape, her eyes are reddish. "You can say yes. You can." She wonders if the neighbors now hear her. Her mumbling through the walls.

"I don't remember." She fishes the car keys from her purse. "I'm sorry to have upset you. Really, I am." She walks to the door and opens it.

Hannah shrugs. "I'm sorry, too." She puts her coffee cup down and clutches the back of the chair. "You would have liked me, I think. Luke said you'd be tough at first, but then you'd like me. I believed him. I thought one day I'd be at your home playing checkers or helping you dry dishes after dinner."

Mrs. Crowley keeps her hand on the doorknob. "Did he? I could hear him say that. I could hear his voice just then." She covers her mouth with her handkerchief.

Hannah stands over the bag. She reaches inside. She finds a small soccer trophy he kept by his bed. "To remind myself I'm a winner," he said once, and laughed. She smiles at the trophy. She touches its gold name plate. *Lucas Crowley. Most Valuable Player.* "It was good of you to bring this stuff. And the coffee. I'm sorry."

Mrs. Crowley looks at her before she leaves. Her eyes behind her glasses look startled but kind. "At some point I'd like to hear about his songs." She pauses. "I do hope to see you again."

Hannah nods. "Yeah." She imagines for a second bringing two coffee cups to Mrs. Crowley's house. Could she ever have the courage to go over there? Maybe. Outside in the hallway, she hears someone walking down the stairs. She hears a door slam shut above her. "It's awful without him, isn't it?"

Mrs. Crowley nods thoughtfully. "Goodbye, dear." She waves and shuts the door carefully. Hannah can still smell her good perfume. For some reason, she wants to yell to the woman that it's her birthday. She can hear her make her way down the stairs. The sun is so bright on the dirty floors of her apartment, and the window that she opened a crack last night makes the sheer curtain flap back and forth. She is sorry. She is sorry about Luke, and that his mother is gone. Sorry about being another year older and not getting anywhere. She hears cars outside and the groaning of the street sweeper. She sees Luke's trophy sitting by itself. Her coffee cup is empty and she is sorry.

15.

The Sound of Time

A Saturday in mid-April and Kay Lionel stays at the window to watch the car drive away. The driver with her ponytail, the man beside her in the passenger seat leaning his head against the window for the long drive ahead of them. Their car is dark gray, and the tires shine. The daffodils are up now in flower beds beside the walkway, and the groups of white tulips and deep purple hyacinth make her sigh. "Fingers crossed," she whispers as the couple pulls away, and she turns to their daughter, who she's watching for two days. She wears a long-sleeved shirt with a sequined mermaid on the front. "So, Miss Addie, I wonder if you'll help me bake some cookies?"

The girl nods shyly. "Sure," she says. There is worry on her face; her gaze is far away. Kay tries to smile, but Addie's sweetly braided hair, her eyes that know more than a girl her age should, defeat her.

Kay watched as Addie hugged her dad goodbye minutes ago. His face—his wrecked face. She had to look away. *Goodbye.*

What if it's the last goodbye? She looks toward the window again, wants to see their car still, to know that this second, they are okay, but the driveway is empty, the street in front of the house only has a mother pushing a stroller, the mail guy parking his truck and hoisting his bag over his shoulder.

She puts her hand on the back of Addie's neck and guides her into the kitchen. "And then maybe afterward, you can help me collect some of those flowers from outside. We could draw some pictures for Mommy and Daddy, for when they come back, right?" Why did she say that? *Daddy.* She doesn't want to jinx it. Damn her well-meaning hopefulness. You can be this way with kids though, can't you? Shouldn't you? This whole procedure could be good, she thinks. It could go fine. Her dad could come home and be better, and they could forget all this and enjoy the rest of spring. An easy summer. Of course a stem cell transplant is a risk, a big one. The side effects alone could kill him, but there are no alternatives. "Otherwise," Freddie said weeks ago with a vacant expression, "we'll just be waiting for it to come back."

The cuckoo clock comes to life, and Addie looks up and stares at the small bird that pops out of the top to announce the time: eleven. After it goes back inside, the miniature dancers play music and twirl around. The water wheel spins. Addie doesn't look away. The pinecone pendulums move up and down.

"Neat, isn't it?"

"Uh-huh." Addie smiles as the clock goes silent again except for the constant ticking sound. She will be here for another forty-eight hours. Dear lord, Kay thinks. Dear lord. This is hard already. What was I thinking? This feels impossible, suffocating. How long can I keep her busy? Will she nap? No, she doesn't think, if she recalls correctly, that seven-year-olds nap.

Maybe they can watch a movie. Maybe Addie will want to take a bath for a while in the garden tub in the master bedroom. She realizes then that she hasn't been alone with a child like this in forever.

She hopes she can do it.

Addie stares up at her. Was Kay the best choice? After all these years, she has never healed completely. She seldom has to engage. She usually drifts away. She has not been right for so long. She has been absent. Her heart flutters. *There is no choice—Greg's parents dead, Freddie's parents far away. Only one aunt (Freddie's sister), but she's in Europe. They need you. Stop this.*

She is glad Alex will be home this evening. He'll at least keep Addie smiling while she gets dinner together. He'll do that trick where he rolls his handkerchief and makes it look like sleeping twin babies. He'll hold up the small hammock and sing *rock-a-bye baby on the treetop.* Then he'll show her how to flip the handkerchief around and fold it herself. Maybe he'll teach her a card trick. He's good like that. She thinks of him doing it with Benny. She wonders for a second if he did it with Iris. The thought occurs to her then: her husband has more experience with children than she does. How odd, she thinks. Sometimes she feels cheated about Iris, feels he's cheating on Benny, but then she shrugs and she's mostly grateful for

Iris. The whole thing is so different. They needed something different.

Kay takes out the bag of chocolate chips, the canister of flour. She pokes the butter to see if it's soft enough and she thinks of Alex many years ago blowing on Benny's belly. How Alex would pause, raise his eyebrows, and furiously do a raspberry on Benny's smooth skin. His tiny belly button, that small little freckle below his rib. How that boy laughed whenever his dad was home. How young and new they all were then. Her heart. Her heart. She forces a smile at Addie. Can she do this? She has to. *Suck it up, toots*. "Do you want to wear an apron? Because I have quite the collection, my dear." Addie follows her over to the broom closet where there are five aprons hanging on small hooks.

"Ooh," she says. She reaches in and touches the different fabrics. There is a ruffled floral one, and one made of linen with *Myrtilles* written on the front underneath a picture of blueberries.

"Pick any one you want." She wishes now she had a small chef's hat. She'd take a picture of Addie in apron and hat and text it to her mother. Then Freddie would know her child was okay. One less thing to worry about, right? She thinks of the two-hour drive Freddie and Greg are making to Boston. She thinks of the parking garage they will leave their car in, and the wind that will blow through it as they walk. Of Greg's hope and worry, his hair a new fuzz on his head, his pale skin as he enters the hospital for the procedure. They are in for so much. Weeks and weeks. First, high doses of chemo (again), then radiation (again) to prime him for the transplant. After the transplant, a risk of infection, and then waiting and seeing. "Believe it or not, the transplant is the quickest and easiest part of this whole thing," Freddie said. "Kind of anticlimactic." Greg is so tough and determined in this fight, but this is his last good hand.

Kay looks down at Addie. It has to work. Please, dear God, let it work. For this little girl. Don't let him catch a cold. Don't let him have one cut. Let nothing stand in their way. She will say the rosary for them. Tonight. When Addie's asleep, she will turn the lights low. She will sit still and say the rosary and pray for them.

She learned these prayers after Benny, after all that time more than twenty-four years ago. She wonders as she has often wondered if she'd prayed more while Benny was alive could she have saved him? A counselor told her that's a ridiculous thing to think, but she doesn't know. She just doesn't know. Maybe she wasn't a good enough Catholic.

She looks down at Addie, who has her hands on the aprons. Can Kay do this? Can she be okay with this child? She wants to lie down. She wants to go outside and sit on the bench she put under the tree that Benny used to climb. It's been over twenty years, and she is still paralyzed in some ways. She has gotten used to it. She has been this way longer than she had Benny. How can that be? But she plays the part well of a woman getting by.

"Um, this one," Addie says, and pulls the red apron free. Plain red. Kay would have guessed one of the more ruffled or lacy ones. She holds her braids gently and loops the top around Addie's small neck. The girl drowns in the fabric. It hangs to her feet.

"Let's get you tied up." She carefully folds the bottom panel up and winds the tie two times around her waist. "Adorable," she says, and Addie poses. "I have to take your picture," she says.

Soon she pulls the chair over to the kitchen island, and Addie helps her measure vanilla and brown sugar. She carefully cracks two eggs into a small bowl. Kay stands beside her, and something about this makes her grateful, makes her melt in a way. She had forgotten about children, which is odd to say because she has never forgotten about her son for a second. But she forgot about how fully attentive you have to be when a child is in the house. They make it more real that way. Without them, you can just go through the motions. But they will not let you phone it in.

It used to be all about Benny. Benny letting the screen door slam. Benny getting their small dog riled up. Benny with his, "Hey, Mom," and, "Uh-oh," and, "Hang on." Benny leaving his headphones and Walkman on the counter, or on the back of the toilet. "Benjamin," she'd say. "Forget something?"

Did she ever bake cookies with Benny? She doesn't think so. Why hadn't she? All she has thought about since he died are lists of things she didn't do with him: let him do the Columbia House CD club, buy him the Super Soaker water gun he wanted, take him to that professional wrestling event a few towns away. And the regrets. So many regrets. She remembers shushing him when she was on the phone. She remembers sending him to his bedroom because he dropped a bottle of apple juice on the kitchen floor, and it made such a sticky mess. Once, as a baby, he wouldn't stop crying, and she let him scream by himself in his crib for half an hour, so red and worked up and sad. Another time, as a toddler, she grabbed his arm too hard because he accidentally elbowed her in the mouth.

God, she hates that she wasn't perfect every single day with him, she hates how she sometimes ignored things he said. She hates that she used to feel a slight dread when the school day ended, interrupting the quiet peace of having the house to herself. But all parents must feel that way. If he had grown up and lived, it would be lost in a sea of a thousand other things, good and bad, and he could have forgiven her for any deficiency. She could have made it up to him. She hates other things, too: that he had clothes in his closet with the tags still on, that he never got to have a girlfriend, that the truck probably dragged him. She winces.

But wait. The feeling of her hand on top of this child's hand as they gently tap the egg against the rim of the bowl—this feeling is familiar. They did do something like this together, she and Benny. Was it French toast they used to make? Yes, yes, she remembers him in this kitchen, maybe on the same chair, cracking eggs.

She savors the feeling of her hand on a child's hand again, and the memory comes back like a paper airplane lazily gliding into a window. She feels a surge of warmth and familiarity. Benny standing beside her. Her body remembers, can feel him there. He loved to plunge the bread into the batter. Then he'd say, "Flip," and he'd flip the bread with a fork before they carefully put it into the hot frying pan. He loved the sizzle of butter against the bread. He would sprinkle cinnamon over it when it was done. He'd say, "Kaboom." Yes, they did that. Yes, yes. Tears rim her eyes, but Addie doesn't see. Kay is thankful for this memory. She feels a release of something, a great relief.

She can see his small hands dripping with egg batter. She can remember bringing him over to the sink and carefully wiping a wet paper towel over his fingers. Another memory comes then: the smell of the top of his head. His clean scalp: *Benny smell*, she used to call it. Like popcorn or bread. She relishes these thoughts returning, and she thinks in that second: *I would do it all again. If I could go back, knowing what I know, I would do it again.* God, he changed her in so many ways. He altered her DNA forever.

She hands Addie a small wooden spoon that is the perfect size. "We need to mix this up," she says, and pats her head. Addie is smiling and looking around. She is having fun. They are laughing together, oohing and ahhing as the batter spills occasionally onto the counter. She wishes Alex could see. Then he'd know that after all these years, maybe she was starting to be all right. Which isn't to say she'd been one of those miserable, bitter people. She was fine, good enough. They could go out with friends of theirs or clients he was entertaining, and she could smile. She could talk about the bluebird at their bird feeder or a story about a hurricane on the news. They could go to Bermuda or to New York City on a mini vacation, and they could sip cocktails and go on day tours and play gin rummy in the hotel room and be okay. They were managing. She has been all right for a while, able to put on a smile and make it okay. But now she feels a difference—a level up, better than she's felt in forever. She remembers how Benny's toys would be sluggish but still work, but if she replaced the batteries, they'd move with a new life. She wants to kiss Addie's head. She wants to hug her gratefully.

How many years she just stared, stayed silent. Alex had his job, his big company to go back to. After Benny's funeral, he stayed home with her for four or five days where he watched the news, the weather, *Jeopardy*, and they ate what people brought them, but then he slipped back to his work. She remembers how she'd whisper things to Benny in the empty house (*Where are you? Are you okay?*), how she looked at Toby, their small white dog, every time his stare went somewhere else. "Who do you see?" she'd say, hoping, hoping he was sensing Benny. She remembers walking outside and staring at the quiet fish pond, and when she couldn't take it anymore, she remembers trudging back upstairs to bed. How the sheets welcomed her, how the pillow felt like the only thing that could save her. When someone called, she usually let the phone ring and ring, enjoying in some odd way its echo in the empty house.

How many days Alex would come home and find her like that. He tried to bring her sister, Ruthie, over to help. He held the phone to her ear with her father on the line. He suggested she take a class in European history at the University of New Haven. Or a knitting workshop at the community college. He brought home brochures for aqua aerobics, for a creative writing group at the library. He'd sit at the foot of the bed and hold her ankle and suggest a trip to Hawaii, a drive to the casino. His sincere eyes. His patient face. How he wanted her to keep going the way he kept going. How he knew sadness could swallow people like them with no other children, with no nieces and nephews.

The affair wasn't her fault. Of course.

It wasn't her fault.

Was it his?

He did what he did. He was desperate, too. She never hated him for it. She hated what he did, but she didn't want him to leave. She couldn't bear losing another person. She sometimes was surprised she wasn't angrier, but their circumstances were unlike anyone else's. She knew he knew it was a mistake. In a way she enjoyed the hurt. It felt good to hold on to it, didn't it?

If her faith taught her anything, it taught forgiveness. She focused on that.

He told her everything: the woman he was with, the child he found out about years later. When she asked him to, he never mentioned it again. She didn't want to rock the boat, she didn't want to change how she felt about Alex. She could pretend it didn't happen if there weren't reminders. He did what he did: visited the girl, sent her money. Whatever. He kept it away from her. They buried all that, too. They could bury anything.

Until months ago when he brought it all up again: the daughter had grown, and was having a baby of her own. He wanted Kay to give her a chance. He knew how it could help her, which seemed ridiculous at first. His love child. For years, Kay felt bitter that this new child got to live instead of Benny. Their lives were connected, she was an offshoot of Benny dying. "Trust me," he said. "You'll like her."

She wants to call him now and tell him something has shifted in her. After all this, after the world ripping their son away, she finally feels something about being alive that she hasn't felt before. Life, this up and down life. What a gift, isn't it? Maybe it's the thought of poor Greg. Isn't it what Greg is fighting so hard for? For life. For this small girl in the kitchen with flour on her hands. This day where Freddie and Greg are doing their best to win. This spring sun outside, the little wishing well in their side yard with the trickling fountain. Yes, she would definitely do it all over again. She and Alex had that boy for fourteen years.

She thinks of Iris then, Alex's daughter, whom she met in December—about Iris's baby on the way. Alex was right, wasn't he? The smart businessman, the risk-taker. He knew they were up for this again, and Addie here, even just for this brief moment, has reminded her of the possibilities. Won't this baby stay with them sometimes the way Addie is here now? Won't they keep stuff like a high chair in the kitchen? Won't they put drawings on the fridge, fill a cupboard with special kid cups and plates. Won't they welcome this child in a Halloween costume, won't they want to start putting up a Christmas tree again? She feels a hint of excitement.

She and Addie drop balls of dough onto the greased cookie sheet. "Can we leave the oven light on?" Addie says. "Can we watch them?"

"Well, sure." Kay wants to hug her. She thinks of Greg changing into a hospital gown. She thinks of Iris rubbing her pregnant belly. Of Benny riding his bike that last day, of all the things he has missed. She thinks of the courage, win or lose, it takes to live. She wants to be more courageous. She closes her eyes for just a few seconds as they watch the heat in the clean oven slowly sizzle the dough and flatten it.

What surprises Kay over the next few days:

The smell of chocolate chip cookies renews her. The scent stays in the house for hours.

Addie. She settles in so quickly. By the first evening, she is opening the refrigerator and carefully pouring herself some cranberry juice. She stays for days and days. She misses her parents, but she is fine with Alex and Kay. The Tylers are grateful. Freddie drives back and forth between Wharton and Boston. She looks tired as she eats Kay's meat loaf. She tells them about the first part of the transplant: conditioning, almost done. The chemo has made Greg so sick, he has such a weakened immune system. He is almost finished with this part. A few days of radiation will follow, and then the transplant. Freddie says he is noble, a soldier.

Alex. He is better than Kay even knew he'd be. He loves having Addie there. He ties her socks in knots while she's wearing them. She giggles. He cuts her chicken for her. He makes her try asparagus. They sit on the couch and watch a show called *Tiny Town* that Addie loves. He helps her build a fort out of the sofa cushions. He leaves work early to get home. It is his idea to have Addie stay longer (Freddie was planning to bring her back and forth to Boston so she wouldn't burden the Lionels). "But only if she wants to," he says.

The weather. It is one of the nicest springs she can remember. The sun is generous over the patio. A robin shakes itself off in the birdbath. Kay has never appreciated a season so much before.

Homework. Addie's teacher gives her assignments that first Monday. Not much. Some math. Some writing. Kay is surprised a seven-year-old gets homework, but she likes sitting at the kitchen table with her, sliding the completed work back into the folder.

The dog. Addie worries about him in the kennel. His name is Wizard. Alex drives there to pick him up. The dog lies by the television and barks when the UPS man comes. He seems to wink at Kay when she walks by. She remembers how sad she was when

Toby died, how he seemed to take more of Benny with him—her last connection to her son. Now Wizard stares at her in the same wise way. She thinks she will tell Alex they need a dog when things go back to normal (knock on wood).

The cat. They stop by Freddie's house to check on the cat, Kitty. She's fine. Addie bends down to kiss the top of her head before they leave. Addie looks around the house and touches Greg's red plaid coat that hangs from a hook in the mudroom.

The big day. The day comes for the transplant. Freddie says the nurses call it Greg's new birthday because it might be the day where he is reborn. Freddie sighs and rolls her eyes on the FaceTime call. Addie blows Greg a kiss. He smiles with the tube hooked up to his arm. He gives them all a thumbs-up. Alex claps for Greg. "Attaboy," he hollers.

"You just want me back at work," Greg says.

It's a girl. Iris is having a girl. She comes for lunch one day.

They have seen her several times, but she has never been in the house before. She hugs Kay when she walks in the door, and Kay holds her a few seconds.

"What a cozy place," Iris says. Kay feels so comfortable around her—as if she's known her longer.

At their first meeting, back in December, in a café near Iris's apartment, she approached Alex and Kay shyly and Kay offered to shake her hand. "I'm more of a hugger," Iris said, and when she reached for her, Kay melted. She had prepared herself to be positive, to be polite, but realized she didn't need any of these preparations. Alex had been right. Kay found herself that day laughing at their similar shirts (polka dots). They both ribbed Alex when he took out his flip phone for a call. They both ordered split pea soup, both snickered when a man at another table called his son the wrong name. Iris looked at her so sincerely that day and said, "I want to know you. I want this to be good for you." Kay felt tears in her eyes, and she nodded and smiled. Within minutes, Alex was sitting back, sipping his root beer, and Kay and Iris were chatting about brands of chai tea and their mutual love of the color orange. Kay couldn't explain the connection she felt to Iris—not like a child of hers, but very much like someone she knew in that deep, always way.

On the day she visits the house, Addie runs to meet Iris, and when she tells Iris about school, about the small footstool she helped Alex build, her eyes keep looking over at Iris's belly. Kay marvels that Iris has Alex's nose. They all eat lunch like some new version of a family. Addie shows Iris her nail polish, reports that Kay said they could plant a garden in the back-yard. Iris tells Kay her tomato panini are the best. Kay is moved when Iris invites her to feel the baby kick. She is surprised she doesn't want to take her hand away once it's there. The baby shifts and twists under Iris's shirt, and Kay closes her eyes and loves the sensation. "Bless the little angel," Kay says.

Panic. Panic comes as quickly as the happiness, like its side effect. Did she forget to pack Addie a snack for school? Lunch money? Is Alex picking her up today? She is too old for this, she sometimes thinks. She panics when it rains one day: rain and rain, over-flowing the roof gutters. She panics that the base-ment will flood from this fast rain. She panics about Greg. These weeks of recovery in the hospital. She knows they will all hold their breath for every blood test. She panics that she is not panicking enough some days when Addie is reading to her, when Iris is texting her an ultrasound picture, when the dog is putting its paw gently on her lap.

The boxes. On the day Addie leaves, after she waves to Kay from the backseat of Alex's car and they drive away, Kay is able to look at the boxes in the basement. She has thought about Benny's stuff so often, but she could never look. Her sister packed up his things. Kay lifts one lid and exhales. His Walkman, a Beastie Boys cassette still inside. She slides the battery pack open because she is worried they rusted, but they are fine. She holds the two small batteries in her hand and looks at them. She sees his stack of *MAD* magazines. The small plaque he made in shop class with his name burned into it. He was real, she thinks. This was all real. She lets her hand hold the key chain from Bar Harbor that used to hang from his backpack zipper. She closes her eyes. "Benjamin Scott," she says, and sighs.

Kay hears a noise and turns around. The dog has followed her downstairs. They are keeping Wizard for a few weeks to help Freddie. "Well hello," she says quietly. His stare is compassionate. He waits for her and follows her up the stairs. She looks around the clean kitchen. The sun makes the granite on the counter sparkle. A vase of pussy willow branches sits on the table. How odd it will be to not have Addie here tonight. She knows she and Alex will feel the quiet. Maybe they can go out for dinner, for a drive in the lengthening evening. Maybe they could walk the dog the way they used to when they had Toby.

Freddie's boss, Darcy Crowley, has agreed to let the cat stay with her for a while. Kay knows Darcy from going to the cleaners over the years, knows her because who in Wharton could forget her? She has thought about Darcy ever since

December when her son, Luke, was killed in a car accident. Whenever she sees Darcy these days, she feels as if they share a terrible commonality they can't speak about. Kay was shocked when Darcy telephoned her one day and asked how she could help, offering time with Addie, offering to have curtains or rugs or tablecloths cleaned. She does not seem to be an animal person, but when Kay suggested temporarily taking the cat, Darcy didn't hesitate. "Certainly I would. As long as it's mannerly."

Kay walks over to the window and picks up her rosary beads. She doesn't say any prayers but holds them, feeling their weight in her palm.

She sees their driveway where Addie sketched birds and yellow suns and whales in sidewalk chalk, the driveway Iris walked up when she visited and timidly knocked on the door, the driveway Benny rode over with his bike and never came home. She is grateful for its cracks, for its shiny black tar. She is grateful for the folded newspaper that sits there, for the squirrel that pitter-patters over it, for the white flower buds that blow across. She holds her rosary and is grateful for the cuckoo clock that Addie looked up at every hour while she stayed here, for the sweet shifting sound time always makes.

16.

Out to Sea

It's been four months since he's seen her.

Four months since she stood beside him in her paisley dress at the wedding, walking slowly with her arm locked inside his, the stars like scattered glitter in the black sky.

Four months since she let him kiss her hand, since she looked at him while he talked in that way a woman hasn't looked at him in so long. Four months since she wore his coat and he didn't care how cold he was. Four months since she came to him, eyes rimmed with red, and begged him to drive her to the hospital. He remembers how she held her hand over her mouth the whole ride, how carefully she buckled her seat belt.

It's been four months since he left her at the emergency room (she said not to come in, that she was calling her parents), and he can still picture her clearly—the whole range he saw that day. Earlier, her smile, how she seemed to hold her breath before she let out a laugh. But then her shock as she gripped his arm and told him about the car accident.

Ahmed Ghannam pulls up to Damon and Suzette's house,

knowing she's inside, knowing the newish Volkswagen with the Georgia plates is hers. He parks his car beside it, and his stomach flips.

He looks down at his gray suede shoes, knowing he ran the brush over them for her, knowing he wouldn't be wearing these pants if she weren't here. Or the starched linen shirt tucked in. He walks up the steps, and there is a wreath of forsythia on the door, and he thinks he can see her through the glass. He breathes and knocks lightly.

He clears his throat. The door swings open. "You dickhead, late as usual," Damon says, and glances into the house to see if the coast is clear. He quickly flips Ahmed his middle finger.

"Man, some greeting, Romeo," Ahmed says, and grips the side of his buddy's arm. Damon pulls him into a hug. He can see the blur of Suzette and Ginger, but he pretends to keep his cool. He looks Damon up and down. "Shit, you're not fat yet," he says. "I was hoping all these months of married bliss would have porked you up."

Damon laughs. Ahmed loves this guy—loves him like a brother. Has known him since they were kids. Tall, lanky Damon with his slicked hair—slicked to keep the curls from getting out of control. Damon with his almost-Boston accent. Ahmed straightens himself, and waves to acknowledge the women.

Suzette with her blond wavy hair, who has set out cheese and grapes, is looking up at him. "A-team has arrived!" she calls. Next to her stands Ginger, who looks even better than she did at the wedding. Not that she didn't look beautiful then.

He just has a thing for women with less makeup. Her hair is tucked behind her ears, and she wears a long, thin cardigan with blue stripes over a black T-shirt, and jeans. He loves a girl in jeans.

"Hi, ladies," Ahmed says. He swallows hard, and Damon puts his hand on his shoulder and walks him in.

"The party can start," Damon says.

"You know it." There are appetizers on white plates. Suzette is pouring wine in good crystal glasses. By the dining room table a big china cabinet is lit up with a collection of white bowls and pitchers inside. He wonders, as he always does when he's there, what it's like to live in this house. To look around at your wife and your big place and know it's all yours, that you've finally arrived. To switch the lights off at night and then come down the stairs in the morning and see the place aglow in new sun. He wants this. Something like this. For years he has.

It's fun being single, but not all he hoped. Not the buffet of girls he thought it would be, the wild trips. In his twenties, he had liked the low expectations, the nothing-special apartment with hardly anything in the fridge, the long, long Sundays, the different dates he would bring to weddings and work functions at his accounting firm. But there comes a time when people stop allowing this. When the college kids on spring break don't want a thirty-year-old doing shots with them. When you're out and all you see is men your age wearing wedding rings and holding kids.

Now he wants kids. He has always wanted kids. There is some opening in his heart for them. He knows it. His brother, who is so much older (Ahmed always wondered if he was an accident—sometimes his parents treated him as though he was an inconvenience), is the version of a son his parents wanted. Ra and his wife are both university professors, and they have two boys, five and three. Ahmed loves playing with his nephews, taking them out and playing soccer. He loves hearing them squeal when he kicks it high and they scramble after it. When they were babies, sometimes they'd fall asleep on him, and he'd think *This isn't bad*. His parents would love if he caught up to Ra. They make constant jabs about him finding a wife, but he pretends he likes his life the way it is. He has done well—important accounts in Wharton and beyond, and he has been told he has partner potential.

Sure it's nice to just watch football and take naps and stay out late at night, but lately he feels like he's just waiting to read a child a book or tuck them into bed, clicking on a nightlight. He wants to go to a huge toy store with a kid sitting in a cart, and another one walking beside him, both grabbing and grabbing for things. He wants to buy Lego sets and for them to spend days on a big Lego building. He wants a wife he can walk through town with, lazily pushing a stroller. Damon and Suzette will have kids. They definitely will. Some of his other friends are on their second and third already. Ra keeps telling him, "Don't worry. You will meet your match, and you'll have what I have." He hopes.

Suzette rushes over and kisses his cheek. She smells like spring—like breeziness and a hint of flowers. The sweetest woman. When she hugs him, there is a genuine force to her body—as if she means it. When Damon introduced her to Ahmed a few years ago, after his brutal breakup with Amanda, Ahmed remembers how nervous she seemed. Her hair longer then, her wide eyes as she giggled at everything Ahmed said. She ordered a beer—the same as them. "You fucker," Ahmed whispered when she got up to use the bathroom. "You miserable fucker, getting her."

"Hey, Suzie," he says now. "This guy treating you right?"

She laughs. "You have to come over more. Damon said you'd be living above our garage after a couple months, so naturally I'm disappointed."

Ahmed shakes his head. "Sounds like him." Ginger stands politely at the counter and their eyes meet. She smiles and waves. He remembers the fake fur cape she wore at the wedding. He remembers her at the hospital entrance, how she shook when she said, "Okay, thanks," and walked slowly inside. How he stayed there at the curb for a minute and watched her. How she looked around helplessly for a sign to point her in the right direction, and then disappeared. He sat and waited. He didn't know why. He remembers the sound of the engine running, the blasting heat that wouldn't seem to get warm. He remembers even feeling sorry for this guy, whoever he was, whom Ginger was running toward. And he felt jealous, too. Jealous of the dead or almost-dead guy who had broken her heart. He let the radio play for a bit, mostly commercials, and when she didn't come back, he slowly drove away.

"Hey, Doc," he says now to Ginger.

"Great to see you!" She hesitates, and then comes out from

behind the counter and approaches him. His heart flickers. He is not breathing, is he? No, he can't be. When she hugs him, he doesn't want to be creepy and hold her too long. He keeps his hands around her lightly and then pats her shoulder blades like she's one of his buddies. Damon or Richie or Topher. What? Why did he do this? She pulls back and smiles. "How's life?" she says.

"Oh, you know. Livin' the dream. Job's a hoot, women won't leave me alone." He winks, and there is something in her eyes then, some recognition of their time together that night of the wedding. Isn't there? "You still down South?" he says. He knows she isn't. Damon told him a month or so ago that she had broken up with the guy in Georgia. That she had sold her practice and was taking over for a retiring veterinarian in Naugatuck.

"Nope," she says, and tells him everything he already knows. Damon watches as Ahmed pretends to receive the information like it's new. Suzette probably thinks since they're guys, they don't talk about this stuff. But they do. He used to be sly about asking for Ginger updates, but lately Damon supplies them willingly. "Man, she's top drawer," Damon said once. "But I don't know how you're going to get through the double hurdle of the dead ex-boyfriend and the recent breakup. She might be out to sea." Ahmed had pictured her in a small boat then, floating away toward a pink and blue horizon.

Ahmed watches her as she speaks. Her eyes are so kind. But they look tired. Her face is thinner. She speaks in a polite voice, a voice that means every word she says. He thinks of her that night. How she was running to the guy she really loved. How devastated and broken she was as he drove to the hospital as quickly as he could on the cold, empty streets, patches of black ice every so often. He remembers how he felt he loved her already, and how he lost her before they could even try.

"So once I unpack the last of the boxes," she says now, "I'll be settled here."

"How's the cat?" Ahmed says.

"You remembered Martin." She smiles. He sees gratitude in her eyes. God, she is the most lovely, real woman he has ever met. He cannot imagine she has one cruel or shallow thought. "He's great. I had to sedate him for the drive up here. He hates the car." She walks over to the kitchen and picks up her glass of wine. Suzette brings Ahmed one.

"Cheers, guys," she says, and the four of them clink glasses. Ahmed looks into Ginger's eyes as their glasses touch, and then he quickly looks away.

"To health and happiness," Damon says.

"To Damon's good looks," Ahmed says. His default mode is to tease. He sees that Ginger is laughing, and he can't get enough of a woman laughing at his jokes. "To Martin the traveling cat," he adds, and everyone laughs. His back is sweating, but he feels looser now.

"Oh my God," Suzette says, her voice a slight screech. She holds her glass by the stem and the wine trembles as her eyes lock on something. She points at the curtain rod above the living room window. "A bat!"

Ahmed feels his adrenaline boil to action. His heart

pounds. He hates bats. And snakes. And mice. He wishes it were a spider. He would pick up the spider without hesitating and bring it outside and let it crawl away. He looks at the thick burlap-type curtain, and sees a small peaceful bat hanging from the rod.

Damon grabs a broom from a long cabinet and holds it like a baseball bat. "I've got it," he says, and charges into the living room.

"Shit, shit," Ahmed says. He wonders if Damon will let it scoot out the door, or if he plans on pulverizing the bat. He is gripping the broom so tightly that Ahmed can see the veins in his arms.

"Wait," Ginger says. She puts down her wine and doesn't look bothered at all. "Do you guys have an empty coffee can or something?"

"Here." Suzette runs to the cupboard, grabs what looks like an expensive can of espresso, and dumps it all in the sink.

"That's like ten bucks," Damon says.

"Hush." Suzette hands the can to Ginger. Ginger holds the can, picks up a brochure from the mail pile by the refrigerator, and tiptoes toward the sleeping bat while the three of them watch. In seconds, she stands barefoot on the dining room chair, guiding the coffee can under the bat, wiggling the brochure over it.

"Got it," she whispers. Damon opens the French doors to the back, and Ginger walks outside with the can, her back straight, her hand keeping the brochure in place on top. She strides across the big stretch of grass to an oak tree and stands back as she releases the animal from its container like a magician. She smiles a satisfied smile as it flies up and disappears.

Later, after a glass of wine, after snacking on figs and cheese and spicy almonds, after Ahmed has fist-bumped Ginger and called her Bat Woman more than once, Damon goes outside to light the grill, and Suzette follows him with a plate of steaks and some kind of fish wrapped in foil. Ahmed looks at them through the French doors, and they don't even realize it, but they are a painting out there. Young and good looking and full of promise. The evening spring sun on them, the stylish deck with two chaise longues. The big rhododendron blooming.

Inside, there is a glass bowl of salad on the kitchen counter, and a basket of sliced bread from a good bakery. He sits on one of the barstools around the kitchen island and Ginger starts to clear some of the appetizer plates. "So," she says. "I never got a chance to apologize for that night." Her words sound rehearsed, as though she has been anxious about seeing him, too.

"What?" he says. This feels like that moment when a roller coaster drops—that light-headed fear rushing at him. It would be easier to not have this conversation, to just keep it light. It's funny that they barely know each other, but already he feels like he's in a serious relationship. She makes him so nervous—the way no other woman has. "Oh, well. Nah, don't apologize." He gulps his wine.

"No," she says. He can see the hint of blush on her. "It was a hard night." Yes. He heard from Damon about how upset she was, how she stayed at her parents' house for a while afterward, how Suzette would take long walks with her and tell her there was nothing she could have done.

"Yeah, I just wish I could have helped you. I stayed in the parking lot for a little while in case you needed me."

She sits on a barstool next to him. "I should have told you about Luke when we were talking. I should have said how torn up I'd been feeling."

"It's your business, you know?" He hates being a guy at that moment, keeping his feelings so close to his chest. He can't stop thinking about the wedding. How he kept engaging her in conversation, how she kept listening to him, the way her arm felt locked in his. It had been a perfect start. During dinner, during all the toasts, he kept hoping maybe at the end of the night she would lean in to kiss him—even if it was a quick one, even if he never saw her again after that. He remembers the nervous excitement and possibility the night seemed to have—before it didn't.

She shakes her head. "I was having a good time with you."

This washes him in something. Joy. Longing. He feels a deep, deep pull. It meant something to her, too. It mattered. He sighs inside. "Yeah. Me, too."

He feels like he's the one out to sea now, out in the blank

water by himself. He glances at Damon and Suzette. Suzette is pointing to something in the yard and Damon is listening. Probably planning a pool. Or maybe a guesthouse next to the barn. "Me, too," Ahmed says again.

"And you were so nice to leave the wedding with me. When I got out of your car, I knew that was the last moment of something." She shrugs.

He remembers looking over at her and her worried face. The darkness and passing headlights outside her window. He remembers wanting to pull her against him, to stroke her hair and say it would be okay. It would all be okay. "What do you mean?" he finally asks.

"I don't know." She bites her thumbnail. "I guess I just mean I knew all the heartbreak I was going toward inside. I knew, I had to know, that Luke was going to die. Like I loved him, I realized I still loved him, and it figures—he's dead. I knew I was going into that, and leaving your car was the last time I would feel joy—just that easiness of a good time—for a long, long while." She shakes her head. "I felt like I was jumping off a cliff, and you were the last person I saw before I did."

He feels a lump in his throat. He will never find someone as good as she is. There is something so whole and decent about her. But he is gripped by a quiet longing now, a pain of regret. She won't ever be over this guy. You don't get over loving and losing someone like that. One way or the other, they needed resolution, and she'll never have it. He hates Luke for a second. Hates what he didn't know he had in Ginger, what he gambled with by doing drugs or drinking or whatever led to that accident. *Screw yourself, Luke*, he thinks, and then regrets insulting a dead guy who didn't mean to die. *Sorry, Luke.*

"I almost yelled after you to come back," he says, surprising himself. He looks at her. At her worried eyes. At her perfect neck with the small diamond hanging from her necklace. "I know that sounds ridiculous. I know it was a hard night for you. But before that, it was one of the best nights of my life." He gulps. Something tells him to keep going. "I like you so much."

She smiles, and her face crumbles slightly—as if she might cry. Her eyes are wet but sincere. Then she puts her hand on top of his. "I like you, too," she says.

His insides get tight. He is on a raft, and she is pulling him in. He almost starts to shiver. He imagines his teeth chattering and how embarrassing it would be. Her hand. Her warm hand on top of his. He never wants this to end. He wants to put his other hand on top of hers to keep it there.

17.

Just That Sort of a Day

After the man she always thought was her father left her mother, Iris stared at his things in her parents' closet for months: a pair of two-toned golf shoes he had worn once, a tweed blazer, and two shirts (one pink, one gray) in a dry cleaning bag. She touched the thin plastic covering his shirts. She put her feet in the barely worn shoes. She smelled the dusty wool of the jacket sleeve. She would look at all her mother's things—the robes, the sequined dress, the shelf on the floor of sandals and shoes—and wonder if he'd ever come back for his handful of left-behinds. Iris remembers reaching into his jacket pocket and finding a ticket stub for a dinner dance he and her mother had gone to. She stared at the writing, the picture of music notes. Then, each time, she would slip it back into the pocket. Doug with the sideburns. Doug with his blond knuckle hair. Doug who seemed to have loved her.

And then it turned out Doug wasn't her father.

And she had a new father.

She was so young then, only four or so, but she remembers everything. She remembers New Dad's car in the driveway, something shiny, expensive. She remembers how cool yet cordial he was to Melinda, who made Iris wear a blue lacy dress that day with the sash tied too tightly. Melinda had pulled Iris's hair into small braids and washed her face with a hot washcloth. Suddenly the moment seemed to be about Iris, her mother, for once, standing back. This man with his kind eyes and worn face, shiny watch on his wrist, shirt so white and starched, a thick gold wedding band. She remembers he handed her a gift: a jack-in-the-box she still has.

She remembers only wanting Doug when New Dad asked her about nursery school. Wanting Doug's song about the bear going over the mountain. Wanting to crawl into Doug's familiar lap when New Dad sat on the living room chair while he folded his handkerchief into something as she stared. But now she has mostly forgotten Doug. One day, she can't say when, she noticed Doug's things were gone from her mother's closet, and she forgot what Doug's voice sounded like. Doug, who her mother said got a job in Florida and that's why he left. Doug. Another casualty of her mother's. Doug, who will forever be thirty-something, broken, shrugging as he blew her a kiss and walked down their porch steps.

And New Dad, who introduced himself as Alex, was wonderful. He would tell her stories about being in the army, which fascinated her (a soldier in real life, and he was her father!). He would do that thing where he made his thumb tip look like it came apart from the rest of his finger. He would give money to her, as well as necklaces and a jewelry box. He'd kiss the top of her head, call her Sunshine in a way that made her heart soar. She found out, years later, he didn't even know about her until that time he first showed up. Another Melinda game, she guessed.

Now, twenty years later, Iris says, "Love you, bye," to New Dad on the phone and hits *end*. Alex Lionel, who lives an hour away but calls to check on her every day. "How are you feeling?" he always says. "Get some rest now while you can." She smiles and takes the portable baby heart rate monitor she got from Amazon out of its package. She looks up at the sound of the door scraping open as Melinda walks right into the apartment without knocking.

"Cold in here," Melinda says, holding a white box from the bakery. "Here, babe, sticky buns." She plops the box onto the table and looks around. Melinda is always looking around. Always a small piece of green gum in her mouth. Always flipping her hair.

"I can't eat those," Iris says. She almost salivates. She feels an urge to rip the box open and push a whole bun into her mouth. Her favorite. She imagines the glazed pecans, the warm dough.

Melinda rolls her eyes. "Oh, they just tell you that stuff." She looks down at the box and starts to pick at the tape with her nail. She tugs and tugs but nothing happens. "What's that?" she asks, and zeros in on the heart rate monitor. Iris remembers Dave made coffee this morning, but she doesn't offer any to her mother yet. Maybe in a minute. Outside, she hears car motors and an occasional horn. The hanging papier-mâché angel she got from Mexico moves with the breeze from the open window. She loves springtime.

"It's a listening device. Now I can hear Phoebe's heartbeat whenever I want." She turns the small white machine over to see if it needs batteries.

"Phoebe. You're still going with that?" Melinda lifts her eyebrows. "Where's Davey?"

"At the store."

"Buying you a ring?"

"Please." Iris opens the battery compartment, and there are two factory batteries already inside. Jackpot. "The stroller arrived at the baby store, so he borrowed his mom's SUV to pick it up." She thinks of Dave leaving that morning. Quiet Dave, with the small ponytail, who broke her rule about men in ponytails. Dave with glasses sometimes. Dave who now kisses Phoebe goodbye, too, bending to smile at Iris's belly.

Melinda's high heels click as she walks. Iris knows her mother thinks the apartment should be vacuumed, that the kitchen counters have too much clutter. Whatever. She's pregnant. She's in grad school with an internship at the hospital. She does what she can.

Melinda sniffs for a moment. She is always sniffing, ready to point out any smell: dust, garbage, the neighbor's cat. She is a good-looking woman for sixty, but her style got stuck at some point in the late eighties. For one, her bleached hair is overprocessed. She wears clothes that are too tight, even though she's in good shape, and today she wears jean leggings and a long-sleeved bodysuit. Dave calls it her *Flashdance* attire. Iris smiles. Once, in a horrible fight, Iris called Melinda trashy, which she regretted immediately. Melinda's mascara smeared with tears as she slammed the apartment door. "Go to your father's up-tight wife then! Go see her on rich bitch lane," Melinda had screamed.

"What are you looking for?" Iris says now.

"Scissors."

"I can't have a sticky bun, Mom. Please don't."

Melinda opens drawer after drawer, clicking her tongue with each one. She finally rummages through the junk drawer and finds the scissors with the blue handle that barely cut. "Honey, don't believe everything they tell you. They always go with the worst-case scenario. Baby diabetes. I never heard of such bull."

"It's not baby diabetes. It's gestational diabetes. The baby doesn't have it. I do, as a side effect of pregnancy. When the baby comes, everything should be fine."

"Tuh," she says, and slides the scissors into the bottom of the white box. "So we'll hear our little girl's heart with that thing?" she says as she breaks the tape. "Imagine: I didn't even know what you'd be or what you were doing in there. I just hoped you'd be happy. *Just be happy*, that's what I kept whispering."

"And healthy."

"Of course healthy."

"We should be able to hear it. It got good reviews."

"Here." Melinda pulls out a sticky bun. The goo from the bottom drips back into the box. The nuts are syrupy and shiny, and the smell demobilizes Iris. Dear. God. She wants to pull it apart. She wants to bite into the sticky soft baked taste. She wants to wash it down with a freezing cold glass of milk. She could shake her mother for doing this to her. "Let me get a little plate." Melinda prances through the kitchen, holding the sticky bun out in front of her and opening cupboard door after cupboard door with her left hand.

"Mom."

"Huh?" She finds a stack of saucers and slides one out. She puts the sticky bun on the saucer and licks her fingers.

"I cannot. I can't *have* one."

Melinda puts the plate in front of her and smirks. "Just a bite."

Iris looks down. She knows exactly how it will taste on her tongue, how her teeth will feel biting into its softness. She hasn't had any dessert in weeks—since the diagnosis. Since the hospital nutritionist gave her a printout of what her daily meal plan should be: a bowl of Cheerios here, a turkey sandwich on wheat there, a small dish of blueberries before bed. She has thought about a sticky bun—just like this one—every day. But she wants Phoebe to be healthy. It's more important. Every time she pricks her finger, she worries her numbers will be too high. She knocks the plate to the side. "Stop. Do you know how crazy this is?"

"Honey." Melinda picks up another sticky bun with her red nails and bites into it. She shakes her head. "You're missing out."

Iris stands. She could have one. This morning her sugar was the lowest it's been since being diagnosed. Back to normal, she could almost say. She goes to the refrigerator and lets ice fall into her glass. She presses the button for water. She watches her mother eat the sticky bun, the glaze around her lips. She hears birds outside and the buzz of a hedge trimmer down below. She comes back to the table and fiddles with the monitor. She slips the headphones on and holds the white wand, rolling it over her belly.

"Let me listen, too," Melinda says.

"I don't hear it yet."

"You're not a doctor, that's why." She taps her fingers and watches Iris. "They shouldn't even sell those things."

"I just want to hear her. I like the sound."

"Don't you need that jelly to make it work?" Melinda's nostrils flare as she talks. She clicks over to the sink and grabs a paper towel to wipe her lips.

"It's not that sophisticated." Iris holds the wand and keeps sliding it slowly. Piece of junk. She is frustrated, disappointed. She hears nothing but static.

"Maybe you need to—"

"Shh. Wait."

Melinda sighs. She crosses her arms and stares at Iris, shaking her head.

Iris's pulse is starting to beat faster. She just wants to hear Phoebe's heart. Every time she hears it, it's like getting a letter she's been waiting for in the mail. It is so quick and constant, so steady and comforting. *Ah*, she always thinks. *There you are.* She has waited for three days since she ordered this device. She wants to hear it between appointments. She wants to slip the headphones on Dave's ears while they are in bed. She hears nothing but the continued drone of static.

Melinda paces back and forth. She finds tape on Iris's messy desk over by the window and seals the white bakery box shut again. "You're gonna make yourself nuts trying to find it with a machine that cost two bucks."

"Fifty dollars."

"Aye yai yai."

Iris glares at her and takes the headphones off. She puts the small machine down. She feels like she could faint, and nausea creeps up her throat. When did she last feel Phoebe move? Iris can't remember. She's gotten so used to the kicks, the twists and turns. Phoebe was always moving. A thump here, a wiggle there. Iris feels the room turn. Her mother seems far away. Last night? Wasn't it last night? But not today. Not one thing today. A cold sweat spreads over her body. "Mom," she says.

"You want me to try?"

"I think something's wrong."

"Nah." Melinda comes and stands by her. She puts her arm around Iris and lays her head on her shoulder. "Don't panic."

Iris puts her hand on her stomach. She cannot breathe. Her belly feels so still. "My sugar dropped really low this morning."

"Because you're eating so well!" Melinda huffs. "Maybe you should have a sticky bun. Bring it up a little."

Iris slips away from her. She grabs her purse. She is going to vomit. She is going to fall over. She feels like her head is in a vise, like her fingers could fall off. There is a painting next to the door that says "Just That Sort of a Day" from the Tribeca Film Festival. It is black with white letters. "We have to go."

She grabs her phone. Dave. She has to call Dave, who will have a brand-new stroller in the back of the car, the price tag hanging from the handle, the car seat bright and new with instructions. He will start joking with her when he picks up the phone. *I'm not getting the swing today*, he'll say.

Melinda stands in front of her. "Now just calm down, honey. You're all worked up. Look how pale you are." She holds her shoulders. "Breathe, baby. Breathe." She smells like cinnamon.

There has to be an explanation, Iris thinks. Maybe babies move less as they get bigger. Maybe she felt her move an hour ago but just can't remember. Phoebe has been growing inside her all this time. Her heartbeat has been boisterous and urgent at every appointment. Why is Iris jumping to this conclusion?

When she found out about the baby in the fall, she felt the way she does now: sick, unable to breathe, paralyzed. She told Dave maybe they should consider an abortion. It was too soon. She'd known him for only a few months. She had school, the graduate degree in occupational therapy. She wanted to go to Europe. She wanted to enjoy her twenties and not have a baby yet. She loved Dave, but she wanted to be sure this was permanent. Look at Melinda. She didn't want to be Melinda; Phoebe to be her. Damn it, she thought. Damn it. For the first few weeks, she wanted to wake up and not be pregnant anymore.

And now what if she isn't? No movement. The lower blood sugar. What if she failed because she didn't love Phoebe enough, because she was ashamed to be pregnant? *What would her professors say?* she thought. What would Melinda say? What would New Dad say? But Alex had been superb. He chuckled. "How wonderful, Sunshine!" he said. It was his acceptance of the baby that made her okay with it. His approval, and then later his wife Kay's warmth, the gift of finally meeting her. Kay so encouraging and nonjudgmental made Iris feel like she could do anything. Alex had always been her best adviser, her barometer. And Kay was another feather in her cap. Even Melinda had been excited. "You little devils," she said, wagging a finger at her and Dave. Now Iris loves Phoebe. She dreams about her tiny face, her future voice. She wants her so badly.

She leaves the apartment with her mother, and notices every detail: the jingle of the car keys, the noise of her teeth chattering as she walks, slowly, down each step of the stairwell, the whistle of the oblivious mailman who nods at her as he opens and closes all those tiny mailbox doors.

A month later, after her final exams are over, after she stands in front of everyone and meekly accepts the master's degree, after she starts her job, mostly doing occupational therapy in nursing homes and treatment centers, after it gets too warm to sleep without air-conditioning—so soon, it seems—Iris is up in the middle of the night looking out at the quiet streets. She sees the dark storefronts with dim lights glowing from inside, the still sidewalks, the row of parking meters, the spots mostly vacant.

The stroller sits in the corner of the apartment. The stupid monitor is in a drawer, never sent back to Amazon. Iris is up, thinking about Phoebe. The image of Phoebe so still and purplish as they handed her to Iris—for just minutes, it seemed— and then took her away.

Phoebe, whom she had to deliver anyway. So tiny and shocked, it seemed. As if she could have never made it in the world.

Iris is thinking about Melinda, who said, "I'm sorry, I'm sorry," and proceeded to declutter her drawers and throw out the box of sticky buns.

She is thinking about Dave, who held her for hours. She heard him weeping in the bathroom that first night. He wouldn't look at Phoebe, but instead shook his head like a sad child and asked them to take her away.

She is awake the way she would have been. She would have been up all the time, tiptoeing around the quiet apartment, the light above the stove glowing, the shadows on the furniture. She waits for the teapot to boil, sits in the big chair and bites her thumbnail as she looks at the black outside the window, and doesn't know what the heck she'll do. She has her job, but it only eats up eight hours a day. Until now she could busy herself with school, with all those final items: the clinical fieldwork evaluations, the extended project for her advanced research seminar that still needed to get done whether she delivered a dead baby or not.

She thinks of Doug for a second. Whatever became of Doug? Melinda said he had a job in Florida, but also that they were just too different to make it work. "He needed to go— for both our sakes," Melinda said, and Iris never asked more questions. She just remembers the way he kissed her cheek before he left, his shy wave as he walked away that day, his head down as if he didn't want to go. His clothes like casualties in the closet. Doug loved Iris—she always knew he did. She wonders if Doug felt the way she does now—if he, too, was lost like this. If loving and losing a child hit Doug the same: the ache, the constant reminders, the part of you broken you know you'll never get back. She feels like she can only limp, like she can't hear anything clearly. She feels pulled down by the ocean's undertow. At some point, she thinks now, in the quiet living room, she will track Doug down. She always promised herself she would. Alex was so good that he made her mostly forget Doug, but she knows this is important. She will say thank you for those years. For the hugs he gave her, for the way he held her hand and they ran outside when they heard the music of the ice cream truck, for the pieces of him he left behind in the closet that comforted her in some way. She stands up and pours her tea over the chamomile tea bag in the thick ceramic mug.

She sips it slowly and whispers *Phoebe* the way she always does when she's alone. Once in a while she absently touches her belly.

Now her phone dings, and she holds the thin throw blanket around her shoulders as she walks to check it. A text from Alex. *Can't sleep. Just thinking of you. Whenever you get this, know I am.*

I got this, she replies. She puts a heart emoji beside her words.

It'll be okay, he writes.

She nods as if he can see her. *Thanks.* There is a long pause. Then a thumbs-up emoji from him.

She smiles. She loves him. She is grateful he came into her life when he did. She sips her tea again, and feels a swelling loss. She can't get Phoebe out of her head. Or Doug either. Why does she miss Doug so much tonight? She feels something unexplainable: a pull toward the man who loved her and had to leave. He knew she wasn't his. He had no rights once Melinda was done with him, and this breaks her heart.

Was he ever up at night thinking of her like this? Did he ever wish he could text her the way Alex just did? She thinks about the difficulty of love, how love isn't enough. Not enough to have kept Doug in her life. Not enough to keep Phoebe's tiny heart beating.

She stares at Alex's words and sits alone in the dark, thinking about how random and alarming the world is. One day her dad left, one day she got a new one. One day she was pregnant, one day she wasn't. She wishes Dave would wake up the way he sometimes does, and they would sit together and say nothing. She wishes she could turn on the radio and hear a sad song. She sees headlights in the distance of a lonely car out on the road.

She feels, some days, she hasn't learned anything yet. She is still that girl looking at abandoned clothes in a cramped closet. She is still, no matter what, that curious girl, rolling a small white wand, looking, always looking, for life.

18.

Life Is Like This

Suzette Savio is pumping gas at Henny Penny on Route 23 on a hot July afternoon when the girls approach her.

It is almost 5 p.m., and Suzette's sleeveless navy blue linen shirt is uncomfortable and stuck to her back, and her feet hurt in these shoes, and her skirt feels tight for some reason, and she just wants to get back to the house and turn the central air as low as it will go and put her hair up and change into a loose T-shirt and pajama pants and ask Damon if pizza in bed with an ice-cold beer sounds okay.

Just one of those days where things didn't fall into place easily, where she had to watch a social worker take a screaming three-year-old named Owen from his mother, who keeps leaving him alone to go score, and all Suzette wanted to do was hold Owen with his messy black hair and red cheeks. He bawled when his mother bawled; even their dog was walking in circles upset. And then Nicole, a client Suzette's been working with for months, met her at Dunkin' Donuts wearing a cotton scarf, trying to hide a new bruise around her neck. "Jesus," Suzette said to her. "What's it gonna take?" And then she felt bad for saying that because she knows about the cycle of abuse, and who is she to judge poor Nicole, whose life has been unfair in so many ways? And to make matters worse, Andy, a nine-year-old for whom she has been advocating, hugged a fourth-grade classmate in the coat closet too tightly, so tight that the girl couldn't get away, and now they want to suspend him and possibly send him to the juvenile detention center, and the poor kid is so sensitive, so beaten down, that she doesn't want to think of what would happen to him there.

So right now she considers taking her sandal straps off because they are pinching her feet so badly and imagines standing there barefoot in the dirty parking lot while the gas gurgles into her car. But all of a sudden these teenage girls walk up to her (Damon always says, *What the hell, do they have radar for you?*).

"Would you buy us a pack of cigarettes?" the taller girl, maybe fifteen at the most, asks, stringy brown hair and freckles around her brown eyes that pull at Suzette.

"What?" Suzette says. She can't digest what the girl is asking. Suzette is lost in her own thoughts, trying to mentally hold Owen in her arms, trying to argue a good case for Andy, trying to drive Nicole a thousand miles away so that guy can't find her.

Both girls' faces are sunburned, and the friend with the light blond hair wears a pink tank top. The brunette girl puts her hands in her jean shorts pockets and tilts her leg to the side. She looks at her flip-flop. "We were just, uh, wondering if you could buy us some cigarettes."

"'Cause we're not old enough," her friend says.

Suzette smiles politely. She has learned to never talk down to teenagers, never make what they say seem foolish. "Thanks for trusting me," she finally says after searching for the words. She hugs her purse around her shoulder. She glances at the friend, tiny in her tank top. Then at the freckled girl. Suzette breathes. A rhythm to her breathing like she will hypnotize them. Breathes like she's breathing out smoke. "But I can't do that, you know?"

She wants to tell them not to get started, that that's what the tobacco fat cats want. She wants to tell them she smoked, too, that she's certainly not judging them, but but but. She wants to give them a number they can call if things are bad at home, her own number even. Her feet hurt, and the sun is still so damn hot even though she's under the metal canopy at the gas pump. "What are your names?" she asks.

"Felicia," says the blonde right away. Her eyes are a permanent squint. Her hair is frizzy. She is one of those girls who gets lost in a classroom. Who the teacher forgets has been out with the hall pass for fifteen minutes.

"And you?" Suzette nods toward the brunette.

The girl bites her finger. Felicia nudges her. "I heard her," she snaps. She twists her fingers together. "Nancy," she says, looking away.

Suzette shakes her head. The gas nozzle thumps that it's full. Other cars back out of their spaces. "That didn't sound natural."

"It wasn't." The girl twists her lip in a pout.

"Then?"

"Natalie." She turns back to Suzette. Suzette notices now she's holding a wrinkled ten-dollar bill for the cigarettes. She thinks of all the dangerous people who could get ahold of two girls like this. She wonders if she should take them to Bobbie at the shelter, or have Carol at Children and Youth look up their situations. But she could be jumping to conclusions. They could be bored kids from Bedford Estates, they could be sunburned from swimming at Oak Gate Country Club.

But their nails are bitten. Their feet look tired. They just have that worn-out look of kids in trouble. "Are you two okay?"

Natalie snorts. "Come on."

Suzette screws her gas cap back on and returns the nozzle to its cradle. In seconds, she hears her receipt printing. Her sweat and her feet and the bad world irritate her. "I asked a question, Natalie." Her voice is firm. Sometimes tough love works.

"We're okay," Felicia says quietly.

"Fuck you," Natalie says. She starts to walk away and turns around and looks Suzette up and down. "Bitch."

"Nat." Felicia glances back and forth between them as though she's a little sister caught in the middle.

Suzette shakes her head. She has been called worse. She remembers being twenty-five, a couple of years after Finland. She remembers the first time she was spit at, the first time someone called her a word her mother said was the worst word you could call a woman. But this hurts. It hurts because she's hot and tired and she thinks Felicia will go along with whatever Natalie wants to do and get herself in trouble. She should count to ten, she should disengage, she is trained to do better. "You think you have it all figured out."

Natalie rushes toward her, and Suzette winces. "Yeah, I do." She is inches from Suzette's face.

"Natalie," Felicia says. She goes to take Natalie's arm, but Natalie swats her hand away.

Suzette locks eyes with her. She feels like she is in high school again when she stood up to a senior girl whom everyone else was afraid of. "Stare her down," her sister Lisa had told her. "Look like you're a mountain she can't climb over." This is going nowhere. "Back off," she says right into Natalie's face.

Natalie swings at her, knocking her hard in the jaw. She is no mountain. She wants to tell Lisa she was wrong.

Felicia screams, and Natalie is scratching at Suzette's face now, her strength ten times greater than what Suzette would have imagined. Suzette pushes back. She feels the burning of her jaw, the burning where this girl's nails are in her arms. She is trying to restrain Natalie, but she can barely breathe. Suzette is unsteady in these damn wedge sandals, and feels herself fall over, bumping her head on the car. She feels blood. She feels Natalie jumping down on her, not giving up. She raises her elbow and thumps it into Natalie's mouth. Her other hand grabs Natalie's dirty hair, and they are face-to-face like two wild wolves. She realizes she's never been attacked like this in all her years. Felicia is pulling at Natalie weakly, and Natalie bites Suzette's arm so hard that she screams. She feels like this girl could kill her right here. *The irony*, everyone would say. She reaches a point where all the pain feels the same, and now Natalie gets to her feet and starts kicking her in the side.

"Stop," Suzette says. "Stop."

Suzette hears a car horn, a man's voice calling out. "Hey!" he yells, and his shadow eclipses them for a second. "Hey, stop or I'll call the cops!"

When Natalie looks toward him, she freezes. Her wild face drains. Suzette sees some fear, some horror in her eyes, and Suzette, bloody and hurt, face throbbing, head aching, body feeling bruised, turns to see who is coming to her aid. A thin man stands over them. His hair is gone, and his hazel eyes look hollow.

He looks like it's his last day on earth.

Natalie backs away. Felicia picks up Natalie's phone that fell out of her pocket. "Let's go." They scuttle toward the Shake Superior strip mall.

Suzette has had the wind knocked out of her. She doesn't know if she should scream or cry or just moan. She squints and recognizes the man. The seamstress's husband, Greg, who works for Alex Lionel. She and Damon saw him at a fundraiser event the Lionels hosted a year ago. He looked like a young George Clooney then. Such smoothness, charisma. He wore a black suit that night. He was smiling, shaking hands. Thick hair, dark and gray. Eyes that sparkled. Now she is speechless. She hurts so bad, but she forgets every injury when she stares into his eyes.

"Greg?" she whispers.

He smiles halfheartedly. "You okay? Let me call an ambulance . . . and the cops, too."

"No," she says.

"No?"

She shakes her head. "I think I'm okay." She holds her side where it hurts the most.

He wears Adidas shorts and a workout shirt. His legs and arms are bare, and she sees a bruise above his wrist. Behind him, a Mercedes is running in the parking lot with the driver-side door open. "What the hell was that all about?" His voice sounds quiet.

He holds his hand out to her, but she feels his frailty, and worries she might pull him down with her. She uses her arm, the one the girl didn't bite, to help herself to her feet. Her side aches where she was kicked. The pain is so bad she can hardly breathe. One of her sandal heels is broken. Her skirt is filthy. She must look like a zombie with the blood on her face.

Greg brushes some pebbles from her arm, and his hands are cold. Suzette wants to weep because he looks so terrible. She wonders if she will soon read about his death, and her heart breaks that on this hot day, he is helping her, and his face and body, so pale, look genuine and calm, as though he is presenting himself to heaven in some way. He holds her elbow and looks at the wound from the bite. "You need a tetanus shot." He studies her face. "And maybe stitches."

She tries to catch her breath. Is it her ribs?

Later, she will think about him saving her, about the way

his eyes looked so far away, and how good his cold hand felt on her ripped skin. She knows she will think about him and just shake her head because life is like this. "It was my fault," she says. "I always think I can save everyone."

"Me, too," he says, and he helps her along.

ETHAN JOELLA

19.

The Time Machine

Darcy was never the type of widow who would set a place for her late husband at the table, or bake him a small cake on his birthday. She didn't keep his clothes hanging in the closet or his toothbrush in the holder. But the one thing she finds herself doing every year without fail at the end of summer, the time of year when he first got sick, is getting angry.

As each year went by, she thought the anger would soften a bit the way she had softened in so many ways with age (not complaining to the newspaper office every time the boy missed the porch and made her hunt in the pachysandra; not shooing the stray cat that would sleep under her porch swing; not chiding Tabby, who worked the register at the dry cleaning business, for failing to put the dollar bills in the same direction), but the general anger this time of year didn't stop. And she welcomed it.

She would feel the end of summer approaching, and maybe it was the intolerable heat, maybe it was the insects everywhere (she couldn't even sit with her tea on the back deck because the

241

mosquitos would swarm around her), but she found herself in a rage every August. And this year she is worse than ever.

"If you would be so kind as to not insult me, dear, we can continue this conversation later," she says to her daughter, Mary Jane, on the telephone before hanging up and wringing her hands. It is a Wednesday morning, and she has told Tabby she won't be in until later this afternoon. She shakes her head, and fills a glass of water from the tap and sips it slowly. She thinks for a minute and can't remember what annoyed her so much about Mary Jane. Something about her saying, "Mother, just relax," or, "You know you can hire someone to do that, right?" Darcy shakes her head. Whatever Mary Jane said doesn't seem that bad now, seconds later. She will have to call her back and apologize.

Darcy rinses her glass and sets it in the drainer. She examines the peel on a banana that she'll eat later. She checks her small stack of bills and places them in her mailbox with a clothespin so the mailwoman will take them. She comes back into the kitchen, sees Ginger's letter on the kitchen table, and attempts to read it once more. Her heart races as she does. She becomes so annoyed. Some phrases stand out: *I think of you often; I sometimes think I see Luke in a crowd; I wanted you to know* . . . Darcy holds the note on its thick stationery and crumbles it slightly—not enough to rip it. "That's enough of that," she says, and sighs.

She walks down the basement steps, tearing her stocking on a loose nail that's been bothering her for months now, only to find that the washing machine has stopped midcycle because her small bathroom rugs were unevenly balanced, and she is so irritated that she kicks the appliance.

"Darn you, you piece of junk."

The basement has a pleasant coolness to it, and she takes a deep breath to calm herself. She thinks of Ginger's note again, about Mary Jane telling her to relax, and her head hurts. She gets flashes of thoughts about Luke—they come to her this way (sharp, quick, vivid) almost every day: *Luke gone eight months. Wrecking beautiful Betsy. His sweet, tired face that day in December, just a few days before he died. It's good to have you back here*, she said. Did she hug him when he came into the house, his last time home? Did she?

They found all sorts of things in his system—alcohol, painkillers, you name it. She refused to look at the autopsy report. She still sees Luke on the stepladder with the Christmas star. *Does this look right, Mom?* he said. *Yes, dear, fine. Fine.*

She rubs her temples.

These old cars weren't made for that kind of impact. Somewhere in the paperwork it said Betsy couldn't even be towed. She wonders if he ever wore Von's sunglasses when he drove. He would have looked so handsome.

I'm trying to wake up. I'm trying, Mom.

She busies herself, reaching inside the washer to align the rugs a bit better and pushing the button again, hearing the machine kick back on and make its satisfying whirring noise. She likes when things are happening, when something is being worked on. She hugs her arms by her waist and doesn't want to leave this basement.

When the children were still young, she and Von had toyed with the idea of making it more of a finished room. They had moved the old living room furniture they were replacing down here—the brown sofa with its floral print and the two blue La-Z-Boy recliners she and Von would sit in after dinner, along with the low wooden coffee table with the claw feet and the television built into the cabinet that Von said still worked "perfectly good." When they had new carpeting put in, she asked the installers if they could bind a section of the old carpet when they were hauling it out, which she placed in the center of the basement.

It was never a musty, typical basement because their house was built into a hill, so it had a wall of windows and a nice door that led right out into the backyard. Against the back of the house sat the wrought-iron bench that Von used to rest on after he mowed the lawn. He would take out a pack of cigarettes and look at the enormous view of the green lawns of Wharton, shake his head, and say, "I tell you what. If this don't beat all."

For a while after Von died, she kept the lawnmower in the corner of the basement where the furnace and water heater sit in their closet, pestering Luke to help her out and cut the grass, but he wasn't reliable, and sometimes he cut the grass too close so he wouldn't have to cut it so often. It was around this time of year, her angry time, that she dragged the lawnmower out to the yard, parked it by the curb, and put a sign on it that said FREE and hired a lawn service. "You're no muss, no fuss," Von would have said. Luke was still living at home then. She felt glad that the worry was gone about the grass getting cut, but also felt as though she was taking something from both Von and Luke.

She walks over to the television now and presses the power button to see what happens, and lo and behold, one of the morning talk shows comes on. This delights her for a second because something has survived from the cable line Von split himself and ran down the wall in the groove of the wood paneling. "We can sit down here and neck all night," he said, laughing.

"You are a silly man," she said.

She lets the television play, even though she notices the dust on the screen, and is distressed by Luke's drum set and two guitars over in the corner. She glares at them. She asked him time and again to get rid of them. He hadn't touched them in so long (thankfully, because the noise would vibrate the whole house, and the cymbals that he clanged every so often would jar her teeth). But how many times did she ask, "Can we relocate these things?" and he'd just laugh her off and say, "Mom, one day I'm going to surprise you, and I'll have a whole band down here singing your name."

"I would throttle you," she said. "Now take out a classified ad. I will be glad to foot the bill, dear."

The drum set with its big bass drum and its extending appendages of other drums looks like some kind of sea monster. She is disgusted that it's here, still alive, and Luke is not.

Why did Luke leave it behind when he moved out? She should have hired Wally, the big guy Von used to have blacktop the driveway and haul cement bags, to load up the drum set years ago. She should have had him bring it right over to Luke's apartment and leave it in the hallway. Now she's stuck with it. Did he know that seeing it would torture her later? Did he care? Did Luke ever care what he did and what effect it had?

If Von had lived longer, if she had told him to cut it out with the smoking years and years ago, she thinks he could have helped Luke. Wouldn't he have said, *No more, kid. You gotta straighten this monkey business out?* Wouldn't he have given him the toughness he needed, grabbing his arm, telling him, if it had gotten that bad, that he was taking him to rehab? Or maybe Von would have said, *Rehab? I'll show you rehab*, and would have dealt with Luke by taking away his keys and making him move home. *You want to act like a baby, well then babies live with Mom and Pop.*

Von was the strongest person she'd ever met. So unafraid of any circumstance. He never seemed nervous. He could laugh while being shot at if he were ever shot at; once, he said during the Cold War, "If any Russians come here, they better be ready to get kicked back a few continents." She loved that toughness, she misses that toughness. She stares at the drum set and wants to break it into pieces.

A commercial for Drano is murmuring on the television now, and she stops for a minute to watch the cartoon dramatization of the liquid dissolving a clog in the drain. Then she walks over to the drum set and sees the drumsticks where Luke last left them. The sun comes through the high windows over in the corner, and it makes the cymbal disk glimmer. There is a music stand, and two guitars propped next to a speaker with a frayed cord. She wants to drag it all away but is surprised how connected the drum set is.

In a second, without really thinking, she picks up one of his drumsticks and hits the cymbal quickly, a noise like someone just told a joke on Johnny Carson. She puts the drumstick back with the other one and stares out the window.

The washing machine is droning, making that nice wet swishing sound, and she looks back at the long basement. What did they envision for finishing it? Maybe sectioning off the washer and dryer. Maybe adding some cabinets, a stove, and a fridge. She remembers thinking they could put a large table in front of the fireplace for holidays. No mess upstairs. And then Mary Jane could have that group of girls sleep down here during her slumber parties, and Luke and those Meddleson brothers he liked to skateboard with could watch their movies and play their video games, dropping popcorn and slurping that Kool-Aid she hated. She imagined opening the door and standing on the top step, listening to the pleasant noise of the young, the girls recounting who said and did what, and the boys giggling and telling each other to shut up.

She wonders now why they let the basement idea vanish.

It seems to her that Mary Jane and Luke were fourteen and ten at one point, and then in seconds, Mary Jane was graduating college. Luke was dating Ginger, and doing his concerts, but still living at home. Sometimes Ginger would come over for dinner, always helping Darcy clear the table, always telling her a good story about her college classes or something her parents had said. Luke had so much respect for Ginger, and Darcy hoped in a way that made her stomach knot that Luke could stay with her forever. Whatever his faults, Ginger softened them. And he made Ginger laugh, and oh, did she look at him like he was a prince. Almost as if Ginger saw something in Luke that Darcy forgot about.

Sometimes Darcy would look out the back window and see them walking around the yard, arm in arm, Luke a half foot taller, Ginger's hair longer then, the weeping cherry tree and white azaleas behind them. Sometimes they'd bring Ginger's dog over and they'd throw the ball to it again and again. Darcy wasn't a dog person, and they never asked to bring it inside. Sometimes, after Ginger had left, Darcy and Von would wake to the sound of the drums or the nasally electric guitar beating through the floorboards. Von would grumble and put his slippers on and march down to the basement, and the noise would stop in seconds. He'd come back to bed and smile. "Noodle head," he'd say. "He didn't think it would wake us." And then Von got sick, and Luke broke up with Ginger, and then Mary Jane was married and pregnant and then and then and then.

She wants this drum set out of here. She can't look at it another day. Maybe she will call Wally. He could bring it to the thrift store. Two or three armfuls and it would be gone. She hears the washing machine draining now, and another talk show comes on with a host she remembers was an actress once, and Darcy perches tentatively on the sofa. Maybe she can just wait until the rugs are clean. She sits back, and her body remembers this sofa, remembers the way the cushions felt against her shoulders, its velvety texture. How many years since she has sat on it? It must be twenty. But she has vacuumed it every so often. She has folded laundry on it.

She sinks back into the couch and watches the woman on the talk show move through the audience surveying them about their end-of-summer bucket lists, sticking her small microphone in an eager participant's face. Darcy hates that phrase, *bucket list*. She hates the thought of doing things only because you'll die. Most of the time, you don't know when you'll die. And items on a list won't save you either way. *Why bother?* she thinks. Why discuss it with strangers on a talk show? Darcy puts her feet up on the coffee table.

She looks around when she wakes up an hour later.

Upstairs is Ginger's letter on the kitchen table. God, that letter makes her angry. She can't say why. She doesn't feel differently about Ginger. She is a dear, dear girl. One of the best people she knows. But she wants to burn the letter. She wants to knock on the door of Ginger's new place and throw it at her, watching the pages scatter on the floor. She stretches and walks over to the built-in phone nook where the black rotary phone sits. "It's like going downstairs to a time machine," Luke used to say, pointing to their old furniture, the type of phone the world barely even used in his time. She picks up the phone. *His time.* Her son has lived and died already. How can that be? His time. How can she still be going through the everyday, looking at the lawn, washing her rugs, rinsing her dishes, when he has already lived and died?

She thinks of Ginger's letter again, and her stomach flips: *I don't use words like "love of my life," but Luke was something like that to me.* Sure, Ginger, she thinks. Sure, sure. Go on and be free, she thinks. And then to invite her and Mary Jane to the wedding! The absolute, absolute nerve.

She feels the sweat bead on her forehead as she dials. Wally, good old Wally, answers on the third ring. She has called him many times over the years: to prune the maple tree at the edge of her yard, to take down the children's old swing set, to lug the ancient cash register away from the dry cleaning store before the new one was delivered. He is always pleasant, always polite. Never charges her much. "I have a job for you," she says.

A few days later, she stands on her front porch as Wally loads the last of the drum set into the back of his truck. She nods at him and hands him a check for his time, along with a twenty-dollar bill ("You don't tip 'em, they'll think twice about coming again," Von always said). Wally nods and thanks her. She listens to his loud engine start up and regards the two guitars, the drums, and music stand on its side, its many legs up in the air, the speaker pushed against the tailgate.

She holds Luke's drumsticks and almost tosses them into the back of the truck with everything else, but then she remembers these were on a Christmas list when he was a teenager, when he still made lists for her.

She remembers going to the small music shop in Middletown, and the man guiding her to a wall of mallets and drum-sticks and all types of cleaners for saxophones and flutes. She liked this set of sticks because they were red.

She holds them in her hand and feels a blast of pain like an ocean wave that nearly knocks her down. She tries to be tough every single day, since Von, since Luke, but these blasts catch her unaware, always hit her so hard. She holds the drumsticks. She watches Wally's truck take her son's stuff, and it rattles in the pickup bed, the cord from the speaker dangling out the back, flapping as the car takes off.

She looks at the lawn and sees dead, dry spots from the heat. She notices a few loose leaves meandering as they fall. She is so sad and empty and disgusted—yes, disgusted, perfectly disgusted. At Luke, at Ginger. When Von died, all she felt was afraid. Afraid and heartbroken. As though someone had stolen everything from her. But this loss is different. She is angry, and Ginger's letter that she moved to the drawer where she keeps the birthday candles and garbage bag twist ties just makes her angrier.

She needs to get to the cleaners. She has payroll to write out, the utility bills to handle. That's what her Saturdays are reserved for. She promised Kay Lionel she'd have that set of linen napkins and tablecloths pressed for a dinner party. She needs to put an ad in the paper to replace her seamstress, Freddie Tyler. She needs to call the company to have them wax and polish the floor.

The air is so warm that she can see squiggly heat waves above the road. She hears the buzz of insects. A car she doesn't recognize pulls into her driveway, and a woman waves shyly at her. She wears sunglasses, but Darcy sees a familiar flick of her hair and recognizes the dimples and cheekbones right away. She is filled with dread.

"I thought I would stop by," Ginger says as she steps out of the car. She is still as beautiful as ever, her hair in a bob above her shoulders.

"Hello, dear." Darcy looks down at Luke's drumsticks. She feels her mouth form a frown. "I would invite you inside, but I'm late for work." She hates being cold to Ginger. She has never spoken one mean word to her in the fifteen years that she's known her.

"Oh." Ginger takes her glasses off. "Okay, well maybe another time." She stands by the car door.

"Okay then." Darcy feels her knees wobble. She feels her heart flutter. She is better than this. *Talk to the poor girl*, Von would say. What would Luke say? She doesn't know. She doesn't know.

"I'm sorry," Ginger says. She holds the car door, and Darcy sees the ring on Ginger's finger. A square diamond. Platinum band. Something that looks like an heirloom, something someone would have given back in her day.

Darcy shakes her head. She knows how ridiculous her anger would sound. She knows how illogical it is, doesn't she? Poor girl. "You shouldn't be sorry. My goodness, why should you be?" But she still feels the anger inside her, the bitter resentment. She imagines scanning that letter one last time, and that's exactly what she thinks: that Ginger betrayed her. Ginger. Luke. She's mad at both of them. *Go to your room*, she feels like saying. *I don't want to look at you.* She imagines Luke's sullen way he would hang his head and slog down the hall. He never slammed his door like some kids might. He would just mope inside and she'd hear him throw himself on the bed.

"Mrs. Crowley." Ginger licks her lips, and Darcy can see how red her face is. "I knew you'd be disappointed. I'm sorry about the way this happened. All I did was think about Luke for so long afterward."

"Come in," Darcy says then, and Ginger closes the car door.

Inside, the house is cool. Darcy is happy she keeps the house clean for this very reason: unexpected company. She wonders how long it has been since Ginger's been here. In a way, she is bitter toward her, but she is also so happy to have her here. *You're back*, she wants to say.

Every time Ginger ever came over, Darcy felt relief and hope. When Luke was with her, she knew he wouldn't get into trouble. Not like with that Chucky, who wouldn't look you in the eye. What will she say to Ginger? She offers her water, lemonade, some cookies, but Ginger politely declines. She sees the puzzled look on her face when Darcy suggests they go to the basement. "It's cooler down there," Darcy says, and Ginger follows her down the steps.

Ginger looks around, and Darcy tries to see what she sees. Does it look like a normal room with the shoji screen she has placed in front of the washer and dryer, with the vase of lilies on the coffee table and her morning paper set there precisely?

Did the new throw pillows she bought for the sofa the other day help anything? The blue curtains Wally put the rods up for today hang stiffly (just pressed at the cleaners), and there are now framed pictures of Luke and Mary Jane as children on the television cabinet.

"I don't remember it being so homey down here," Ginger says. "How nice."

Darcy nods pleasantly. "It's a shame we never used it much."

Ginger points to the corner. "He used to have his music stuff over there. I'd sit on a folding chair and listen as he played."

"I don't know what became of all that," Darcy says, surprising herself with the lie. She hardly ever lies, but she realizes how heartless it seems for a mother to give away something so precious to her son, especially after the son dies. Why does she only realize something like this after the fact? Why is she missing that sentimental gene other mothers seem to have? Ginger's expression as she stares at the empty corner haunts her. Darcy stares at the drumsticks in her hand guiltily and places them on the sofa.

"Those were his, right?" Ginger says.

She nods.

"He was so talented."

"He was." She hears the words and realizes she never knew this. Was he? His singing mostly sounded like shouting. Darcy found herself distracted by the drums, the blaring speakers. How could she not feel his songs in the tender way that others seemed to? How could she have cared so little? What did that do to him? She only saw him perform a few times: once as the opening act before a high school play when he sang something by Elvis. She just never liked Elvis, so she didn't know if he was good. She only wished when he played that he would have combed his hair better, tucked his shirt in. *He was so talented.* She stares at the corner, and everything feels so far away. Luke was a stranger to her when all was said and done. *Who are you really mad at?* Von would say.

They stand in silence. Ginger finally sits down on the edge of one of the La-Z-Boy chairs, and Darcy sits beside the drumsticks. Darcy clears her throat. "So the . . . wedding . . . is when?"

"October."

"Big? Small?" Her chest is tight. She keeps her teeth pressed together.

"Medium-sized, I guess. But my mom just said there's not much family to invite anymore. It seems like everyone . . ." She lets that sentence trail off.

"Well, good. Good, good, Ginger." She crosses her legs and holds her knee. She knows her face must look so cruel as she says all this. "You deserve to be happy. You were always a wonderful girl."

"Thanks." She straightens herself. "And, as I said in the letter, if you and Mary Jane want to come . . ."

She sighs. She wants to say, *Are you really that naive, for pity's sake?* "Thank you, but I don't think so."

"Oh, okay." She looks down.

Darcy feels agitated again. "Don't worry about us. Just be happy."

Ginger looks directly at her. "But you're angry." Darcy is reminded why she always loved her. She is not only smart, well-mannered, and beautiful. She is brave.

"No."

"You are."

"Stop, Ginger. Give me a break." The central air system comes on, rumbling in the closet, and Ginger startles.

"I'm sorry."

"Stop saying that. I mean, why *should* you be? What did we all think we'd do, just sit around and light candles for him forever? Go through his high school yearbook nightly? I don't know what else there is to do but move on." Except this mourning, this devotion, is actually closer to what she wants. *Now* Ginger moves home. Now of all times. *Where in heaven were you years ago when you could have come back and changed things?*

Ginger looks at her. "Then why are you angry?"

Darcy stands. "I can't have this conversation."

"It's no one's fault, Mrs. Crowley."

This punches her. "I don't know about that." She is furious. God, she hasn't been this angry in forever. She wants to shake Luke as hard as she can for doing this to her, for making her miss him this much. She wants to scream at Ginger for moving back now, doing it for this new guy. She could spit.

"Please don't be angry with Luke. Please forgive him. It was an accident. Just bad luck, or something." Ginger starts to cry, and her voice changes. "I've forgiven him. I've tried to forgive myself for not helping him."

"He played by his own rules, didn't he?"

Ginger stands. She looks for a second like she might hug Darcy, but she stays where she is. Lord, she knows Darcy well.

"I wanted better for him," Darcy allows herself to say.

"I know."

"But you go get married."

"What does that mean?"

"It means I *am* angry with you. And I know I shouldn't be. I'm just a bitter old woman who can't make sense of any of this."

Ginger shrugs, wipes her tears. "You feel like you're being loyal to him if you punish me, right?"

Darcy puts her head down. She can only see the lackluster rug. "I'm one of the last things left of his life, I guess. Who even will remember him?"

Ginger looks at her, her eyes wet. "We all will. He was special."

"I guess I missed that."

"No, you didn't." Ginger wraps an arm around Darcy's back. "You knew." She holds her tightly. "You knew."

Then the tears come. Darcy feels uncivilized. She feels foolish, but she is safe with Ginger. They are safe down in this basement, Luke's time machine. "God, I loved him." She sobs as she says this. "I couldn't help him. I couldn't ever understand . . . he was so lost. I kept pestering him, but I didn't understand."

She wonders about her makeup. She must look so ugly.

"I never clapped for him. I never saw him sing the way a nice mother would. My dear, he thought about you so much after you went away. He was lost without you, and then Mr. Crowley died, and Mary Jane and I were there for each other, and he was all alone. I should have told him to go after you. I should have let him be messy with his feelings, let him tell me how he felt."

"You loved him," Ginger whispers.

She nods. "But I wanted better."

They don't say anything. They stand there in the quiet basement, and Darcy feels her anger lighten a bit. What would Luke say if he saw them there? She looks at his red drumsticks, and wishes she could give them to Ginger.

But she wants to keep them. To hold them where her son's hands were.

20.

Highways

If you fly over Connecticut in a helicopter, you might be surprised to see all the rivers: the Naugatuck, the Connecticut, the Farmington, the Housatonic. Rivers everywhere, blue and brilliant among thick green trees and spreading hills, like blood vessels splitting up the state.

Connecticut could be a dozen sets for a dozen movies because it has everything: acres of farmland, thick clusters of woods, cities and towns, bridges and houses, red and white, with stone chimneys. There are churches, tall buildings, stretches of coast with sturdy lighthouses with fresh paint, the rocky shoreline, white triangle sails of boats on the water. You could get lost looking at Connecticut.

You wouldn't notice Wharton right away because it looks like so many small cities, but late summer is its best time, with its rows of marigolds in orange bunches in front yards, the patches of sedum and Limelight hydrangea turning pink by the elementary school. Everyone is out during this time of the year, soaking it all in. *It's almost through; this is almost it.* Late August in Wharton is daring green, full blue. Late August is the Firefighters' Carnival at Woodsen Park, with the snack bar serving hot dogs and hamburgers. Trucks parked in a neat row selling waffles and ice cream and fresh squeezed lemonade. Kids laughing as they try to win goldfish or pull a prize lollipop from the lollipop tree. Adults pushing strollers and stopping to say hello to people they haven't seen probably since last year's carnival. "Oh, look at you." And, wagging a finger, "Hope to see you before next year!" You can hear the clicks of the spinning wheel from one booth or the ding of the penny pitch as the coins hit old glasses and mugs.

If you look, in the open field where the kite club usually flies kites or where the junior high kids play soccer, you'll see the bright lights on the Ferris wheel and the slick yellow of the potato sack slide or the sea dragon ride for small children creeping in a circle. In the air is the scent of cotton candy and the last of the summer flowers: honeysuckle, roses. The Wharton firefighters are everywhere: volunteering at the dunking booth ("Oh!" as the bench collapses) or holding a spatula while sausages and peppers sizzle on the grill.

Tonight as the cars creep through town, past the Regent Theater, past Let's Bagel, past the apartment building where Luke Crowley used to live, past the Mildred Vines statue and wishing fountain, past the Garroway & Associates building, past the Wharton Library with its drooping willow trees and green metal benches, there is a certain radiance in Wharton, and everyone who lives there wishes it were always this alive, this sparkling.

Alex and Kay Lionel stroll slowly home from the carnival. Alex looks down at the spot of mustard on his gray Ralph Lauren shirt. He shrugs and smiles and reaches for Kay's hand. Kay wears a light cotton sweater over her shoulders and holds a caramel apple for later. She always brings something home for later, to delay gratification, and Alex pictures her standing in the kitchen in her white eyelet nightgown with her bathrobe over it tonight, slicing the apple on a white plate and bringing some to him. "What a treat," she'll say, and when he thinks of her now, he still thinks of her that day they met in college, so animated and beautiful, such a straight head on her shoulders. When he looks over at her, he smiles because she still looks so much the same as she did fifty years ago. When she takes his hand, he feels in her fingers something that makes him warm and grateful.

At home, his daughter, Iris, is waiting, there for a weekend visit. She wasn't feeling well tonight, so she and Dave skipped the carnival. He worries that Iris doesn't sleep enough, that Dave doesn't seem to know how to help her. Is there always someone to worry about?

He looks down at Kay's polished nails, a dusty pink, and they walk down Maple Street, toward the neighborhood where the Tylers lived. Alex thinks of Greg for a second, and wishes they could stop by the house. How odd to think of that house being empty: the refrigerator unplugged, the mail forwarded. How odd to know that Greg and Freddie and Addie aren't inside it, like perfect dolls in a dollhouse.

Greg. Alex thinks of his face—before the illness, during the illness. What a damn fighter.

Kay looks up because there is a rush of movement next to them, and she gasps as a boy darts by them on a bike, barely missing scraping them as he says, "Sorry." In that second, they release hands, and stare longingly at the boy's fine hair that bounces as he rides, his small legs and the blue jersey he wears.

Alex puts his hand on Kay's back as together they watch the boy glide his bike onto the sidewalk ahead of them and pedal, pedal, pedal until he is just a blur. Both of them keep hearing his *Sorry* echo in their heads. Alex wonders what the boy is rushing toward. He imagines a sweet quiet house with the porch light on and parents who smile when he walks in the door. "I was getting worried," the boy's mother will say, and kiss his head.

Iris sleeps in the Lionels' guest room (she went to bed even though it's early evening because she can't sleep when she should sleep) and dreams about one of her clients in the nursing home, who loves to sit at the table and put puzzles together, and all of a sudden, right next to her client, she sees Benny in her dream, the half brother she never met.

His picture is on the wall next to the cuckoo clock in Alex and Kay's kitchen. She is surprised in her dream, for she knows he is dead, but she reaches out and touches his arm, and says, *I've always wanted a brother.* In truth, she thinks about Benny quite often, and in dreams, those things come out, she supposes. There is Benny, wearing the yellow and blue striped shirt he's wearing in a photo album she looked at today when her dad and Kay left for the carnival.

"Good news," Benny says to her, his voice so distinct and

unfamiliar, and she wakes and the room spins. She feels a quick rush of dizziness and nausea, takes deep breaths. She sits up in bed and braces herself and wonders about the carnival. She hopes Alex and Kay are having fun. She imagines everyone stopping to talk to them.

"Oh, you're not coming?" Kay had said earlier.

"I'm not feeling great," Iris said. And that was half true. She does feel odd, as though at the very, very beginning of a stomach flu, but she might be imagining it. She could have gone. She would have probably been fine.

The whole truth is she can't stand to think of all the children she'd see there—running around with cotton candy, riding the rides and laughing. The toddlers with sweaty foreheads and tired faces reaching up to be held by their parents.

She thinks about Benny coming to her in the dream. Why did he say *good news*? She doesn't believe in messages from the universe, but that dizziness feels like something she remembers, and hope, like a sensation she'd forgotten, warms her for a second. She looks out the open window and sees Dave walking the yard, his hands in his pockets, his thoughtful expression as he checks the Lionels' birdfeeders and sits down on the small stone bench under a big tree.

Yes, she is late. Yes, she felt similar with Phoebe. Half of her will not allow the feeling of possibility, but the other half has a thousand excited questions. *Could it be? Could it possibly be?*

She watches Dave outside. His tranquil eyes. His hands folded on his chest. His glasses slipped down to the edge of his nose, his ponytail loose. Dave with the birds and trees around him. His kind face not broken, still believing good things can come. She should get dressed, rush out to meet him, tell him about the dream, about the feeling. Life is always possible, she thinks, and she doesn't bother to get dressed. She knocks on the window, and he looks up and grins. "I'll be right out," she mouths to him, and she hurries out of the room.

Two miles away, Hannah Johnson leans against her new boyfriend, Brandon Giorio, on one of the benches outside the library. She sips her strawberry milkshake from Shake Superior as she reads a book of poems by Sharon Olds, and Brandon nods and sighs the way he always does when he's lost in something good, as he reads the biography of J. Edgar Hoover. She can feel his breathing against her, and every once in a while, his stomach makes a noise or she adjusts her head and hears a few thumps of his heartbeat.

She sips the sweet shake and revels in the honesty of this woman's poetry—the boldness. *And what they did to you / you did not do to me.* She read the other day that Olds once refused to go to a luncheon at the White House to protest a war, and she likes that. She wants to be that brazen. In the last light of the evening, it gets harder to see, and she slides her bookmark back into place. She reaches up to touch her new pixie cut, her blond hair all one color now, and makes a slurping sound as she finishes the shake. She puts the cup on the ground and settles into Brandon, his familiar smell like sandalwood. Brandon will not want to admit the light is fading, and he'll keep reading for at least another ten minutes, even if he has to squint, and she will lie against him and close her eyes and open them just in time to see the last blue and pink of the sky.

Now, Suzette walks upstairs to the bedroom she shares with her husband, Damon. In a gray T-shirt and her comfortable jeans, she notices lately that she can no longer feel the tenderness of the fractured rib from where that girl kicked her. That girl who the police found quickly, whose friend Felicia was a runaway from Virginia who was returned home. She wonders about Natalie and where all her anger came from. "Go easy on her," she said to the cops that day in the hospital, even though Damon said, "Screw her. Let her meet a cellmate who'll teach her some manners."

She feels the place where her ribs were sore for so long and remembers her sister Lisa telling her once when Suzette was waiting for a headache to go away that the body notices pain, but not the absence of pain. "That's why you keep feeling the headache when it hurts, but when it goes back to normal, you don't even realize it's gone." She likes that explanation. She thinks of Lisa every time she hurts and then the hurt disappears.

She crosses her arms and looks out at the mowed expanse of lawn, the thick patch of trees outside her window. These days, she thinks constantly about Owen, the toddler in foster care whose mother has a heroin problem. He has been in foster care since that day in July, and Suzette inquires about him all the time, imagines bringing him here and letting him never feel pain again, letting him run across their backyard and cutting up French toast for him in his high chair. Damon has come around to the idea lately, and she wonders what the process would be like to foster him, wonders if the mother could ever stop doing drugs and if she and Damon would be okay if they had him and then had to lose him. She thinks of pain and the absence of pain and pushing Owen on a swing at the park and letting him climb into their bed every time he had a nightmare. She looks outside, and the moon sits like the bottom of an anchor over the rows of trees.

She sees that Damon has flicked on the porch light. She thinks of Ahmed and Ginger coming over in a few minutes, and something about the four of them sitting around the living room together makes her giddy. The laughing, the talking. Perhaps a card game or some Yahtzee. The wine. The scoops of ice cream in bowls. Giggling with Ginger as they go back for more ice cream and start raiding the cupboard for tortilla chips and salsa. Maybe tonight she will tell them about Owen and see what they say.

Not far away, the dark roads make Ginger Lord nervous as they always do, but Ahmed is singing Frank Sinatra to her in the old Saab convertible he got at Classic Motors last week. Yes, he's singing. The car is pale blue, and when he showed up in it at their house, he beeped the horn, stood in front of it, arms crossed, Ray-Bans on, and said, "Hey, baby. 'Sup?" She shook her head and smiled. So this was his surprise? She didn't say how impractical it was. She didn't say maybe, with the wedding coming up, they should discuss big purchases like this. She didn't even think any of this, because Ahmed's charm just crept over everything. "You won't be able to keep the chicks away," she said. "How can I compete?"

He took out a small bag with a new pair of women's Ray-Bans in it and handed them to her. "These will stay in the glove box, and you're the only chick allowed to wear them," he said. "Keys to the kingdom, baby." Now they drive, top down, and the stars are out as they head to Suzette and Damon's. She looks over at him as he watches the road and sings. *This man will be my husband*, she thinks. Less than two months until the wedding, where they will stand in her parents' garden and she will wear a simple dress and he a tan suit. She still can't figure it out. How did this happen? She remembers walking with him outside Suzette's wedding. She remembers him driving her to the hospital that night in December. And she remembers finally kissing him months later and thinking, yes, yes, he is what I want. Nothing has ever happened this fast and unexpectedly for Ginger.

She hates to drive these roads at night—the back country ones that lead to Suzette's—because they remind her of Luke's accident. All she can think of was how helpless he must have felt—did he cry out when he swerved? What did he feel as Betsy smashed into that big, solid tree, the tree that still stands? It is odd that Luke will forever be that boy whom time can't touch. When she pictures him, he'll always be in that toy store that day. She will spend the rest of her life seeing him like this.

Even when she's old, even when she and Ahmed have children and grandchildren, Luke will always be somewhere in the back of her mind. She doesn't know what to do with this, and neither does Ahmed. They never talk about him. Except that one time when he stood in the bedroom of her apartment getting dressed, and she had that faraway stare she would get, and he said to her, tears in his eyes, "Am I enough?" And with that, she snapped out of it. She stood and kissed his forehead, then his lips, and said, "Yes, yes, you are more," and she meant every word.

She rests her hand on his leg as he drives, and they hear crickets faintly amid the music, and some branches from trees hang low over the car. Ahmed looks at her and lip-synchs to Sinatra, and he rests his left arm on the window. In the distance, when the song is about to change, she can hear someone singing from the bandstand at the carnival, and there is that tug of something in her that thinks of Luke, but only for one second, the way Luke will always ever be there: in flashes, in bits, in the notes of a song.

On the other side of town, hours later, Darcy Crowley has a song in her head and cannot sleep. One her husband used to whistle: "Baby Face." She keeps replaying it over and over in her head: *Ain't nobody could ever take your place.* She wishes she could sleep. She should have left the air-conditioning on, but she thought she detected a nice breeze before bed. Now her bedroom feels stuffy. She hopes Mary Jane and Alvin put the ceiling fan on in Mary Jane's bedroom. They are staying over tonight with Lizzie (and their standard poodle) because they are having their carpets shampooed. When Mary Jane asked if they could stay, Darcy clapped her hands. "For as long as you want," she said. Mary Jane was surprised she would allow their dog, but Darcy has surprised herself in the last year. She had the Tylers' cat here for a while, and she pet its head and changed its litter and even brushed it, so one night with a well-behaved dog is nothing.

Lizzie wanted to sleep with Darcy, which Darcy looked forward to (she imagined whispering back and forth and giggling together and hugging the sleeping Lizzie close to her), but when Lizzie fell asleep on the living room sofa watching that special on pandas, Mary Jane covered her with a sheet and placed a pillow under her head. "Let sleeping dogs lie," she said, because Lizzie was a terrible sleeper. Just like her uncle Luke, Darcy thought.

Darcy opens her eyes and takes in the dark room, the nightlight from the hall bathroom sending a reassuring glow. She runs her hand across the summer quilt she switched to in May, the tulips and blue rings stitched carefully into the squares.

As her eyes adjust to the dimness, she sees everything as it should be: the matching crystal lamps on either side of the bed, the tufted bench at the foot, her oak dresser with the carved mirror and the framed pictures of her children on either side. Long ago, she had their senior portraits put into nice frames, and they remain her favorite photographs of them. She loved that time: the world still full of possibilities, she and Von in their prime, each of their parents still alive. Mary Jane with her longer hair then and the strand of pearls around her neck that Darcy insisted she wear, her straight white teeth from those years of braces, her promising smile and sincere brown eyes.

And Luke with his sweet smirk of a smile. His white collar and tie. How he shrugged out of that sports coat immediately after the portrait session was done. How he yanked off the tie.

If she looks closely at the picture, she can see those two freckles on Luke's cheekbone, and now, as she lies in her floral sheets, she wants to flip on her light and look for those freckles. She doesn't know why. Oh, Luke. *My wittle Wuke*, she used to say when he'd get hurt, even though he grimaced at her baby talk. She hates when her mind comes back to what she's lost, and she hears him playing his drums in the basement. She hears him shutting his bedroom door after Von died in that slow, painful way. She sees him that day they put Von's car in storage, driving behind her, his mouth so hangdog. Now she turns in bed and flaps the sheets to get some breeze.

Tomorrow she is taking Mary Jane and Lizzie to the festival of kites, the day where the retired men who run the kite club encourage all the people in the town to show up, and they help the children fly whatever kites they bring, whether it's a cheap kite from the five-and-dime or an elaborate box kite. She has bought Lizzie a perfect kite from the toy shop on Walnut Street: a classic red one with a rainbow tail and thick line. She imagines standing behind her granddaughter and watching the kite climb into the sky. "Now you've got it," she'll say. She imagines Lizzie's eager eyes as she runs with the spool reel and watches her kite in the air, one of the kind old men nodding or whistling as it takes off.

Every time she sees those men and their kites, she thinks of Von. Would he have been the type to join that club? Would he be watching his granddaughter tomorrow leading her kite into the air? *Go get 'em, tiger*, he'd say. How can it be he never met Lizzie? How does he not know this new part of her life—the part where she's a grandmother, the part where she's a widow, a mother who lost a son?

She lies still and tries to count something: imaginary kites in the sky, a school of fish, one at a time, swimming by. She starts to settle. She pretends Von is in the kitchen, pouring Hershey's syrup into a tall glass of milk the way he used to do when he got hungry late at night. She pretends she hears the sound of the spoon against the glass, and she can see the white milk turning dark. My God, she can see him so clearly, standing there in his blue pajama pants, his V-neck undershirt. Something about this image of her husband standing there, the light from the refrigerator, the glass he will leave in the sink, soothes her.

She thinks of the kite in its bag sitting on the kitchen table. She likes plans. She likes that Mary Jane and her family will come back to the house afterward (maybe they'll decide to stay a second night?) and she'll pour fruit punch for Lizzie and put coffee on for the three of them. She stands now and slips into her robe and walks the hall. She feels like a night watchman at a museum. The house is so silent. She faintly hears Alvin snoring from the bedroom, and tiptoes to the living room where she sees Lizzie sleeping, the dog on the edge of the sofa by her feet. Darcy smiles at how peaceful she looks, her little mouth open, her head back, her wrist moving slightly as if in her dreams she's already flying a kite.

Lizzie scrunches her closed eyes, and Darcy is startled because there is an echo of someone else in her expression: a little Von, a bit of Luke. The beauty of science. A hint of a feature just continuing on and on and on, and this satisfies her. Her chest heaves, and she is sad, but she feels grateful, too. She will hopefully have years to tell Lizzie all the good things about these men their family lost. She will say they were golden, one of a kind. She will make them unforgettable.

Suddenly, Lizzie's eyes open, and she looks up to see Darcy standing there. She worries her presence will scare Lizzie, but Lizzie smiles and sits up.

"Grandma, I was supposed to sleep in your bed tonight."

Darcy reaches down to smooth her messy hair in place. "You were indeed, dear," she whispers.

"I fell asleep before I could."

Darcy holds out her hand and Lizzie takes it. "Then let's get to bed," she says, and smiles, and side by side, the dog following them, they make their way down the hall, Lizzie asking her questions about the kites. *Will there be enough wind? Will the sun shine? Will the kites climb and climb?*

"We'll soon see," Darcy says, and they settle into bed.

Freddie Tyler holds the wheel of her husband's Mercedes as she drives in the middle of the night, only big trucks on I-80 West as she switches lanes and sips her coffee. She has the radio on low, and it's just mumbling the way Darcy Crowley's radio at the cleaners does, and she stops to think for a second that they are over eight hundred miles from Wharton—eight hundred miles and counting as they breeze through Indiana.

She has never seen Indiana before. She tries to look around to get a sense of it, but it looks the same as Connecticut, as the Pennsylvania and Ohio highways looked.

She loves the middle of the night. She loves this open road. Her mind keeps putting phrases together that she could write, and once in a while, she'll reach her hand into the empty cup holder next to her coffee and pick up her cell phone and record an idea she has: *In the last year, I have thought of nothing but highways: their long stretch, their openness, the way they take you away from what you know.* She knows the ideas are rough, but she feels a certain accomplishment that she can put these words down. She can say them all now.

She glances back at Addie, her head slumped to the side, her arms so limp, her small stuffed penguin just out of reach. Wizard is curled up beside her, his head resting near her lap. For a second, she thinks of Kitty, their old cat who died two weeks ago. Freddie is surprised how often she thinks she sees the cat now, but it's just a pillow on the sofa, a bag on the floor. She feels regret that they never gave Kitty a proper name. They meant to, but all of a sudden years had gone by, and she was still Kitty.

Freddie watches Addie's parted lips, her resting eyelashes as the passing lights illuminate her, and she can't wait until they get where they are going. Addie has never seen Iowa, and Freddie imagines how exciting it will be to move into the rented town house, to take a walk into the downtown district and sit at a sidewalk café or wander through one of the markets with its umbrellas and fresh produce. Freddie reaches back and squeezes her knee lightly.

She cannot believe she got into the Iowa program. What were the chances? The last time she looked, their acceptance rate was in the single digits. Did Lance Gray's recommendation help her? He was on the faculty there at one point, and he told her those years ago at that conference in Vermont that she had potential. He didn't seem at all surprised when she emailed him, and he said he remembered her poem. How could he have? But he did.

And now she's going. A full fellowship, too. A marvelous opportunity with the best faculty. Will she be able to do this? Compete with young, eager writers in their twenties? She thinks she can. She has so much raw stuff these days, and a new honesty she never felt before. Classes start next week. She is nervous and exhilarated. She keeps her eyes on the road, then thinks of something else she can write. She hears the words come together. Something about grief and hope—how they are two vines of the same—no, not vines. They are, they are what? She thinks about the right words, and she is startled by his voice.

"Want me to drive?" Greg asks, sitting up next to her. His hair has somewhat grown into a buzz cut, and a new mustache sprouted that he didn't want to shave.

"I'm fine, Tom Selleck," she says, and smiles. The gray shirt he wears says All I Care About Is Fishing, a present Addie got for him for Father's Day because he promised her fishing lessons at Lake Macbride in Iowa.

He wipes the side of his face and groans. "I slept like a bear in a cave," he says. "How we doing?"

"Breezing through Indiana. Next stop: Illinois." She offers her coffee to him, and he sits up and takes it. He sips, and she sees the line of muscle on his arm, the way his throat moves when he drinks, and she is stunned by this man sitting so close to her. She wants to pull the car over and kiss him. Every day she is still shocked by the gift of him.

"I like you driving," he says. "I might just sit back and let you get us all the way there."

"I think I've got at least another two hours until my head falls off," she says. She looks at the road, the yellow dashes, the steady gray. "Go back to sleep if you want."

He nods, and turns over, and in a few minutes she hears the sound of him snoring, her husband who battled for his life—and won. His arms crossed in front of him, his long legs stretched. His chest rising and falling. This is still real, she thinks. Nothing, nothing, has happened.

Acknowledgments

To Rebecca, who I met in third grade when we were paired up to write about our summer plans. I don't know who I would be without you, and I couldn't ask for a better partner. Our long walks have kept me sane, and you believed I could do this when I didn't. I love you, and I love our life. Little did I know thirty-five years ago that you were the summer I was hoping for.

To my daughters, Gia and Frankie. Thank you for teaching me everything I never learned. Our talks, our playing, our little and big traditions. I am so, so proud to be your dad.

To my parents and siblings and cousin June, who all loved me and let me be sensitive and odd. Thank you for the books and the laughing and the Tenenbaum lifestyle. To my wife's family, who I love like my own, who always had a place at the table for me.

Thank you to everyone in the Rehoboth Beach Writers' Guild: the exact group I needed when I was a tired teacher with young kids who just wanted to write more. The readings and classes and community of writers have been everything.

To Maribeth Fischer, novelist and friend, who made the guild what it is and always encouraged me. Thank you for your early reads of this book and sound character advice. You have taught me so much, and I am a better writer because of you.

To Gail Comorat, my poetry workshop co-teacher and one of my best friends. I am so glad I met you, and I love that we share poems and share a brain. Also to Irene Fick, Sherri Wright, Ellen Collins, the email group that shares writing, commiserates over rejection, and celebrates acceptances.

To Walter Cummins, who taught me so much about writing and teaching and generosity.

So much gratitude to Madeleine Milburn, my agent, who is worlds too good for me. I cannot tell you how lucky I feel to have you by my side. You saw what I always hoped someone would see in my writing, and you cared so much about my characters. To everyone at the Madeleine Milburn agency, especially Rachel Yeoh, who was an early reader and is always so kind and helpful. Also to Fiona Mitchell, for her early valuable reading.

To Kara Watson, who is as skilled and insightful as any editor could be. Thank you for acquiring this and for helping me tell these characters' stories so eloquently. Your checkmarks are nourishment. Thanks to Sabrina Pyun for the early read and excellent suggestions. To Nan Graham, Mia O'Neill, Ashley Gilliam, Jaya Miceli, Katie Rizzo, and everyone else at Scribner: how is this even true? I used to look up at the Simon & Schuster building whenever I visited the city, and I wished then for exactly this. Thank you will never be enough.

Thanks to all the students over the last twenty years who

remind me how much hope there is. It has been an honor learning from you.

And finally thank you to my great-aunt Stella, long gone but still so present, who demanded the local newspaper publish my poem when I was eight. Thank you for making me feel like I had something to say. This might all be because of you.

"A comforting companion for difficult times."
—*People*

Ethan Joella's deeply moving yet ebullient novel about residents of a Connecticut town facing everyday fears and desires—a lost love, a stalled career, a diagnosis—pulls at the heartstrings and provides hope.

Freddie and Greg Tyler seem to have it all: a comfortable home, a beautif[ul] young daughter, a bond that feels unbreakable. But when Greg is diagnos[ed] with a rare and aggressive form of cancer, the sense of certainty they on[ce] knew evaporates. Throughout their town, friends and neighbors fa[ce] the most difficult of life's challenges and are figuring out how to surviv[e] thanks to love, grace, forgiveness, and hope.

A Little Hope is a deeply resonant debut that immerses the reader in [a] community and celebrates intimate moments of connection.

"A quietly powerful portrait of small-town life."
—MARY BETH KEANE, author of *Ask Again, Yes*

"A heartfelt, life-affirming novel."
—ALEXANDRA DADDARIO, Book of the Month

ETHAN JOELLA teaches English and psychology [at] the University of Delaware and specializes in comm[u]nity writing workshops. His work has appeared in *Riv[er] Teeth*, *Cimarron Review*, *The MacGuffin*, *Delaware Beac[h] Life*, and *Third Wednesday*. He lives in Rehoboth Beac[h] Delaware, with his wife and two daughters.

© ETHAN JOELLA

SimonandSchuster.com
f ✕ 🅞 @ScribnerBooks

COVER DESIGN BY ELIZABETH YAFFE
COVER PHOTOGRAPHS: KITE BY DIANE DIEDERICH/SHUTTERSTOCK;
BACKGROUND BY PLAINPICTURE/FRANK KREMS; BACK COVER PHOTOGRAPH BY
JERRY AND MARCY MONKMAN/ECOPHOTOGRAPHY.COM/ALAMY STOCK PHOTO

SCRIBNER

ISBN 978-1-9821-7120-9 $16.99 U.S./$22.99 Can.